BOTULISM ROMANCE

Botulism Romance

This is a work of fiction. Names, characters, places, and incidents either are the product of the author's imagination or are used fictitiously. Any resemblance to actual persons, living or dead, events, or locales is entirely coincidental

Copyright © 2024 Tyler H. Jolley

Cover Design by Jolene Perry
Cover Art by Canva Creator 独家插画
Interior Typesetting by Melissa Williams Design

Published in the United States by Tyler H. Jolley

ISBN: 978-1-958734-26-1 (paperback)
ISBN: 978-1-958734-30-8 (hardcover)
ISBN: 978-1-958734-31-5 (eBook)

BOTULISM ROMANCE

A SCIENCE EXPERIMENT GONE WRONG, OR VERY, VERY RIGHT...

TYLER H. JOLLEY
WITH JOLENE PERRY

JOLLEY CHRONICLES

I DEDICATE THIS TO ALL THE HOPELESS ROMANTICS OUT THERE AND HOPE THEY DON'T DIE FROM BOTULISM TOXIN.

I don't believe people are looking for the meaning of life as much as they are looking for the experience of being alive.

—Joseph Campbell—

ONE

I stared at the screen on Mom's phone as a pale brown desert flew by the car windows. The little Ford Escort rattled a bit on the eighty-mile-an-hour highway.

Payout: $12.13 stared back at me from my online account.

Well, the hope of covering expenses by being a YouTube star was diminishing each week. If I hadn't killed my phone on my last urban exploration, I may have had a chance. We were moving next to a mostly shut-down army base, rife with opportunities for cool videos, but again, a dead phone meant dead video production.

Mom coughed again. Swallowed. This was what she did before trying to talk after a long period of silence.

The twisting helplessness in my gut was familiar.

"I'll get you a new phone as soon as I can," she said. Her voice rasped like a ninety-year-old who had spent their life smoking, not like a barely forty-year-old mom of one.

"I broke the phone. I'll figure it out," I told her as I logged out of my account and slipped her phone back in her bag. "Town looks small enough that I might be able to find a job within walking distance."

"Our housing is close to the military base, Chuck . . ." Her lips pursed. "Town is a bit . . . far."

It couldn't be that bad. Maybe I could find a cheap bike at a pawn shop or something. "Okay."

And if Mom said "a bit far," it meant quite a ways. Dad would have rolled his eyes or let out an overdramatic and exasperated sigh at her generalization, but I generally attempted to do the opposite of what I thought he'd do. We hadn't spoken in almost a year—when he called me on my sixteenth birthday.

She coughed again, a rush of air roiling with mucus, and my stomach tightened. I'd had two fears in the last few years since she'd finally kicked Dad out. First, that Mom would get so sick she'd send me to live with him, and second, that this genetic lung disease, the one that was so rare no one knew what to do with her, would take her life.

Nobody got what it was like to live with someone who was chronically ill until they'd been there. So many nights I was in bed listening to her rasp, making me grateful for the only thing I wasn't afraid to admit I'd gotten from my dad—my lungs.

The tires created an endless hum, and the brown landscape was never-ending in every direction. With Dad in the navy, we'd generally lived on the coasts, so this was all new to me. Even the Arizona desert had more variation than here.

"I'm sorry we had to move again," Mom said, as if sensing my trepidation at this blah landscape.

"It's fine. I get it." And I did. She'd gotten a federal job, which meant federal health benefits. With her health, it wasn't something she could turn down—even if she'd be cleaning toilets on what was left of an army base just outside of Twin Falls, Idaho.

Idaho. You-da-ho. Like, the only thing I knew about this place was that they grew potatoes, but as I stared at the endless brown, I couldn't imagine growing anything in this dirt.

Mom tucked her hair over her shoulder and twisted it with one hand while holding the steering wheel with the other. She'd had this nervous habit since I could remember.

I scratched my forehead, making my dark hair fall over my eyes again. I needed a cut, but a new place meant finding a new person to cut my hair and money we didn't have—everything always came back to money.

With money, Mom could have kicked Dad out long before she did. With money, Mom could be in a fancy medical clinic while someone tried to figure out what was wrong with her lungs and not have yet another doctor who simply sent her on her way with a stupid inhaler. With money, we wouldn't be driving this POS car to a job that I wish she didn't have to do.

"I'll get a bike or something," I told her. "And I'll get a job. Fast-food jobs always have free meals." My bank account held a pathetic two hundred and thirty-three dollars. That wasn't enough for even one specialist appointment when we were in Arizona. I couldn't imagine Idaho would be much different. Though, the insurance that came with her new job was supposed to change all that.

She nodded a little, but the way she worried her fingers over her dark hair said she was only half listening.

I slouched lower in my chair. I couldn't believe I'd broken my phone. My books were on there. My few friends from our last house in Arizona were on there. I'd jumped wrong through an open doorway, and the thing found its way through a crack in the floor of an abandoned factory and dropped about thirty feet to a concrete floor. To be fair, it was better the phone dropped than me. I wouldn't have survived a thirty-foot fall either.

A few spots of green began to appear alongside the road, and I sat up taller as I started to see signs for exits. At least we'd passed the dry landscape.

"We're a ways north of town," Mom explained as we pulled off. "So don't get too excited that we've arrived."

I slumped lower in my seat but stared out the window, trying to get a feel for the place that I needed to hope was our home until I graduated. Maybe longer if Mom could get the insurance she needed to fix her lungs.

Twin Falls had all the usual stuff—fast-food places near the highway, a couple of grocery stores, and then we passed through a little downtown area. All old brick buildings, a large square around a fountain, and a massive library with a modern front. The short street felt like something out of a small-town Hallmark movie.

A McCallister's restaurant appeared on the left. I'd worked at one before, so I could do that again. But then we passed a taco place, and who didn't want free tacos while they worked? I'd try there first. Once I figured out how much time homework was going to take—each school was a little different on that front. Well, and once I figured out if coming into town was even a possibility for me.

We passed the high school on our way north, and I released a sigh. The windows on a wing of the school with darker brick were mostly boarded up—at least on the roadside. Mom had said that the town had shrunk since part of the military base had closed.

Checking in for the last two months of junior year almost felt pointless. If we'd been able to stay in Arizona for even a month longer, they'd have called my school for grades and I'd be done for the year.

Again, a problem a little money would have solved.

But the town dissolved behind us, and we drove and

drove and drove, and it was about three miles before we reached the townhome complex—just outside the decommissioned area of the base.

Acorn Townhomes—the cheesier the name, the worse the low-income houses were. I stared at the faded sign that welcomed us into the neighborhood. I mean, if I was willing to call the tragic two-story fourplexes a neighborhood. There was a park with trees on the right, weeds growing out of planter boxes. The left side held a row of figure-eight offshoots with housing.

Mom's turn to release a sigh. "We're 4345 B."

By the look of the dust on the windows and the weeds growing through the cracks in the pavement—there were green things here!—we were the only ones living in this particular building. A few cars sat parked under the carport of some of the other "houses," but only in front of maybe a third. It was a Tuesday, so maybe the other people were at work.

Or maybe this place was as dead as it looked.

The light-blue paint was peeling a little and the screen door was missing a chunk out of the bottom right corner.

"They said they'd leave the keys in the mailbox," Mom told me.

I flipped open the lid of a rusting mail slot next to the front door, and sure enough, there were two keys on a keyring at the bottom. My big hands barely fit into the mail slot, but my fingertips finally caught the edge of the keyring, and I slid them out.

"Thanks," Mom said, but she coughed a few times once the words were out. The clear air was supposed to help with that.

The door creaked open, and I braced myself as I followed her inside.

The kitchen was a weird hallway thing to our left,

then stairs, and once I moved past the stairs, I was in our living room. One of those big empty wooden wire spools acted as the coffee table. The two couches were an olive green and . . . shiny? I ran my fingers over the surface. They felt plastic—like the old seats on a truck Dad used to own.

"It's better than nothing." Mom exhaled loudly. "Just needs a good cleaning."

The only other furniture in the room was a horrid, flowered chair whose orange and pink blossoms had been shredded enough to see the springs underneath.

I wasn't sure I agreed with Mom's lease that this place was furnished. But at least there was an ancient flat-screen TV plugged into the wall.

A large bank of dusty windows let patterns of light into the room, and I peeked through one of the panes to see a small and weedy backyard with a shed and a six-foot privacy fence. There was sagebrush-covered desert behind us, followed by another circle of houses. But the privacy fence was something.

"Whichever room you want is fine," Mom said. "We'll be sharing the bathroom."

I jogged up the stairs, my worn Adidas creaking more steps than not. Even upstairs, the floor was these weird tiles that weren't real tiles, but like linoleum tiles. The bigger bedroom looked over the driveway and had a large closet. A few hangers sat on the bar and there were a few shoeboxes that sat empty, aside from one that held a handful of random pens and pencils. Okay, then.

Of course I'd take the smaller room. I had almost no clothes anyway. A few pairs of jeans, a few T-shirts, and a couple pairs of shorts. Mom could use the closet—though she didn't have a lot more than me.

My new room had a mattress on the floor, an old milk

crate for a nightstand, and a lamp with no shade. Yeah, I definitely didn't call this "furnished." But it wasn't the worst place we'd ever lived. When I opened the closet, I leaned inside. The space wasn't deep enough to be a walk-in, but too deep to feel like a regular closet. I stepped half inside and grabbed a string, lighting the dingy space. A dusty box rested on the floor, just out of sight of the opening left by the rickety bifold doors. I stepped back out, eyeing the doors. One of them was off the track, making them look like broken wings.

The place was a total dump, but two floors at least meant that I could maybe watch TV or something while Mom rested upstairs without keeping her up. Before she could try to unload our stuff, I ran back down the stairs to the car. We each had two roller suitcases with our personal things. Well, and we had one box of random kitchen stuff.

With the state of my mattress, I was just grateful for the sheets Mom had made me clean at the laundromat before we left Arizona. I took the small wins where I could get them.

"There's a small store on base, and I'm allowed to use it, so I'm gonna stock up a little." Mom gave me a small smile. "Why don't you settle in?"

I should have offered to go with her. I knew I should have. But I'd been in that horrible little car since Arizona. I couldn't. I just couldn't. "Thanks."

At least I'd put her suitcases in her room first.

I wheeled my two suitcases in. I didn't mind living out of them, and all I needed tonight was my pillow, some sheets, and maybe a blanket.

Instead of unpacking, I wandered back over to the closet and flipped down part of the top on the large box that rested inside. Books. Huh. I dragged the big box from the closet and over toward the bed. Without my phone, this might save me. I sat on the ancient mattress and started to go through them.

Chemistry? Biology? Biochem? I dropped each one on the floor. Seriously? Science books? What a waste of paper. Not that I had anything *against* science; it's just that I'd wanted fiction. Anything to keep my mind occupied.

I dumped the whole box over, and yeah, aside from a boxed set of C.S. Lewis, which I'd probably reread only because they were what I had, this sucked. Nothing good. I'd started placing the dusty books back in the box when my fingers wrapped around the end of a simple black book. No writing on the outside. I flipped it open and saw handwriting.

Some kind of journal?

Now, I knew I was at a kind of juncture here. Like, clearly whoever wrote this left it behind, so it was their fault if I read it. That being said, if I were to leave a journal somewhere, I'd really just want it back and to know that whoever found it did NOT read my words.

I settled for flipping to the first page.

Name: Sam Miller

Date: Junior year

I liked this Sam already. I'd probably do the same and just put junior year rather than a date, though I kind of hoped I knew *when* this Sam was writing in here.

Flipping the pages from beginning to end, I stopped at the end to see some kind of patch taped to the back cover, with the word "Chemistry" on the top and "Boy Scouts of America" on the bottom. Scouts?

With books strewn around me and my two suitcases

next to the bare mattress, I sat on the floor and tentatively flipped back to the beginning and opened the journal to the next page.

You know what prompted me to start this? #$%^&% younger siblings and parents who work too much. That's all. Sometimes you just need a place to vent. Honestly, I don't get why my dad let himself get in trouble. We went from living on the nice side of base to this crap hole next to base because he has a big mouth.*

All I could think was how many times Dad had come home saying he'd lost his job because his boss was an idiot, but in the end, it always came out that Dad had mouthed off and gotten fired. Just like when his time in the navy ended abruptly—which, for the record, wasn't his choice, and he was about three F-bombs from that discharge being dishonorable. My situation wasn't exactly the same as this guy's—I was guessing the journal writer's dad was demoted—but I could relate.

The first few pages were endless rants and anger about how much Sam had moved and how this place was supposed to be better, but was clearly worse because when his dad lost rank, he also lost pay, and his mom was pregnant again.

Mom couldn't have kids after me, so I couldn't relate on that front. I was a C-section, and she was so unhealthy that they made sure she wouldn't get pregnant again while they were in there taking me out. The bottom line is they repo'ed her uterus.

And I didn't think I'd even ever have the guts to write down what this Sam guy had written. I'd hate for Mom to know how frustrating our constant moving was, and how hard our being endlessly poor was. None of those things were her fault, and she already carried those burdens. We both did. Mom working forty hours was like a healthy person working seventy. It was brutal. But we needed the money, and we needed the insurance, and teens didn't get paid jack.

"Chuck!" she called. "I got the TV on, and there's dinner! This old microwave still works!"

I hadn't even heard her come in or unload groceries.

Two stories of house would definitely be nice. I got to my feet and tucked the journal under my arm. If Sam didn't want me reading it, he should have taken it with him.

Two TV dinners sat on the wooden spool in the living room—a bottled root beer in front of each.

"Thought we'd celebrate," Mom said as she lifted the root beer to her lips.

We only bought the bottled stuff for special occasions. I eased onto the plastic couch, the cushions squeaking a bit as they rubbed together. We'd need a blanket for this thing or something. No one wanted to sit on squeaky plastic for any amount of time.

She turned on some PBS show where people were in some kind of historical clothes. Not my thing. I grabbed one of the "chicken" bites from the meal and flipped open the journal again.

Well, Dad said he and Mom are in counseling, but I can feel the end coming already . . .

I remembered that conversation with my parents as well. Though at that point, I just wanted Dad gone. He never had any patience with Mom's illness, and I had no patience for someone who couldn't see beyond their own needs. None of Dad's misfortunes were ever his fault, and I found his constant blaming of other people exhausting.

Mom hardly said a word, and Dad tried to act like all of this was no big deal. But it's totally a big deal.

12

"Whatcha reading?" Mom asked when the TV switched to a commercial break.

"There was a box of books in the closet," I explained as I popped another nugget into my mouth. "And a journal."

Her brows rose. "I'm surprised anything was left behind here."

"Really?" I asked, glancing around at the obvious neglected state of the place.

Mom laughed a little. "Okay, I shouldn't be surprised."

But in a way, it was kind of strange. We weren't left with a proper nightstand, but somehow, a deeply personal journal was included in our subsidized housing. I'm guessing they didn't do a very good walkthrough when people moved out.

"It's what I have to read right now," I told her.

Her frown was immediate. "Your phone. Your books."

I shrugged. "It's fine." Then I lifted the journal. "I have this to read for now."

Mom released a long sigh. She felt the lack of funds every bit as much as me. There was just no way to get ahead. People didn't get how expensive it was to be poor. Costco membership? No way. You couldn't buy in bulk when you didn't have money to back it up. What happened was you bought the big can of cheaper peanut butter, but then you couldn't get most of the other stuff on your list, so poor people ended up paying more for a scoop of peanut butter than wealthier people did because we were always buying the smallest jar to make sure we could eat more than just peanut butter sandwiches for the next week. The system was rigged. But if we could just get a *little* bit ahead—just a little—our money would go so much further.

After the small dinner, I jogged back up the stairs with the journal under my arm, almost unsure if I wanted to know what happened next in Sam's life. I stood at the entrance to my room, looking at the mess I'd made on the floor, the suitcases leaning against the bed, and my shoulders dropped. I might not have had a lot of stuff, but it didn't mean it wouldn't take me a while to get this disaster cleaned up.

But the night before starting a new school meant I probably wouldn't be able to sleep anyway, so I might as well make this room livable.

TWO

I leaned over the console of the small car and stared at the odometer as we stopped in front of the school. The morning sun shined just over the blue metal roof of my new prison. The "new kid" experience never got easier the older I got. Besides, my body still felt a bit numb and hazy from the lack of sleep that always happened in a new place.

"Three point three miles," Mom said.

I nodded. Just over three miles from school to home. "I can walk."

She sighed. "The bus will—"

"I can walk," I said again. Being the new kid with only two months left made me enough of a curiosity. The last thing I needed was to end up on a school bus with the military kids. Been there. Done that.

"I'm not set up for you to get free lunches at the school yet—I'm still waiting to hear back—but you have a lunch."

"Yeah," I responded. We'd already been through this at the house, a sure sign Mom was nervous. "I got it in my bag. Thanks."

She tucked her hair behind her ears, even though she'd already pulled it up to prepare for her first day at work. "Here we both go."

"Yeah," I said again as I stared out the window at the parking lot littered with students and cars.

A few guys and two girls stood behind a huge truck, sporting cowboy boots and belt buckles. Most of the girls wore denim jackets, but the boys braved the chilly March morning with bare arms. The ranchers' kids. Maybe a wannabe or two.

Two other girls stood at the trunk of a guy's car, black boxes that held instruments in their hands. The guy pulled drumsticks and some kind of drum in a black bag from the back of his car before they moved into the school together. Another group was all dressed in bright tracksuits with the school's logo on the pantleg.

Almost every high school in the country, and some outside, would probably have a very similar scene. Though the parking lot wasn't even half-full, and school started in fifteen minutes.

"The counselor is expecting you for your schedule," Mom said.

"Thanks for the ride." I glanced over at her and the worry lines on her forehead. "I'm fine, Mom. Good luck with your first day."

Her shoulders convulsed, but only a slight rumble came up her throat. She was trying to hide her coughing from me. "You too," she whisper-rasped.

I climbed out of the car, knowing that if she'd spoken fully, she'd have ended up in a coughing fit. She shouldn't be working anywhere. But even if I worked full time, I couldn't support the two of us. No diploma. No special skills. Just a subpar YouTube channel and no phone to maintain it.

My fingers itched for my phone, for my headphones, for something to drown out the noise in the hallway. For something to show that I didn't care about being the new kid. Instead, I was forced to listen to the chatter that happened between friends who had known each other their whole lives.

"Prom tickets! For this Saturday at the fairgrounds!" a voice called.

Fairgrounds?

"Gag," a girl said next to me. Her long blonde hair covered most of her face and shoulders. "I'd rather be riddled with bullets while escaping with a load of cash. Am I right?"

"Uh . . ." My brain had shorted out with being spoken to as if I belonged. And seriously? That's where her thoughts went first thing in the morning?

"Chuck!" My attention snapped toward a wide woman with red hair and thick eyeliner. "I have your schedule!"

A couple of kids glanced my way, but I moved for the main office and the woman flapping a piece of paper in the air. Of course she'd know who I was. There weren't that many kids in the school, and I wasn't familiar.

"Welcome to Northern Twin Falls Middle and High School!" she chirped.

I paused on the hallway side of the counter. "Uh, thanks."

"I have your locker number right here with the combination." She pointed to the backside of the paper, where she'd used a bright purple marker to announce my locker and combo. "And your schedule is on this side."

"Got it." I reached for the paper and glanced at my schedule.

"Give it a look over," she said. "Just in case we need to change something."

My computer programming from Arizona hadn't been available here, but at least they had an IT class. That was something. Math same. English same. Government same. "Weight lifting?" I asked.

She shrugged. "You needed to finish your PE credit."

Whatever. "I don't have clothes to dress."

"It's your last class of the day." She shrugged again. "So you can wear whatever you want. Coach is pretty laid-back."

Brilliant. "Okay, I think I got it."

"Classes are all in the two hallways—above and below—just over there." She pointed a brightly painted nail in the direction every student was headed. "Your locker is on the second floor to the left. Almost on the end near the windows."

"Great," I told her, hating the nerves twinging in my stomach. *Two months. Two months. Two months.* I could handle a new school for two months. Then I could disappear into work and TV for the summer.

"Anyone on the student council would be happy to help you find your classes." She nodded as she spoke.

The last thing I needed was to be led around like a child. "I think I can manage." One thing I knew was that teachers were pretty forgiving about tardiness on your first day of school.

She smiled, and the skin around her eyes crinkled. "Drop in if you have any questions."

I might have questions, but I wasn't sure how much I'd want to drop in. Running under the radar until the end of the school year felt like my best option. That, and finding a job so I could replace my phone and help cover groceries.

There was no point in going to my locker when I had nothing to put in it and nothing to take out, so I headed up the emptying hallway toward math.

The morning passed with me introducing myself four

times in four classes, getting four new textbooks. Shoving said textbooks in my locker. And now lunch.

After living in Germany, and on the East Coast and then the West Coast, and then Arizona, I should have had a routine for eating lunch in a new school. *Should.*

The echoing voices in the cafeteria made me walk right by that room. After seeing the boarded-up side of the school, I felt my feet leading me past the gym and the small theater, where I found double wooden doors holding a laminated, typed sign:

SUPPLY—NO STUDENTS
WITHOUT PERMISSION

New kid would be permission enough for today. I pushed through the old wooden doors and into the smell of ancient library and commercial cleaners. From the way the glass cabinets sat against the walls of the hallway, and the antique-looking drinking fountains, this place reeked of the 1940s. The first classroom was locked, but the second was open, and I slipped inside. These windows weren't boarded up, but they looked toward the running track and football field rather than toward the road.

I swung my backpack off my shoulder and sat next to an open closet in a classroom with those miniature chairs attached to desks. Antique stores on the East Coast would charge a fortune for the small wooden desks, even though a normal-sized human could never use them.

My Lunchables sat in a bag with a lukewarm cold pack next to it. At least there were Oreos. I started with those as I pulled out Sam Miller's journal.

At that point, I knew I could have gone to the library and checked out a new book, but I'd read too far into his story not to continue. I made it through my crackers and cheese as I caught up on his days at what was then Northern Twin Falls High School—not Middle and High School.

Twin Falls is sucking hard, but Mom signed me up for Scouts. I was so pissed at first, but then I started doing the research on how fun it can be to earn new badges, and I can legit get a badge just for learning about dentistry or microbiology. Like, there's a merit badge for this one small area of study. I think they might have a merit badge for everything. The leader said I'd get an extra something if I presented what I learned to the rest of the guys.

I can become a mad scientist and have adults praise me for it.

This is what I've got so far:

5 common bacteria that I think I could use and purify to make a toxin:

> *1. Staphylococcus*
> *2. Micrococcus*
> *3. Bacillus*
> *4. Pseudomonas*
> *5. Botulinum (soil) or food*

All the science books in the closet now made sense. Sam Miller's journal wasn't in that box by accident. Those were his things. The dude must have really wanted that merit badge. This was all getting super interesting. I was taking a biology class now, but not until after lunch. And toxin felt . . . strong? Ominous? Curious? That one word had definitely made Sam another level more interesting. Or two.

Just then, the bell rang, because of course it would ring just when things were getting good.

I hauled myself to bio and slumped in an open desk. Another introduction of myself to the class, which felt redundant at this point, considering how few students there were at the school. I got another textbook. Signed another student-teacher agreement.

The teacher began talking about genetics and the Punnett square, which I'd done as part of my first unit at my last school. This was going to be so great. Easy A.

Weight lifting was basically a chance for the guys in sports to flex, but they all gave me a brief nod and smile. Five guys and three girls in the class. Small school. The coach asked how seriously I wanted to take the class, and I gave him a shrug. I was generally in decent shape just from being out and filming and stuff. Though no phone, no filming.

"Wouldn't mind earning some more muscles."

Coach chuckled. "Hey, Brock. I got another project for ya."

Before I could protest, a huge guy jumped off the weight bench and reached out his hand to shake. I took it.

"Can I set you up with a workout plan?" Brock asked, his excited-kid voice not matching his broad shoulders and military-cut hair.

"Uh . . ."

"I wanna be a personal trainer after I graduate, and the more workouts I can set up, the better it'll look." If a huge human could look contrite and pleading, it was this blinking, wide-eyed Brock guy.

"Yeah. Okay." As long as he didn't make it too hard. I couldn't afford extra meat or supplements or anything— not by a long shot.

"You just made his day," one of the girls said. "He's always wanting to redo our circuits."

"It'll help me later," Brock said. "When I'm trying to get a job. You all know that."

"You keep track of everyone's progress?" she asked as she lay down on the bench press.

His dark brows pulled together. I guessed he was at least six inches shorter than me, but a lot broader. Though I was a hair over six feet, so being shorter than me at this age was pretty common.

"Of course I keep track," he responded. "Otherwise, what would be the point?"

"Well . . . thanks," I offered him.

Brock nodded seriously. "Let's go over your goals, and then today or tomorrow, we can find your max weights and work out a circuit from there."

At least I now had a simple laid-out goal for this class. Should make it go faster at the very least.

Finally, the last hour of the day was behind me, and I started the walk home. Even with the distance, I'd have an hour or two before Mom got home where I could read uninterrupted. And she'd be exhausted anyway. She always was after a full day of work.

Not long into my walk, a small older truck pulled off to the side in front of me. Brock stuck his head out. "Acorn Townhomes?"

I nodded, slightly embarrassed, and he waved me to his truck. With sustained twenty-mile-per-hour winds, I wasn't gonna say no.

"Anyone walking this way is at that housing," he explained as I climbed in. "The ranch kids have trucks and drive."

"Oh," I responded. "Which one are you? Poor or a ranch kid?"

He laughed. "A little of both. But I live on a ranch."

His train of thought continued from the weight-lifting class. Macros and protein. None of it stuck. My mind was already settled on the journal in my pack rather than the exact things I knew I couldn't afford.

Brock dropped me at the entrance of the townhomes before driving on. His dad worked on the actual base, but they lived on a ranch—a detail I filed away for possible filming opportunities later. If he could get me on base, I could film the kind of video that generally did fairly well, as long as I was careful to not show anything that could be considered a breach of national security. I'd seen videographers go down hard for that.

Though after a year of videos and not nearly enough views, I wasn't sure how best to move forward there. I'd have to see what the old parts of the base had to offer. And how long it would take me to get a phone.

When I was finally home, I went straight to my room, pulled the box out of the closet again, and began to sort the textbooks by topic.

Biochem, toxins, purifications . . .

Then I used the empty shelves in the closet to stack the books. This was Sam's world, and I wanted to have some part in it. Figure out what had him so interested. The textbooks, which had been a terrible disappointment yesterday, were starting to have a purpose.

I flipped open the journal again and learned that Sam had started with *The History of Killer Diseases: A Look at Manmade and Natural Pandemics in the History of Mankind*. I scanned the page and flipped to the next—not reading much but noticing that one word populated those pages most: "Botulism."

Botulism was a rare and potentially fatal illness caused by a toxin produced by the bacterium Clostridium Botulinum.

Morbid. But with the way the book was sectioned off, I fell into it in minutes. I couldn't imagine fighting an illness before understanding what spread disease. Black Death? No thanks.

"Chuck!" Mom called up.

When had she come home?

"Dinner!"

Already?

I brought the book downstairs with me and settled in front of the TV with another TV dinner resting on the spool/coffee table.

"How was school?" she asked.

"Everyone's nice," I told her, knowing that was what she'd most care about. "How was work?"

She smiled a little. "Everyone's really nice."

But only two bites into her dinner, I watched her eyes droop. Listened to her cough around her Salisbury steak. After a moment of coughing, she got up, went into the kitchen, and I heard the faucet turn on. She came back with a big glass of water, as if that had ever done more than give some temporary relief.

My gut twisted. She needed to get in with a specialist again, and soon. She couldn't keep putting off appointments because of money. I had to do something. I couldn't just sit here and watch Mom get worse.

THREE

First period math, and I finished the homework while the teacher gave the lesson—benefit of being a unit ahead at my last school.

I had flipped open the journal when a small snort sounded behind me. Just as I started to turn, the teacher began speaking again, pulling my attention to the front of the room. I scribbled a few notes, which was stupid since I'd already finished the homework.

"Okay," Ms. Metts said, "go ahead and start on your assignment. I'd better not see a book or a phone until it's done. I'll be available for questions, but not rants about why you'll never need to know how to graph after leaving school."

"What about our math books? Since we can't have books out until we're done?" a guy asked. Two guys near him laughed quietly.

Ms. Metts just stared. "I'm going to assume you're smarter than that, Connor. Also, remember that I run with your mother in the mornings."

His grin fell, and I didn't even try to suppress my smile.

"He's always like that," a distinctly female voice whispered.

I turned to see wide gray-blue eyes framed by white-blonde hair with ash-colored roots. Just above her ears, her hair was shaved on both sides, showing off several piercings in each ear. Soft pink lips curved into a wry smile. My mouth dried out.

"Do you know that you and I have every single class together?" she said, a grin widening her cheeks.

Not possible. "I'd have noticed." *I think.*

One of her brows danced upward. A sly smile ticked on thin lips. "That's a terrible pickup line."

Heat flashed up my neck. "No, I just . . . it was . . ." *It was what?*

"I just kept expecting you to notice yesterday," she whispered.

"Stella?" Ms. Metts warned.

Teachers, I could handle. "I just did this unit in Arizona," I explained to Ms. Metts. "I was helping her with the slope on number twenty-one. That one was tricky."

Ms. Metts's shrewd teacher glare went back and forth between us. "Best to shift your desk a bit if you're going to help, then."

Ignoring the warmth on my face, I shifted my desk, and Stella did the same.

Stella . . . Old name, but also new and interesting.

"Good save," she whispered. "But the slope is seven over nine."

"Yeah," I whispered back. "I finished. Wait, you're not in my weight-lifting class."

"Yeah, that doesn't count. I would never, ever take a class like that. What are you reading?" she questioned.

"Nothing."

"Well, you've been here for a day, so you're not reviewing notes." She squinted at the worn cover. "Is that . . . your diary?"

"No, it's not mine. I mean it is, but I didn't write it. It's just a journal."

"Hand it over, I want the goss." Her eyes brightened. "Actually, never mind, that's a pretty big invasion of privacy. So whose is it?"

"It's no one who goes to this school."

"Oh! Then no harm, no foul. What deep, dark secrets are lurking inside?"

I rested a hand over Sam Miller's journal, feeling suddenly protective. "We just moved into the—"

"Low-income housing, yeah," she interrupted. "I overheard you in one of the classes yesterday."

"Paying attention?" I teased. I wasn't stupid. The new guy was extra interesting for about a week, maybe two. Then everyone went back to their groups, and I could disappear again. I half expected a blush or an apology.

"I deserved that," she said instead. "So . . . the book? When are you going to make time to tell me about it?"

"Really?" I asked.

"Sure." She smiled in a way that made my stomach flutter. Why was she so interested in Sam's journal? I guessed she was looking for excitement anywhere.

"Today? I'll show you at lunch? Old wing?" I couldn't imagine heading to the cafeteria with a journal and a girl on day two. There would be no flying under the radar after that kind of display.

"Are you asking because you know people sometimes go there to make out, or are you asking because it's quiet and you're avoiding getting to know anyone so you can maintain your quiet, mysterious vibe?" One of her brows arched upward again.

Of course I should have known that without those doors being locked, students would use that space once in a while. "Just looking for quiet."

"It's a date, new guy." She winked at me just as the bell rang.

Her pants were baggy and rolled up to show off a well-worn pair of white Doc Martens, and a plaid shirt that looked like a granddad shirt hung from the back of a worn green backpack.

She'd left the room before I realized that I should follow.

And yup. Stella was in each and every one of my classes until last period.

In math, I noticed her hair and piercings. In English, I stared at the wear on her Docs. In government, the way she wound her rings around her fingers. In IT, I noticed that she finished her coding in less than five minutes. For the rest of the class, her thumbs flew across her phone, her pale gray-blue eyes focused on the screen.

She nudged my shoulder once the bell rang for lunch. "Take me away, cowboy." She laughed as she spun out of the room.

Cowboy? I glanced down at my worn Vans and snug jeans. *It's a joke, you idiot.*

The hallways filled up as much as they ever did in a school that was nowhere near capacity.

"Stella!" a girl with dyed-black hair called from the top of the stairway. "Eat with us, betch."

"Got plans with the new guy!" She used both hands to gesture to me as if I were a statue or an oddity—I wasn't sure if I should be flattered or offended.

The girl flipped Stella off, and then her face turned into a smile when her attention moved to me. "Welcome to hell, Chuck!"

"Thanks?" Not the most original line, but at least I now had three other students I'd talked to.

The black-haired girl left.

"She used to have the center dyed green like Billie Eilish, but then Billie changed to blonde, and Cheyenne can't stand blonde."

"Okay." Because what else was I going to say? What girls did with their hair was foreign to me.

We passed the main office, and Stella whispered, "Go on in. I'll meet you there."

I glanced toward her as I moved to the doors to see her chatting up the front-office ladies who had a partial view of our entrance. Once again, I slipped through into a hallway that smelled of old dust. As much as I wanted to dart into a classroom, I didn't want Stella to waste lunchtime looking for me.

But now I felt like an idiot walking up the short hallway—three classrooms on one side, two on the other. Bathrooms with sinks that hit me mid-thigh and mini toilets. The tiles in there were a weird, faded peachy-pink color. How had this ever been an option for a public bathroom?

"Bathroom?" Stella asked, her voice echoing in the space. "Is that seriously where you're spending lunch?"

"N-no," I stammered as I spun to face her. "Sorry. I was looking around."

"Well, Ms. Parker at the front office kept watching me, so I had to pretend to go to the cafeteria before coming back this direction through the band room."

"Which classroom is never used?" I hitched my pack higher on my shoulder.

"Supplies are stored on the same side as the bathrooms, and students go to the third classroom on the other side to make out."

I stepped around her, realizing only when I was leaving that I'd been in the girls' bathroom. The door to the next classroom sat propped open. "You've lived here a while?" I asked her as we sat on the floor, stretching our legs out in front of us.

"My parents have been stationed here for, like, five years." Her eyes rolled, and her head matched the movement.

"So long?" We were never anywhere longer than two.

She let out a sigh that was more like a groan. "Yeah. My parents volunteered to stay here longer when they had a hard time finding higher-ranking officers to help keep the base going." Both hands were shoved through her long hair, pushing it off her face.

I almost told her about my dad, but that wasn't a topic I wanted to touch yet. "So, what's there to do around here?"

"Well, the part of town near the base is all but dead, so there are a lot of cool buildings around there to explore."

"I have a YouTube channel I used to do that on."

"Oohhhh." She immediately pulled out her phone, and I instantly regretted bringing it up.

"It's terrible. My videos." This was the worst. I should have never said anything. "I tried to monetize, but my phone was old, so my videos were crap. Also, I know the videos are just missing . . . something."

"Probably you don't like them because you're a beginner with good taste. Takes a while for your taste level to match your talent level." Her eyes were still on her phone. "Wait. Your phone *was* old?"

"It broke just before I left Arizona," I explained.

"That is terrible." She rested a hand on my arm and her face went solemn. "I'm so sorry for your loss."

I released a chuckle, trying not to think about her fingers against my arm. "Nah. It's fine. I just need a job so I can save up. I have a little over two hundred bucks now, but . . ." But sometimes I used my money for groceries,

30

and I wasn't about to blow it all on a refurbished phone from eBay or something.

"But that buys you a crap phone," she finished.

"What should I do for jobs?" I asked. "Like, is there a place that wouldn't be terrible?"

"Ha!" She nudged me with her elbow, and I was learning quickly that she didn't have a big zone of personal space. "All jobs suck. I'm gonna be a famous writer one day. I don't want someone else making my schedule for me."

"What do you write?" This didn't seem super feasible for me, even though I read a lot.

"Fanfic mostly, but that's what people are reading, you know? And I heard this author who makes bank say that she started with fanfic."

"Oh." I'd read my share. *Blade Runner* cyberpunk fanfiction mostly.

"You know Bonnie and Clyde?" But before I could answer, she kept talking. "They were horrid criminals, but people were, like, totally behind them. Didn't want them to get caught. When their car was towed through town with their bullet-ridden bodies, people wept and grabbed souvenirs. Isn't that wild? Like, the watch Clyde wore when he was killed sold for over a hundred thousand dollars in auction."

If I didn't already understand that Stella was different, this was my best clue.

"Oh!" She pulled up her phone again. "What's your YouTube channel?"

"LegendCityVids." And then I sighed because Stella was exactly right—I had good enough taste to know that my videos weren't as good as I wanted them to be.

"Ahh." She tapped on one of the videos. "Cool. But

yeah. We have better buildings around here. You gotta find some funds for your phone."

"And I need to make better videos." More than she knew.

"Oh crap!" She reached over and tapped the journal sitting in my lap. "You were gonna tell me about your diary."

"It's not mine." I shook my head. "I found it in the house where we live."

"Oh," she said.

"Well . . ." I set Sam's journal on my lap. "This guy is big into toxins and some other science stuff."

"Toxins?" The look in her eyes was close to . . . excitement?

"Yeah. He started because of a Boy Scout thing."

"There are a lot of those here." Her head fell forward in a partial nod.

"But he got his badge and then kept going. I'm just reading and along for the ride." I started opening the book. "It was left in my room."

"Cool."

The bell rang. Lunch had passed in a blink.

"Well, I'd ask for your number, but you don't have a phone." Stella stood. "And I'd write my number on your arm or something, but weight lifting would probably rub it off."

"After school, then?" I offered. "Or you could just . . . use paper."

Her face twisted up in an odd sort of smile. "What's the fun in that?" she asked as she sauntered out of the room.

Well, there was no fun in not having a phone either. So.

FOUR

Brock gave me and Stella a ride home. She got dropped at the gate to the base—apparently, she'd taken her mom's BMW off-roading and was no longer permitted to drive. Given what I knew of her so far, this wasn't surprising.

I had him drop me off at Guerra's, the taco shop. I was excited it was on the edge of town, so it would make the walk to work less terrible than McCallister's. But still, it was two miles each way.

When I walked into the taco shop, it smelled like deep fried dough and spiced meats. The floor was a little greasy, like all good hole-in-the-wall restaurants. Colorful walls and mariachi music that blasted over the speakers gave it an authentic feel.

"Hi," said a small-statured woman with graying hair and a tag that told me her name was Saya. "What can I get you?"

"Um, how about an application?" I asked, suddenly feeling very unprepared. "Are you hiring?"

"Sure," Saya said, "but by the looks of you, I'm guessing you're only available evenings and weekends."

I rubbed the back of my neck. "Yeah, I'm still in high school. But I have food service experience."

"All the high schoolers think they want to work here, get free tacos, and hang out with their friends that stop by. Oh, and they hate giving up their weekends. Never works out.”

“I’ll take all the hours I can get, I *need* this job.”

Just then a family of three walked in, the bell at the door announcing their arrival. Saya handed me an application and pointed to an empty booth with a chipped Formica tabletop. When I got to the phone number portion, I paused. That was going to be tricky. I could give her my mom’s number, but somehow that felt like I was already unreliable. She wouldn’t be able to call to have me cover extra shifts. I wrote “TBD” instead. Once the counter was free, I handed it to her.

“Okay.” She reviewed it. “What’s this?” She tapped where my phone number should have been. “How can I call you for an interview?”

“I . . . I don’t have a number right now. I’m saving up to get a phone.” I cringed. Money. Always money. Never enough and always unreachable. Everyone had cell phones. But not me! Everything about this was humiliating. I’d constantly smell like fried food, I’d have zero free time, and best of all, it would all be compensated at minimum wage. The absolute minimum.

“I never do this, because it never works out. Teens these days, they barely work and eat so many tacos, I end up losing money. That’s of course if they even show up!”

“I won’t be lazy. Or eat on the job,” I said, though I knew the last part was a lie.

Saya cocked her head sideways, sympathy etched into her face. “Do you know how to run a register?”

“I think so, I just need to see your POS system.”

“Come on back.” She waved me to the side of the counter and opened a door. “I’ll need you three days during the week. Weekends vary, but plan on most of them. I could use an extra hand. I'm getting a little too old to be running this sun up to sun down."

"Thank you!" I said with a little too much enthusiasm. "When can I start?"

"How about now? I'll train you today, then you're on your own tomorrow. First full day will be Saturday. And I'm guessing you had gym today. You'll need to be showered next shift."

"I promise. I won't let you down."

She spent the afternoon showing me which buttons to push to place each order. Which ones to press if someone wanted no onions or tomatoes—which in my opinion was insane. Who wouldn't want onions or tomatoes? Apparently a lot of people. After three hours, she sent me on my way, and I walked the two miles home.

* * *

When I got home, my arms still felt stiff after arm day in weight lifting, but my first couple days in school hadn't been as terrible as expected.

I opened the almost-empty fridge, but figured I could just wait until dinner. My stomach rumbled, but it didn't pay any bills around here, so . . .

With only a little reading for English, I could waste a few minutes and read a little more of Sam's journal.

Earned my merit badge today, but I'm not ready for the toxin project to be over. How many people can say they understand how to turn a bulging and compromised can of Big Boy Beans into something deadly? I don't wanna kill anyone or anything, but I need to play with this a little more. I know too much now to walk away. Thought of watering it down a bit—maybe make a sleep aid for my old cat or something.

I was glad he got his badge—and yeah, I didn't want to walk away from my LegendCityVids YouTube channel either. I'd put a lot of time into it. But now I kinda wanted to know if he'd been able to help his cat.

It would be a bit before Mom would get home, and there was nothing to clean because we had almost nothing in the house.

Dad would hate this place, but I didn't have to listen to him complain about it anymore. I didn't have to listen to him complain about anything anymore. I glanced up toward the backyard from where I sat on the vinyl couch. We'd need at least a weed whacker or something to keep up with the grass back there. It was dry and wild. The shed sat untouched.

As I stood from the couch and stretched, I found myself wondering what it would feel like to carefully work with something mostly benign—like a bulging botulism-infected can of generic beans—and turn it into something deadly. What would it be like to know how to put normal things together to make something extraordinary?

Mom and I hadn't yet managed to take something normal and make it amazing.

The handle of the door to the backyard stuck when I tried to turn it, so I re-gripped with both hands until the stiff handle gave way. Maybe there was a weed whacker out there. Or after what I'd found in my closet, maybe there was stuff in the shed, too.

I watched for snakes as I moved through the grass— they generally ran away, but no one liked to be surprised.

Fortunately, I ran into no snakes, but the second I opened the old shed door, I knew the place had to be filled with spiders. There was no law that said I had to clean this place out, no one offering to pay me a thousand bucks to dig around in this mess, but the stacks of old boxes and haphazard yard tools begged to be dug through.

An old army rucksack sat on a shelf that was bolted to the wall—the green of the pack layered with so much dust, it blended into the wood.

A weed whacker sat near the front, looking a little more usable, so maybe I could turn the yard into . . . something. But after the boxes in the house, I had to know if anything out here belonged to Sam. He'd messed around with all sorts of cool stuff, and he had to have tools for that kind of thing.

Leaning into the shed as far as I could without fully committing myself to the miserable space, I grabbed a box and jumped back outside. Snakes, I could deal with. They were generally terrified of a human and fast enough to get away. Spiders could jump. On me. And had too many legs for something that was alive. No thank you.

Two more boxes rested inside, and I stood in the doorway, trying to force my eyes to adjust to the dim light let in by the few cracks in the wood walls and the doorway that I filled. Craning to the right, I peered up at the ceiling. I mean, cobwebs freaking everywhere!

You got this, Chuck. You got this.

At least no one from school was watching me dart in and out of there like a three-year-old stealing candy from the corner store. I grabbed another box, spun, and set it outside next to the first. One to go.

You've done two, you idiot. Get the last box.

I rubbed my hands together, jumped in, slid my fingers under the box, and nothing happened. *Holy crap, what is in here?* I hefted, my arms and shoulders still aching from weight lifting, and stumbled back out of the shed with the heavy box in my arms.

Bug spray had to go on the grocery list. Once that old shed got a good dousing, I could get in there and clean it out for real. For now, I just wanted the contents of the boxes. There was no way I was bringing the dirt-crusted cardboard into the house, not with Mom's lungs and her already spending all day cleaning.

The box tops were just folded, not taped, so I pulled open the smaller one.

A towel. Another towel. Another towel . . . I tossed them in a pile. We could wash those up for sure. And then an old keyboard. Like the light-tan ones that came with the ancient IBM computers. A faded piece of tape was pasted across the top of the plastic, and I could barely make out an "S" and "Mill."

No idea what I'd ever use that for, but still, I paused as I held it. Sam was more real now that I might be holding something else that was his. If the keyboard was his, the journal might be older than I thought. I pulled out a few more towels, a bleach-stained sheet, and a few T-shirts.

Nirvana, Atari, Sega ringer tees . . . Were these Sam's? Or did they used to be?

The second box looked like piles of the crap that were left behind when someone cleaned out a room. Lint. Random desktop organizers. Two bags with an assortment of pens, pencils, markers . . . and at the bottom was an old computer tower, open and with some missing components.

My heart raced a few beats, and I tore into the last box. A decrepit *Star Wars* blanket was wrapped around a bulky old monitor and a few random internal computer bits.

Was this the rest of the computer?

As carefully as possible, I put all the computer parts in one box and hefted it to my room. I went back for the towels that seemed usable, as well as the T-shirts, and threw them in the wash before sprinting back upstairs to see if I could get the computer put back together. Even if it was terrible, it was better than the NO COMPUTER I currently had.

I'd need small screwdrivers and probably some canned air to blow the dust out of the thing, but I still got the pieces spread out on the rickety desk in my room. The chances of the thing working were slim, but it'd give me something to do. I sat down and got to work, using an old T-shirt to carefully wipe the dust off the smaller pieces. Time faded as I concentrated on what went where.

"Chuck!" Mom called from downstairs. "Dinner!"

The light outside had dimmed, and while I still had a bit to go, the computer was coming along. I tromped down the narrow stairs.

"Pizza tonight," Mom said as I hit the bottom.

My mouth watered, even though I'd seen the frozen pizza box on the counter. I'd come to embrace the crappy frozen pizza for dinner, and I looked forward to it.

She set a slice on a napkin, her features looking sunken and . . . tired. This couldn't go on. She couldn't go on like this. I couldn't get a real job until after high school. Feeling this helpless was terrible on so many levels.

"You okay?" I asked.

"Oh, I'm fine." But her voice had that tired, scratchy quality that said she was not fine.

I should probably be looking for more work rather than putting what was hopefully Sam's computer back to life.

"Work gave me a phone," Mom said with a smile. "I wiped mine. You can have it."

Well, a day sooner and I could have avoided the awkward conversation with Saya. But also, I think she only gave me the job because she pitied me. Pity for the poor. In that moment, I decided not to tell Mom about my job. It would just make her sad, too, that I was working. I could only handle so many sympathetic looks in one day.

"Oh," I said, though I nearly choked on that one word. I didn't think I'd be able to have a phone for months. "Awesome. Thank you."

I'd have my books again and a way to contact people. Mom's phone was a small step up from my last one, so maybe I could check out some of the abandoned parts of the old military base that were no longer fenced in. See if I could squeeze a few more bucks out of YouTube. Figure out how to make better videos.

But that night, after pizza, and after downloading my apps and resetting every stupid password—because who could remember those things?—I used a fork and a butter knife to put more of the computer together and then I kept reading in Sam's journal.

Sam earned his badge for microbiology.

He didn't stop working on the biochem projects.

His parents tried to stay living in the same house. They did not argue less.

I wondered if having a project those last few years my parents were together would have helped me feel better or maybe made them pass faster. Too late for that now.

* * *

The next day at school seemed to fly by. Stella was gone, so I actually concentrated on my classes. Plus, I needed to get all of my homework done every chance I got. Working while in school was tricky.

After weight lifting, I asked Brock if he'd wait for me to shower before heading home.

"Oh, dude, I'm sorry, I can't," he said. "I have an orthodontist appointment that I can't be late for. Broke my retainer. Need a new one."

"No worries," I said. But I was worried. It was now raining buckets. What was worse, show up wet or dirty? I chose wet.

The walk to Guerra's was miserable. I could walk in heat, snow, wind, cold—anything but rain. Each step threatened to soak my shoes completely through. What would Saya say when I walked through the doors sopping wet? I shoved my hand into my pocket, retrieved my cell phone, and glanced at the time. I was going to be late. I couldn't risk it getting ruined, so I slipped it deep into my backpack.

The sidewalks were dangerously close to the road, no shoulder to speak of whatsoever. If this had been a movie, a car would have driven by and sprayed me with a massive puddle. But if this were a movie, I'd somehow hit the jackpot and find my mom a cure. A jackpot. That's all I needed. Fiction was always better than real life.

I stood under the awning, shaking off like a dog and debating if I should even go in. My first day of work and it felt like I'd blown it. Time to face the music.

The bell dinged behind me and Saya looked at me with wide eyes.

"Chuck! Don't come one step closer. You're soaked!"

I stepped back onto the mat. "I'm sorry, my ride canceled."

"And late." She frowned. "This is why I don't hire teenagers. Unreliable and always with an excuse. You failed me on what was supposed to be your first day."

"Supposed to be?" My stomach dropped. "Please I—"

My phone rang from inside my backpack. Saya

cocked her head to the side like she had when she felt sorry for me and hired me. This time her expression was decidedly different.

"I thought you didn't have a phone. That was all an act to gain my sympathy, wasn't it?"

"No." I shook my head, silently pleading with whoever was calling to hang up. "It's not like that. My mom, she gave me her old one last night. I swear."

Saya held up her hand and shook her head. "I have zero tolerance for tardiness. And even less tolerance for *liars*."

"I'm not lying!" I didn't know why I was still trying; she'd made up her mind. "My mom, she got her work phone yesterday and gave me her old one."

Saya opened the cash register and pulled out a lousy twenty-dollar bill and walked around the counter. "For yesterday."

I accepted it because I certainly wasn't too proud to say no. "I really am sorry," I said, then walked out, that stupid ding announcing my departure.

The evening had been a sad disaster. I got home with barely any time to spare. I took a hot shower and slogged into bed. I didn't even bother saying hi to my mom or eating dinner. I was actually excited for school to take my mind off things the next day. Plus, Stella would be back.

As soon as Ms. Metts stopped lecturing about graphs and assigned our homework, Stella scooted her desk next to mine.

I slipped my phone from my pocket and flashed it to her under the table.

"Moving up in the world, eh?" she whispered with a smile.

Pale blue eyeshadow today. She shoved her white-blonde hair back off her face, showcasing the shaved sides of her head and the large black spots of her earrings on petite ears.

"Mom got a phone from her work," I explained.

Stella snorted. "Yeah, always be skeptical of that. If they want you to have a phone, they want to be able to call you."

I hadn't thought of that. I'd just been glad to have my own phone. I stared at the dark screen. Was this a good or a bad thing?

"You could make more videos," Stella suggested. "I

could show you some of the cooler spots to film. There's nothing else to do in this town, and there are a lot of abandoned places."

My attention snapped from my phone to her face. Was she just thinking we'd hang out, or was this something else? "Uh, yeah."

She leaned over her desk and started in on the first homework problem, writing out the equation in small, tidy handwriting that didn't quite match the rest of her. "How goes the spying?"

"Spying?"

"Snooping, journal reading . . ." Her smooth lips curved upward, but her attention remained on her paper.

"Oh yeah." I'd been so consumed with letting Saya down and losing my job, I hadn't even found time to mess with the computer. "I found some stuff in the shed."

The bell rang, and in two quick moves, Stella had her stuff packed in her old backpack.

I was two steps behind—though that seemed to happen around her.

"What kind of stuff?"

"An old computer. T-shirts. Towels. Some office crap. Tools."

We walked side by side down the hall to government together. Easy when we had the same schedule.

"Were the T-shirts any good?"

I turned sideways and pulled out the bottom of the Atari T-shirt.

She nodded approvingly. "Nice."

I shrugged. Clothes were clothes. But it did feel good to have something different. "I need a few smaller tools to finish putting the computer together."

"Oh!" She grabbed my arm, her slim fingers stronger than I was expecting, despite what a force she was. "Let's ask Mr. Lester if we can take a few tools home. I bet he'd even give us extra credit if we could get it working."

"That'd be cool." I hadn't thought to ask someone if I could borrow tools. I'd only been wondering where and how I could buy what I needed or use what Mom and I already had.

"Sweet. I'll just follow you home today after school. Brock won't mind giving us a ride again."

Stella stopped to chat to a girlfriend in the hallway, and I flopped into my seat. She was coming home after school with me. To my house. Stella.

She swung into the classroom a few minutes later, her hair swooping in behind her, her T-shirt tucked into her jeans, showing off her waist, and I stared at my lap. Probably a lot of guys had been taken in by her at one point or another, and she was far too smart to be oblivious. The thing I wondered was how obvious was it that I had a hard time *not* staring when she was in the room? The end of school couldn't come quick enough.

* * *

Brock waved at me and Stella as he pulled away, his little truck humming along the road. My heart dropped a little as we passed the turnoff to Guerra's. I'd told Brock during weight lifting that I didn't get the job when he asked about needing to be dropped off there. Last thing I wanted to do was tell him I got fired.

"Wow. I always forget what dumps these places are," Stella said with a sigh, her eyes taking in the pathetic rows of townhomes.

Heat rushed up from my chest, up my neck, and covered my face. "Yeah."

"But whatever. We have better things—" She turned

toward me, and her face fell. "Crap. Put my foot in it, huh?"

I shrugged because there wasn't much else to do. What could I say? It was a heck of a lot nicer than the last few places we lived. The last thing I needed, or wanted, was Stella's pity. I knew enough to understand that if both her parents were officers on base, her housing situation was far different than mine.

"Okay, Chuck. Let's look at the hunk you found in your shed." She slapped my arm before walking up the short driveway.

Right.

"So," I said as I shoved my key into the lock, wiggling it around to find where the key would catch. "When do you get your car back?"

"Soon, I think." She folded her arms. "I just don't like stopping for the MPs when they're in a mood and don't just wave me through. Dad got in trouble, and I got my keys taken away. That, and I like driving on the canal roads and the fields. Mom doesn't like her precious car going there." Military brat through and through.

"Ah," she continued. "Man, these are *all* the same." Her attention moved over the worn space. "There are a couple of these loops where no one lives. You can imagine the parties that get thrown there."

Yeah, I could imagine. Not my scene. I had spent too many nights listening to my dad slur and slobber and rant to ever want to go down that path.

She started up the stairs. "Which room is yours?"

"The one that faces the back." If I were a normal guy in a normal house, I might be scanning real quick through my head to remember if I left out anything embarrassing, but I really didn't have a whole lot. One suitcase of clothes. One of bedding. And the rest was Sam's stuff and the odd mash-up of things that came with the house.

"This thing is ancient!" she called, and only then did I realize I still stood at the bottom of the stairs and Stella had to be in my room staring at the old computer.

I grabbed two Shastas, feeling a twinge of guilt I was raiding our meager stash of soda from the fridge, and walked up the stairs like I wasn't freaking out that Stella was in my room. I hoped she wouldn't turn her nose up at the off-brand soda.

"Like, I've always wanted to do my writing on a type-writer, but this is just a little step above that, huh?"

"Yeah," I answered. Even the monitor was one of those old boxy ones.

Stella already had the tools out of her pocket. She sat cross-legged on my office chair, both knees sticking out of the holes in her jeans.

"Stop staring and get over here," she said as she blew off one of the circuit boards.

I set a soda on the desk and then sat on my bed—so much lower than where she sat.

"I super hope this thing runs." She bit her lip as she gently slid the circuit board into the computer. "It would be so sick to have a vintage computer. Hey, maybe you could even make a video of this old clunker for your channel."

"How do you know where things go?" I asked, taking a long drink.

Stella shrugged. "Mom's in tech. She's always built computers, so I used to think they were for taking apart."

"Did you ever take one apart that—"

"That I shouldn't?" She paused and looked at me for a moment. "Oh yeah. Mom had to take a day of leave, and she made me help her put it back together."

"How old were you?"

"Ten."

When I was ten, we were in Germany. Mom spent a lot of time in and out of the hospital. That's just before Dad decided he no longer wanted to be in the military, though it really wasn't up to him, and we lost Mom's health care. "Wow," was all I said.

"Ever since then, Mom's been bringing old parts home to me—once she got permission, of course." Stella scoffed as she attached a small fan. "Top-secret stuff is imprinted on some of those things, you know."

"Ever find anything cool?" I asked.

She shook her head. "They never let Mom bring home anything that holds memory. Just the other pieces."

Of course, that made better sense.

And then I found myself wanting to know all the places she'd lived. About her mom. Her dad. "Do you have siblings?"

"Oh no. I wasn't even planned. I'm all they can handle."

Her brows pinched together, and she took a picture of the insides of the computer with her phone before pulling up the outer casing to the machine.

I stood. "Need help?"

"Just if you'd hold this while I screw it in?" she asked. "Also, there's a strange attachment thing in there. That's what I took a picture of. I think it's a special messaging thing—like dark web kind of stuff."

"You're kidding." That wasn't a real thing.

"Totally not kidding." Her brows waggled. "If this computer was Sam's, he was maybe into some shady sh—"

Her phone shattered her sentence with "The Imperial March" from *Star Wars*.

Stella answered. "What's up, Mom? At a friend's . . . helping with some tech stuff . . . Yeah, a new guy at school who needs a computer . . . I don't know . . . She works on base or something . . . You cannot be serious . . ."

I held my breath.

"Now?"

Instead of staring *and* listening, I took another long drink, so I was just listening.

"Fine, but I'm gonna need a ride if you want me there on time." Her voice was so calm while saying things to her mom that I couldn't imagine saying to mine.

There was no way to make out words, just tone, so the only thing I could tell from the other person on the phone was that she was not happy. So much for making a decent first impression on Stella's parents.

She shoved her phone back in her pocket. "Gotta head. Doctor's appointment. I forgot. Mom's pissed."

"Thanks for your help."

"Just screw the outside on—if you want. It's not like the cover is necessary. There are a few loose connections, so I can solder it if we need. Maybe don't screw on the outside yet and we can get some smaller tools from school."

"I'll keep off the top."

"Thanks for the soda." She held up the can as if giving me a salute, and I followed her down the stairs. Some kind of fruity smell wafted behind her.

"I'll walk you out."

"Such a gentleman," she teased as I held open the front door.

"I could walk you to your—"

"Oh no. You do not need to meet my mother," she answered as she continued down my driveway. "And don't forget that you didn't do your math in class today."

As soon as she left, I texted her a thanks. She responded back with a link to one of her fan-fiction sites and her profile.

My friends read my stuff and tell me they're sure I'll be famous one day. Just so you know what friend qualifications are.

That felt easy enough. I sat down to read one over a cup of noodles—my stomach was not going to wait until Mom got home—and plowed through it. She'd mentioned Bonnie and Clyde, and she hadn't been lying. This one set them in an alternate universe with lasers and armor, but the basics were the same.

Screw over the people with money, give money to their families, kill more than they intended in the process. Like a Robin Hood type of story.

Her writing was good, but I couldn't help but wonder how she'd gotten started writing in the first place. I finished dinner, then made my phone read me another one of Stella's stories as I sat at the computer, blowing out the last few attachments and plugging the thing in.

Then I sat back and flipped the On switch. The screen buzzed to life—a green hue over the gray background.

But . . . nothing else.

Maybe the thing had no operating system.

The windows of my bedroom were dark. Stella's second story had wrapped up. Mom coughed in her room down the hall. My whole evening had been a blur.

Maybe tomorrow's lunch would be spent with the IT teacher. Now that I knew the computer turned on, and that there was an extra something inside of it, I had to know what was on the thing.

"Sam, was this yours? Why do I feel like this is yours?" I asked the room.

I sat in front of the computer. Where was he now?

What had happened to Sam Miller? How long ago had he lived here? Why were some of his things left, but no one else's?

If I could just get this computer talking to me, I might be able to get some answers. Also, I needed it to be Sam's in a way I couldn't quite explain. Just a few days of reading about his life had me wondering what else he'd faced, what he'd done with his time, and if I could use his life as a blueprint for mine.

After willing the computer to roar to life, I finally gave up and went to YouTube for answers. There were a lot of suggestions, but nothing that got me more than the same blinking cursor.

I rubbed the sleep from my eyes as I shuffled through the hallway before first period. I'd stared at that computer screen for hours the night before, but all I'd gotten was a small blinking green cursor. And then I'd laid in bed, feeling almost as if I were doing the same thing. Stella had said there were probably still missing connections.

Fourteen YouTube videos and too much caffeine had gotten me nothing but a crap night's sleep and a blinking box taunting me. Brock waved, and I think I nodded back, but the lights were too bright, the talking too loud, and the lockers slamming felt like cymbals between my ears.

"Morning, sunshine!" Stella chirped as I slumped into my seat.

"Mmph," I responded.

She leaned across the aisle. "I showed my mom a picture of that computer part."

"Oh." I slipped my math book from my backpack and dug around the bottom of my bag for a pencil. Only pens. Of course.

"She got all—"

"Stella?" Ms. Metts snapped as the bell rang.

"After class," Stella mouthed to me.

After Ms. Metts started lecturing about parabolas,

my mind finally focused on Stella's words. Her mom got all *what* over the small box? What?

I'd nearly forgotten that Stella's mother was a tech person. I figured the thing was just old. That it was a part people didn't use much anymore or something.

I'd left my last school in the middle of parabolas, and between Stella's half-spoken revelation and my lack of sleep, Ms. Metts was about as useful as the YouTube videos I'd watched the night before. The bell rang before she stopped showing examples of curvy lines on graphs, and my pen fell to the floor when I jerked to attention.

"And Mom got all uptight, like where did I find this picture and what was it for, and I had to tell her it was for a school assignment because her eyes got all big like parents' eyes sometimes get, right?"

We'd made it to the hallway, only my brain was just now catching up.

"Anyway." Stella turned and walked sideways, facing me. "Mom said it was a thing for covert communication. It encrypts messages. Super-old junk. Ha!"

"Interesting," I said automatically, even though I now vaguely remembered Stella bringing that up the day before.

Her brows just rose, and her eyes didn't move from mine. "That's what I thought too."

"Not just for movies?" I guessed.

"Handsome *and* smart," she teased with a laugh.

But her words wrapped themselves around a totally different part of my brain. The part that found Stella more interesting every time we talked. That still thought about her teasing touch the first day we had lunch together.

"So apparently that box is something that helps a computer attach to a different part of the internet, even with regular internet connection."

We turned into the government classroom.

"Wild, huh?"

"Wild," I agreed. *Handsome and smart.* She thought I was handsome and smart.

"Do you have internet?" she asked.

"Tomorrow," I said. "Mom talked to someone who said we should be able to get online tomorrow, but we won't have Wi-Fi for a while."

Stella snorted. "That old thing won't have connections for Wi-Fi."

"Right." That's something I should have known. Probably would have known if I hadn't been up all night. And if Stella hadn't been walking so close to me. "I was literally up half the night on YouTube trying to get the computer to do anything."

We sat. "You really want the computer to be Sam's."

No question. "Yeah."

"Why?"

There it was. The thing I wasn't exactly ready to admit to her, let alone myself. But she was so blunt, so direct; she put me on the spot in a way that made me feel like I *had* to spill my guts. She'd make a great cop if she weren't so anti everything. "He is—or was, I'm not sure—kinda like me. His dad royally sucked and made Sam's and his mom's lives . . . hard. Eventually his dad was gone, and it was just Sam and his mom. She wasn't sick, but his cat was. And he lived in my place. It's like we shared a room, like brothers."

"You know, he might not have even lived there."

"Yeah." I felt stupid. I shouldn't have said anything.

"The books and his journal have some borderline shady stuff in them. He could have put them in a house that wasn't his." Instead of her voice dropping in worry, it rose in excitement. "Your house was where he hid all this stuff."

"I mean, I guess, yeah. Makes sense. If he was into some shady crap, I don't see why not."

She slugged my arm. "You're worthless without sleep."

Maybe a little, but it was more than that. Mom's coughing, new house, new school, new and spectacularly failed job . . . it felt like I hadn't taken a full breath since just after Dad left.

A woman I didn't recognize stood at the front of the class. "Mr. Bagley isn't here today. I have a packet on introducing bills in the House and how they get passed on to the Senate. Phones are okay to use for help. Your teacher said you can work in pairs."

"Perfect." Stella scooted her desk next to mine before the sub could take attendance. "You have the journal?" she asked.

I nodded, but the teacher came by and set a packet on each of our desks. As she moved around the room, I slipped my hand into my backpack and felt around for the leather book.

There was no good way to read the journal without it being obvious, but five minutes into our packet work, the sub was behind her Kindle at the teacher's desk.

Stella held her hand out, palm up, and wiggled her fingers. I took the journal off my lap and handed it to her. Immediately, she slid her lithe figure lower in the chair and rested it on our desks.

I glanced at the sub, knowing the last thing Mom needed was for me to get in trouble at school, but clearly whatever she was reading was really good because her eyes didn't veer up from her Kindle.

"Check this out." Stella pointed to the next journal entry.

I've done it. I've purified the bacteria and ended up with crystalized botulism toxin. Bet my parents had no idea Boy Scouts would lead to this. But I think it's more. I've used a combination of hot and cold and made this stuff into small crystals. My uniform of choice is a bandanna with a medical mask over it. I duct-taped my long-sleeve shirt cuffs to rubber gloves and I taped the ankles of my jeans to Ziplocs over my shoes. This stuff can't be eaten or breathed in. Death will follow.

A skull and crossbones drawn in thick black marker bled through the bottom of the page.

"I've heard of that. Isn't it, like . . . deadly?" Stella asked.

"It's for sure dangerous. What was he thinking?"

Stella shoved the journal my direction and pulled out her phone. She turned a page in our packet just as the teacher peered over her Kindle. Stella won at being sneaky. After nudging my arm, she flipped her phone toward me, showcasing the definition she'd found on the cdc.gov website.

Botulism ("BOT-choo-liz-um") is a rare but serious illness caused by a toxin that attacks the body's nerves and causes difficulty breathing, muscle paralysis, and even death. This toxin is made by Clostridium botulinum and sometimes Clostridium butyricum and Clostridium baratii bacteria.

She switched to another window in her phone's browser.

Although **botulism can** cause severe and prolonged symptoms, most people recover completely from the illness. Early treatment reduces the risk of permanent disability and death. However, even with treatment, **bot-**

ulism can be fatal. Without treatment, more than *fifty percent of people with* **botulism would** die.

And someone let this guy do this for a Boy Scout project? Maybe the Scouts weren't quite what I thought they were. I opened Sam's journal wider. The more I learned, the weirder his journal and the books and the computer and everything became.

I'm going to look into selling this to some research facilities, universities, that kind of thing. Mom and Dad say I need college to go somewhere in life, and I'm about to prove them wrong.

Sell it? To research institutions? How much money could someone make doing that?

He had my attention now. I flipped through the journal and scanned the pages, but didn't see more mention of universities or research institutions. That was fine. I could use a computer at the library to look some stuff up. Maybe not the school library, since every other search led to a dead end of *RESTRICTED CONTENT*, but we'd passed a small library coming into town. The public library's searches were always far better than school ones. I needed to get a card anyway.

"I can't believe you just found this in your room," Stella whispered. "I wanna know this dude."

Her and me both. The journal felt like far more than a journal now. Now, the words on these pages felt like a road map to the way out. Mom's way out. Money could fix anything, and this journal was showing me just how simple that fix could be. Basically, a step beyond a Boy Scout merit badge, and I was in. And Sam had mapped a lot of it out for me. I wouldn't know until I'd read the whole journal, but still.

"I wanna come over so bad and figure out that computer, but Mom is still pissed at me for forgetting my doc appointment yesterday. Military, man. She's like, it looks bad if you're late. But why not Dad? Why doesn't it look bad for him and just her?"

I didn't have any answers for her, so I just shrugged. "Oh. I read the Bonnie and Clyde with lasers. It was really good."

"Aw," she said, a teasing edge to her voice. "You *do* wanna be my friend."

I did. I just stared in response, but Stella didn't even pause. Clearly my input wasn't fully needed.

"Call me, though, okay?" She began twisting her hair behind her head. "Like, I'll see if I can figure out how to get that computer up. Oh. Tomorrow. Because internet." With a slip of a pen, her hair magically stayed in the twist and up off her neck.

I was learning that Stella's nonstop talking was her excitement taking over.

So, I could do the library after school, but it would mean a lot of walking.

During lunch, a text from Mom came through.

> *Mom: Lungs not cooperating today. Fighting with insurance over a disease they don't have in their database. I'll be at home. Let me know if you need a ride.*
>
> *Chuck: I'm good, thanks.*

Unfair. That's all I could think through the rest of the school day. Because we didn't have enough money to just pay for her visits, we had to have the insurance on our side, but we rarely did. Plus the ninety-day waiting period for insurance from her new job was too long.

In weight lifting, I added extra on to every circuit. My body ached by the time I finished, and I'd soaked through my clothes. At least it was the last class of the day. I'd need to take my gym clothes home to wash anyway.

And even though I told Mom I didn't need a ride, the old Ford Escort sat in the pickup line anyway. I opened the passenger's side door, but Mom climbed out of the driver's side. As soon as she was standing, coughs curled her over herself again.

"Can you—" But she was cut off by another round of coughing.

Too many nights I'd sat in my room listening to her lungs trying to drown her. Way too many nights.

Without a word, I got out of the car and held the passenger's side door until she got in. I took a long breath in to prevent myself from slamming it in frustration. No way was I going to try and glance around to know if I'd been seen. If Mom had been seen coughing as if she were out of air. I didn't want to see pity or worry or disdain. I got behind the wheel and started toward home, Mom wheezing the whole time.

"I'm gonna get us Taco Bell," I told her as I turned around. Truthfully, I wanted to try Guerra's and pay with the same twenty she'd given me. But I wasn't ready to show my face there. "No one has to cook or do dishes or whatever. I have money," I said before she could pull out her bag and wallet.

Every dollar in my account was important, but tonight, I just wanted to do one stupid thing to help take care of it, and if Taco Bell was what I could afford to do, that's what I'd do. God and everyone knew I was helpless most of the time.

One day, I'd be able to set her up somewhere nice. With good doctors who had a chance to actually get to know her before we moved again.

When we got home, our stomachs already filled with

quasi-Mexican food, Mom went to her room, and I went to mine. I grabbed Sam's journal out of my backpack and started reading.

If he was working toward creating a toxin to sell to researchers, there was no reason I couldn't do the same thing. Tomorrow would be spent trying to get this computer working, hoping it was Sam's, and finding a way to contact possible interested parties for a toxin I was determined to learn how to make.

SEVEN

Sam had accidentally killed his cat. He'd been going for just enough toxin to help it rest longer, and the cat had stopped breathing. In the journal, Sam said the cat should have been put down already, but that his mom couldn't do it. Still . . . he'd killed his own cat. And he seemed sad, but not devastated. *The cat was old and sick*. But it had still been Sam's pet, and he didn't feel *any* responsibility. No guilt? He just moved on?

But, like Sam, a part of me realized what a big thing this was. Sam Miller had created a toxin powerful enough to kill, and he'd done it in or near his own house after reading some books. This couldn't be right. It didn't compute in my brain. I lifted the journal and pinched the unread entries in between my fingers. There was a lot more to this Sam Miller. I was drawn to find out, but I vowed never to kill a cat.

The day flew by and by period four, there was still no Stella, and we'd been so busy I hadn't had more chances to finish Sam's journal. But with lunch to myself, and with me forgetting to pack anything, I sat in an old empty classroom and kept reading it.

Would it just end? Would I know what happened to him? I flipped to the back where the badge was taped and then slowly turned pages until I saw writing again, but quickly shut the book. Even with someone's journal, going to the end felt like cheating. I was more than two-thirds of the way there anyway. I quickly turned back to where I'd stopped reading.

I used the toxin to kill the rats that were coming into the yard around Mom's compost piles. I can't believe I made this poison. This all started for a stupid badge, and now we don't need to call for an exterminator. I know that universities study this kind of thing, so I'm hoping I can maybe sell some of it to them for research. I know they can make it on their own, but maybe that's against some rules or something? I also know that different strains can have different results, so yeah . . . if I could earn enough that I don't have to go to college, that would be amazing.

Besides, my process is just a little different than anything I've seen. The crystalline bits at the end don't feel normal, but are clearly effective, as the rats are now dead. So I'm still sad about Mr. Whiskers, but at least I was able to use that same toxin for good.

I read over the paragraphs again. And then again. I just needed enough money for Mom to see specialists who could help her lungs. That was all. And yeah, Sam talked about the financial possibility before, but not in such specific terms. I could reach out just to see if some research institutions or universities were interested.

With so many thoughts and ideas and wants spinning through my head, there was no way I'd make it to the end of the school day, so I slipped out one of the bathroom windows in the old wing of the school. With all the movies that used those as escape or break-in routes, you'd think people would check the bathroom windows, but they didn't. I'd gotten into a lot of old and abandoned buildings that way.

The library was a two-mile walk, and the wind pummeled me the whole way. But I wasn't going to let this idea slip away. I could create a new email and check universities that had programs for biochem or something. I hadn't made anything yet, but I had Sam's instructions in my backpack. He'd done it. If he could do it, I could do it. He'd started with just an idea. I was starting with an idea *and* his step-by-step instructions.

The walk into town was windy and the spring blossoms made my eyes itch. I was used to this after Arizona, but it wasn't like I'd lived there all that long, and the heat bothered me more than anything.

By the time I made it to the glass doors of the library, the wind had died down and I paused for a moment in the two-story-tall foyer. After a few long, pollen-free breaths, I headed toward the help desk.

A woman with chunky glasses and fewer wrinkles than I expected from a librarian was stacking books on a cart behind the counter. She was probably younger than my mom.

"Excuse me?" I leaned on the counter.

She paused and caught my eye.

"What do I need to do to get a library card?" I asked.

The woman's eyes narrowed. "You a high school student?"

"Yes, ma'am."

Her eyes narrowed further. "Shouldn't you be in school?"

"Uh." I swallowed. "I'm a senior. My day ends at lunch."

She sighed and pushed her brown hair over her ears. "Your student ID works as your library card."

"Serious?"

"Serious," she answered with a smile.

"I just need to, um . . . use a computer for a bit?"

She gestured to the large sign showing the way up to the public computers. "If people start to line up, be mindful of how much longer you stay on, okay? But it's usually slow this time of day."

"Got it." I moved through the area with the lofty ceiling—large origami structures hung from the skylights. The stairs were open to the children's reading area and the help desk below. Old brick on the outside. Modern on the inside. Very cool library for a sleepy town.

I sat at a computer with a screen that faced a wall with no windows, opened Gmail, and then stopped.

What kind of username should I have? Not my name, but a made-up name? Something else? I had to be taken seriously by universities and research places. This step forward could be the step that would change my life. Mom's life. No more counting pennies for things like Taco Bell, full-coverage insurance, and much fewer doctor's appointments.

Raymond . . . Cartwright?

That seemed respectable enough. Sounded older. I had Google make me a fake person with graying hair to use as an avatar for the new account.

Once the address was created, I sat and stared at a blank email. What was I supposed to write? How was I supposed to ask if they wanted to buy a deadly toxin from me? One I hadn't started making yet? One I wasn't even sure I *could* make.

I opened a new browser window and started researching universities that might find the botulism useful. There was no point in asking more than four or five—at least at first. But if I could use some old canned-goods or something and make money off it? That would be way easier than breaking into abandoned buildings for YouTube videos that no one watched.

I had to just write the email already and get this thing started.

To Whom It May Concern —

I am the owner of a small business interested in supplying your university with strains of botulism for use in study. My lab is equipped to supply any amount needed. If this is something you have need of, please respond to this email.

Thank you,
Raymond Cartwright

Simple. Easy. And hopefully would be a way for me to move forward. I'd figure out how to deliver the stuff later. Maybe I could hire someone to be Raymond or something. Maybe I shouldn't have used a Google-made face for the avatar.

Too late now. The batch of emails had gone out.

My phone vibrated on the desk.

Stella: Mom gave me a day off of school. I have the car. You think we can get that computer up and running?

Chuck: I'm at the library downtown right now.

Stella: I could give you a ride home? That's a walk. What are you doing there?

Chuck: Long story. Would love a ride. Thanks.

My body vibrated from nerves about the emails I'd just sent, from Stella picking me up, and also from the possibility that she and I could figure out a little more about the computer in my room. But also the fact that I didn't feel safe just texting her what I'd been doing. Breaking into buildings that were never used was one thing, but creating an online identity to sell a toxin I wasn't sure I could make felt like a whole different level. This whole thing seemed illegal.

But I was doing it for good causes. Wasn't I? Selling it to reputable universities and using that money to help my mom. Little did I realize a battle was beginning in my mind. Fortunately for now, the illegal stuff was weighed down by my mom's sickness and curiosity of what came next for Sam. I was in a living Choose Your Own Adventure book. Suddenly I sat forward as panic welled from deep within. Was there a way to get the emails back?!

As I walked to the front door of the library, I wondered what on earth I was starting.

* * *

Sunshine came sideways into my room, thickening the air with heat and making it seem as if my overhead light wasn't on at all. The blade of light swathed over my bed and onto the floor.

Wisps of hair fell over Stella's face as her brows wrinkled together in concentration. The tip of her tongue played with her top lip as she tightened a screw with a screwdriver that looked as if it were designed to work on glasses.

"Almost there," she partially grunted. "Did you read more of my stuff?"

"You'll be rich and famous any moment," I said. "I liked the one in the alternate universe."

She snorted. "Of course you did. There was less love story and more action."

"Should I be offended?" I teased.

Her bright eyes focused on me over the back of the

computer tower. "Nah. And thanks. I'm glad we can keep being friends."

Me too. But there was more than that. I stared at her hands, wondering what the strength of her would feel like as our fingers tangled together. What it would be like to be the guy who could tuck her hair behind her ears. To text her in the middle of the night for no reason. I hadn't ever bothered trying to get involved with anyone—our life had always been too fluid. But now . . . we might have a chance to stick around. *Idiot. You just met her.*

"What's up with you?" She nudged my arm again.

I shook my head, wishing it was enough to clear my thoughts. "Oh. No. I'm, um . . . good."

She snorted. "Don't get weird. Guys get weird. Don't be that guy."

"I don't know what you mean." But really, I did. My thoughts had shifted toward her in a way I hadn't intended, and really, we'd only had a few conversations.

"Whatever." She turned back to the computer and flipped it on. The thing hummed and sputtered a bit before the screen gained the same greenish hue, the small square cursor blinking at us from the top left corner.

"This is where I got stuck."

"But there were two missing connections." She pulled a slender knee up to her chest and leaned on it as she stared at the screen. The keyboard's clacking noises echoed in my empty room. "Now there are no missing connections."

I tugged on my lower lip as the computer whirred and sputtered.

Five messages popped on the screen. Strange font. Green.

MPG: Thank you, Sam.

SAM: No problem.

MPG: Looking forward to meeting.

SAM: Me too.

MPG: You missed our meeting. Please advise.

"It's Sam's computer," I said as I felt my mouth pull into a smile. Only in this moment did I realize how much I wanted it to be his.

"You called it, it really is his computer." Stella laughed a bit. "I can't access any more messages. I don't know why. And as far as I can tell, there's nothing else on this computer."

"No information or anything?" I asked.

She shook her head.

"Five messages." And no information. I knew the computer was old—probably even old for Sam's time—but I'd still hoped for a little more than this.

"Who was this guy talking to?" Stella sat back in my small chair—both boots now on the seat, her knees tucked against her, making her look smaller than I ever thought possible.

"No idea."

"But he said in the journal that he was hoping he could sell the toxin to someone. If he's talking about meeting up, do you think that has something to do with it?"

There was no way to tell. "I think you like true crime."

A smile lit her face. "This is true. But what else could it be?"

"Meeting someone new online?" I offered.

"Through an encrypted messenger? That's what this is." Her face twisted into a type of incredulous look. "You get that, right?"

I rubbed my hands over my head. She was right. Of course she was right. "Could this be real?"

Her brows danced up and down as her body did a sort of side-to-side dance in the chair. "One way to find out."

She started typing.

SAM: Sorry I've been silent. Are you still there?

"No!" I twitched forward, but Stella laughed as she hit Enter.

"Too late. It's sent."

Blinking, I stood and stared at the computer, my heart drowning out every other sound in the room. "But what if . . . I mean, what if . . ." I'd always been cautious. Checked out my options before moving forward. I wouldn't just . . . "I can't believe you did that."

"I can." She shrugged. "This is typical Stella. You have to know it's taking everything in me to not reach out and ask them if they're there again."

"Please don't." I shook my head. "I don't know what this is, or what we've maybe started here." Sending out a fake email from a fake name was one thing. Sending out a message when they expected Sam felt like something far different. What if they had codewords or something or . . . We didn't even know who was on the other end of this chat. I'd known exactly who each email had been sent to this afternoon. "Military encryption likely means something high-key shady, right?"

"Chill, Chuck, chill." Stella stood and stretched an arm across her body one way, and then another arm the other way. As if we were just hanging out rather than messaging some mysterious entity, pretending to be someone we weren't. "They think you're Sam, and you're clearly *not* Sam. Also, even if this computer was old when Sam had it, this series of messages is still super ancient."

She did have a point. "I'm paranoid, that's all."

Just then, the front door opened and closed, and Mom's coughing filled the downstairs. My heart twisted in defeat as the sound continued.

"You look like you're in pain," Stella said softly.

"I can't help her." I shrugged, but I didn't feel like shrugging. As Mom's coughs continued, my muscles tightened—in my shoulders first and then down my arms until my fists clenched. My head grew light as the coughing continued throughout the main floor of the house.

Stella glanced toward my open door and the sound of Mom's continued hacking. "What's wrong with her?"

"Rare genetic thing. I don't have it." I was leaning against my wall, my head tilted back, having very little idea of how I'd gotten there.

"I'm sorry." She stood in front of me. Her strong hand wrapped around my wrist. "I'm sorry."

"Yeah, well. Her job here is supposed to have good insurance. They're being lame now, but she'll get it sorted. It's why she took this job."

Stella nodded. "I should go. But you'd better tell me if someone answers back on that chat."

I pushed myself back off the wall and stood. "I can walk you out."

"I'll follow you so you can introduce me."

Right. It would be weird for her to slip out without meeting Mom. Each step down the stairs twisted my stomach into more knots. This was just Mom meeting a friend from school. Nothing else. But the message. But Mom's coughing. But the emails I'd sent out that day.

"Chuck, could you—" She stopped when Stella and I were at the bottom of the stairs.

Mom's two hands were under her nose, blood slipping between her fingers and staining her shirt. This wasn't uncommon for her, but I was still frozen.

"Sit and lean forward," Stella said. "That way, the blood comes out your nose rather than running down your throat."

Mom sat, her eyes going from me to Stella to me to Stella. But Stella was already in the kitchen wrapping paper towels around her hand before going back to Mom.

"I'm Stella," she said as she handed her the towels as if this was how she always met people. "Happy to get you a washcloth, but I'm new here and don't know where they are."

A corner of Mom's mouth lifted, despite the blood coloring her hands. "Tracy. Nice to meet you . . . sorry." But then the coughs came, and she leaned forward, pressing the paper towels to her face.

I ducked into the small bathroom and stuck a washcloth under cold water for a moment. When I came back out, Stella was sitting and talking with Mom like nothing was out of place.

"Yeah, I got loads of bloody noses when I was a kid. I learned a million tricks to help them stop, but really, none of them work. Your nose just has to decide it's done." She crossed her legs, putting one boot over the other. "Chuck was just helping me with computer stuff."

Mom nodded.

I handed her the washcloth. "So, this is Stella."

Stella snorted. "We covered that a few minutes ago."

Right. My thoughts just weren't forming the way I was used to.

"I gotta head." Stella stood and tilted her head toward the door. "Hope you two have a nice weekend. And welcome to Twin Falls."

"Thanks," Mom rasped, which just sent her into another coughing fit.

I started for the door, but Stella waved me back with a short head shake. "Text me later."

I would. I wanted to.

And then Stella was gone, and Mom dabbed at her nose, which was now a slow trickle. "Was that her car out there?" she asked.

"Her mom's." And yeah, there weren't many new BMWs in this part of Twin Falls. Or probably any part, really.

Mom adjusted the washcloth on her face.

"Why don't you just lie down on the couch or something?" I offered.

"Just a long week," she said. "You know, after a long drive. I'm okay."

But that was the thing—at the heart of it, Mom wasn't okay. Her lungs weren't going to get better without some specialized treatment. And this job might have come with great insurance, but it didn't mean there were specialists here who knew how to do more than help relieve her symptoms rather than get to the heart of the problem.

I had to do something.

EIGHT

Mom coughed on and off all night while I lay in bed, staring at the stained ceiling. Occasionally, I got up to see if anyone had responded to Stella's message. Nothing. At the first hint of light, I grabbed my "new" phone, tiptoed down the stairs, and went out into the near darkness.

This was the kind of light that gave old buildings that something *extra* videos needed to get lots of views. I needed *lots* of views. Like, hundreds of thousands if I was gonna help Mom. I took a few side shots of some of the fourplexes that weren't being used. Some hopefully artistic shots of weedy backyards and old signs.

At the end of the row of figure-eight neighborhoods sat what looked like a small shop—abandoned. This was the kind of thing viewers went for. The sign had been taken off the facade, leaving a patch of darker brick beneath. When I walked around the side, the door had been left open. This meant nothing would be left to explore and that the place was probably trashed. Viewers of urban exploring loved seeing places that had no marks of being used by anyone or anything besides the previous occupants.

I slid sideways through the door into darkness. When I flipped on the light, a trashed back room met me. The place even had power. What a drag. Random wrappers, soda cans, takeout containers, pizza boxes . . . this was clearly just a place where people came to party away from homes and parents.

Still, I kept videoing as I worked my way to the front of the store, which had been stripped of everything. Even shelves. Only a plain floor and bare walls greeted me. Well, bare aside from the pathetic attempts at graffiti.

It was all I had, and I was in desperate need to upload a video, so I just kept it going. This was just a nothing place. But with the cool light filtering through the front windows of the used-to-be store, maybe there was enough to be interesting here. With a lot of work, and a ton of editing, I could follow the old fence line and do a thing about the shrinking of the military base, but how many would care?

I kicked a stray can across the floor, letting it skitter over the tiles.

What a waste. I could text Stella to see if she was up for some exploring, but it was only six in the morning on a Saturday, and no one should have to be up at six on the weekends.

There was an open gas station halfway between my neighborhood and school. I had a few bucks in my pocket and needed something to do. Mostly just work-looking trucks passed me as I headed to there. And really, only a few of them. The world felt asleep. Layers of guilt came with the relief that I wasn't home and just sitting there listening to Mom cough. Each rasp made me feel more helpless and frustrated than the last. I could only take that for so long.

After buying an overpriced fountain soda—hey it was cheaper than a bottle—and bag of chips, I started home. I thought about maybe trying to find another job, but I had

74

a feeling Saya was a talker, and I was sure she'd warned the other businesses not to hire the *liar*.

Two honks were followed by Brock's familiar truck pulling over in front of me. "Hey! Want a lift?"

"What are you doing up so early?" I jogged for his car and climbed in the passenger's side. As much as I didn't want to be at home, I also was about done walking down this farm road.

"I was at the gym," he said, as if I should have known. "I have work at ten, so I had to make sure I got home in time to shower first."

"Where do you work?" I asked.

"Soda Palace." He sighed. "It blows, but at least there are tips. And everyone comes through there at some point so it's not boring."

I'd seen that little building on our way into town. I probably wouldn't love working in that tight of quarters either. "Thanks for the ride."

"So, why are you up so early?"

There were a lot of answers to that question, but I gave him the simplest one. "Couldn't sleep."

He nodded, his short hair not moving as he shifted. "So . . . I was gonna tell you . . . about Stella . . ."

My shoulders tightened at the low tone of warning in his words.

He glanced over at me before focusing on the road. "She's cool, but . . ."

And then silence. One beat. Another beat. Another.

The hum of the tires on pavement filled the car. "But?" I prompted.

"But she's reckless. She doesn't care about getting into trouble. Like, at all. It's like there's a piece of her that's missing. That piece of self-preservation. She doesn't have that." His attention was more fully on the road than I'd ever seen it.

"Noted," I told him, though I wasn't sure what to even do or say about that information. It wasn't like I had super-cautious plans for my near future, but then, Brock wasn't as desperate as I was for life to change.

"Look, she's hot, and she's super fun, but I'm always on guard around her, and you probably should be too." He laughed a little. "I sound like my dad. That's . . . that was terrible."

"Nah," I told him. "I appreciate the warning." But honestly, I wanted someone who could help me get into cool buildings. Someone not afraid to see what was going on with that computer. Someone as interested in Sam Miller, who made toxins in his bedroom.

Brock pulled to a stop. "A few of us are getting pizza to take to the corner stop. That's, uh, the old store up the road."

"Found it this morning," I said.

"Cool." He nodded. "Anyway. Pizza there on Sunday night is sort of a thing."

Maybe I'd learn a little more about the people who lived around here. Could find better places to video. "Thanks, and thanks again for the ride. I'm gonna have to give you gas money or something."

Brock shrugged a shoulder. "My granddad pays for my gas. It's his way of pissing off my dad."

I laughed a little.

"My dad wants me to work for every penny I spend, and my granddad said my dad didn't have to—" Brock just stopped and shook his head. "I'm rambling. It's a whole family drama thing."

"At least you come out on top," I told him.

He tapped the steering wheel, grinning. "That's right."

I closed the door and gave him a wave.

The moment I opened the front door, Mom's coughing wafted down from upstairs. Thick and raspy—a sign she might end up in the hospital again.

She'd only worked four days last week. How could this go on?

* * *

The credits rolled on another *Indiana Jones* movie because Mom always loved watching those when she felt sick. Another round of thick, wet coughing went along with the music. Sunday afternoon, and this was all we'd managed to do all day.

"How about I do the grocery shopping?" I offered. Anything to get out of the house, and I knew Mom planned a trip, so I'd both be helping and giving myself some distance. This weekend was going to last forever.

She just nodded. "Keep it under eighty and—"

"I know. Check prices. Think ahead."

"I have car registration to worry about, and we'll both need new licenses." She pushed herself up on the couch, paused, and then lay back down.

"Eighty. I can do that." I handed her the remote and half ran out the door. How did anyone take care of a sick family member for long? Before Dad left, I felt like a buffer between the two of them and didn't have the space in my head to think as much on how sick Mom was. With that pressure gone, and just Mom and I at home? I couldn't drag my thoughts away from her failing lungs.

I slowed at the library, but I wasn't going to leave Mom for longer than necessary. The email would have to wait until at least Monday. But that could be my other way out. I'd been working on videos for over a year and only made a few hundred bucks total. And since the video I uploaded yesterday did so poorly, there was no way I was going to even start thinking about what I'd made an hour. I mean, it was way more fun than working at some random fast-food restaurant, but pennies an hour wasn't going to work.

If I could somehow reproduce what Sam had and find a place to buy that stuff from me, there was a chance my hourly rate would go way up.

As I walked through the grocery store, I stared at my favorite cereals, all twice as much as the generic ones. Generic won. It almost always did.

I mental-mathed my way through the grocery store and came out at $78.20. Just under Mom's limit. Getting the groceries was a blatant reminder of why we did so many frozen meals. Buying all the stuff to make a dinner with potatoes and real meat and gravy and biscuits would cost a small fortune.

Instead of packaged Lunchables, I'd gotten ingredients. And as much as I wanted to eat Oreos by the handful, I planned on sectioning out the pack so it lasted the week. More would be better.

Again, I slowed as I passed the library. But once the main part of town was behind me, I hit the gas, wondering about the message Stella had sent on Sam's old computer. Wondering if I should text her after I got home. Wondering when I should tell her about those emails I sent. If she'd be one of the people there for Sunday night pizza.

When I got home, the house was silent. I slowly put the groceries away as my mind spun through scenarios. Mom had died. Mom was finally sleeping. Mom had felt good enough to go for a walk. A quiet house should have calmed me a bit, but instead, the possibilities began to scream.

When I walked around the corner to the living room, Mom was crashed on the couch, her blanket pulled up and over most of her head. The house wasn't as silent as it had felt from the other room.

A subtle rasping sound came and went as she breathed.

I ate all my Oreos for the day, plus one from tomorrow's planned Oreo amount. Then I sent Mom a text saying I was out doing pizza with friends and then hoped a five-dollar contribution would be enough.

When I texted Brock to ask him what time to meet up, he responded immediately.

Brock: We hang for a while. Pizza's on its way because Cheyenne works there.

Chuck: See you in a few.

I jogged up the stairs and clicked a few keys to bring the computer to life.

The message Stella had sent still rested at the top of the screen.

SAM: Sorry I've been silent. Are you still there?

But underneath her words was a new message.

MPG: We are still here. It's been years. Where do we stand?

My fingers shook as I stared at the computer. How did I answer? What would I say?

They'd responded.

Who was Sam talking to? What did they want? Was this a university? I racked my brain to try to figure out which university used the initials MPG. The attempt was futile, plus I was too impatient to figure it out.

As much as I wanted to respond now, I couldn't. Not before talking to Stella. Not before reading the rest of Sam's journal. I grabbed the soft leather book and sprinted down the stairs, out the door, and up the street.

I had to figure this out, and I had to do it now.

Where do we stand . . .

By the time I made it to the corner store, I was gasping for air. I couldn't just run in like this because everyone would want to know what was going on, and there was only one person there I could tell.

Music pulsed through the windows, but not so loudly that any neighbors would notice. Three cars were parked directly behind the place—Stella's mother's car being one of them.

I reached into my pocket for the five and folded it around my fingers. I stepped through the back door and held up the money. "Who needs this?"

A girl snatched it from my fingers. "Cheyenne. That's me. And thanks, new guy."

"Chuck," I said automatically.

She turned to face me, and I immediately recognized her as the girl who had yelled at Stella my second day at school. "We all know your name. You're the only face we haven't been staring at for years."

Right.

"You know Brock," Brock said with a grin. "And that's Cheyenne and Ammon and Connor."

Stella sat on the counter, her legs stretched out on the surface in front of her and her back resting against the far wall. Her headphones were on, her eyes were closed, and she mouthed words to a song I couldn't hear between bites.

My heart flipped.

"You drooling over the girl or the pizza?" Cheyenne whispered before opening a pizza box in front of me.

Maybe both, but I wasn't gonna say that.

"Thanks," I said instead, and picked up a slice of pepperoni before walking toward Stella.

I nudged her boot with my elbow, and she immediately scowled. Her eyes opened, and her frown turned into a wry smile. "Hey there."

"I got a response," I said.

"Uh, okay?" Then she froze. "Wait. Like . . . on the chat?" she whisper-yelled.

I glanced over my shoulder, but everyone seemed to be in their own conversations. "Yeah."

She twisted on the counter and let her feet drop off the side. "What did it say?"

"We're still here. It's been years. Where do we stand?" I took my first bite of pizza; the salt and spice of the pepperoni filled my mouth. At least Twin Falls had good pizza.

"Ho-leee . . " She trailed off.

Yeah, that had been my first thought as well. "I brought his journal."

She peered over my shoulder. "We can't do that here."

Yeah, the last thing we needed was questions we didn't want to answer and didn't know how to answer. With a coded chat room open on the internet, which I was still wrapping my head around being real, and talk of making deadly toxins—best to not be discussing this with anyone else, or even *around* anyone else.

Slipping off the counter, she grabbed my arm and dragged me toward the door.

"Hey, Stella—headed off to make another notch in your bedpost?" Cheyenne teased.

She turned just as we reached the door. "New guy stuff. Don't be weird."

And then we were outside. And then she opened the back door of her mom's car. And then we sat on either side of the back seat, and I finally took another bite of the slice of pizza that had cost me five bucks.

"We need to read the rest of the journal and figure out what to say back." Stella slumped in the seat, pushing her pale hair up in a mess behind her.

"What if this is all . . . shady?"

She snorted. "Of course it's shady." She snatched the book from my hand. "Otherwise, it would be Facebook messages or something. And honestly, even old-person Facebook is used for some seriously shady shi—"

"Okay, okay," I agreed.

She opened the journal. "You read ahead?"

"Just a little."

"Okay." She flipped until she reached the small strap that was used as a bookmark.

We read more about Sam's family. More about his mom and dad. Some school stuff. Searched for anything that would give us clues as to how to talk to these people online. Nothing.

"Imma gonna get more pizza," she said abruptly, then left and came back a couple minutes later with three slices balanced in her hands. At least my five bucks had gone for more than just one slice.

I was still reading about Sam's failures and successes. How he started. How his toxin formula was working.

Big Boy Beans. Like, who would have thought that those cheap, crappy cans of generic beans would be the key to the crystalline toxin? Between that, my hand-

*done flask, and the heating and cooling being timed just
right . . . I think I have something totally new. Or almost
totally new. A new strain of something old.*

Success. Real success. Again.

*Took me a while to figure out how to get this old
clunker of a computer online, but it didn't take me long
to find a buyer for this stuff. Not sure who MPG is, but
I was sent pictures of cash—close enough to see serial
numbers. I'm there.*

*Later I realized that MPG could be an overseas uni-
versity. I couldn't figure out which one.*

And then . . .

"That's it?" Stella flipped through to the end. Nothing but blank pages—one of them had the microbiology
merit badge tapped to it with yellowing clear tape.

"But that's them." I rested my head back, staring at
the spotless ceiling of the BMW. "That's who's in that
message thing."

She turned to face me, grabbing each of my forearms,
pizza forgotten on the center console between the two
front seats. "We have to figure out what to say back. Do
you see what this could mean?"

Money. This could mean money. I was out of options.
My YouTube channel had failed almost as spectacularly
as I had at my short-lived job. What other options did I
have? Mom wasn't getting better on her own, that was for
sure. I could do this. Sam did. He was my age. A junior in
high school. He'd developed a toxin from botulism using
simple supplies. He had them all listed. All his trials and
successes and failures. His final formula for success.

But what about the dead cat? This toxin could kill.
My mind glitched as the battle of what to do ensued. Get
money and save Mom? Or get caught and go to jail?

"We need supplies. We need Big Boy Beans. We need

to . . ." She flipped back through the book and took a few pictures with her phone. "We need to figure out where to get this stuff. Maybe from the old wing of the school or something?"

"Yeah." It wasn't really stealing if no one was using the equipment. Besides, if I could work this out . . . the theft would be to help a life. My mom's life.

"Oh, but the universities and stuff." Stella paused. "What do you want to do?"

"Move forward on all fronts." What else could I do? Eighty bucks a week for groceries wasn't going to even keep us fed, much less pay for doctors. I knew that our moving expenses were digging into the money now, but even after . . .

"Here's what I think you should say to MPG."

I shifted in my seat to face her more fully.

"Let me know what you need, and I'll see what I can do." She nodded decisively.

It did fit in with being open to anything without giving away information. "Smart."

Stella tilted her head to the side, exposing her neck. "I can be brilliant once in a while."

I knew. And I couldn't stop staring at the shaved sides of her head, her earrings. Her soft lashes.

Our eyes connected, and her excited expression softened.

I held my breath. We were so close. My knee touched hers, and the warmth radiated up my leg.

"Oh wow . . ." Stella breathed in deeply, her eyes never leaving mine. "We're having kind of a moment, huh?"

Maybe. I swallowed and nodded. My eyes strayed from hers again to notice her pink lips and lean neck.

Her gaze flickered to my lips.

The whole time we'd sat in the back of this car, I hadn't worried about my breath or my body odor or anything, but now . . .

"You wanna kiss me?" she asked.

"A b-bit." My voice cracked.

She turned her cheek toward me and pointed.

The move was so perfectly Stella that my nerves settled as I leaned toward her and pressed my lips against the soft skin of her cheek.

"My turn." A finger grazed my jawline. "If you're okay with a kiss."

I mimicked her, tilting my head and pointing at my cheek.

Her warm breath floated over my face before her lips touched my cheek, almost on the corner of my mouth.

We'd just stepped over a line of some sort, or maybe now we were standing on it, and we could shift back and be friends, or we could shift the other way and spend more time in the back seat of this car without a journal between us.

"Tomorrow we meet to see what we need to do this thing, and tonight, you send back that message." She sat back and opened the car door. "This is gonna be big, Chuck."

Big. Big. I wasn't sure I wanted big except for the money part.

"Are we really doing this, Chuck?" she asked.

I wiggled in the seat, wishing we could just go back to kissing. Maybe more than a cheek this time. Thoughts of everything reeled in my mind. My whole life. This whole "joyride" of a life I'd been on. Now was my chance. Crack my emotional vault.

"Uh, yeah, we're doing this." That's it?! That's cracking the vault?

Stella rubbed the tops of her thighs and rocked a couple of times. "Okay."

We sat in silence for what seemed to be an eternity's worth of uncomfortableness. But just as the nervousness was about to sabotage the night so far, I found my voice to speak. "Stella, I'm glad you're helping me with this."

"You couldn't do it without me." She smiled. Her perfect teeth gleamed in the moonlight from the driver's back window.

"I mean, I need to do this. My mom . . ." I blinked. "My mom is really, really sick. Like she's going to die if we can't get treatment."

Stella just stared at me, her soft eyes beckoning me to continue.

"So I guess this is the way to get the cash so I can help my mom, you know?"

"I understand."

"We have to be careful. I'm sure this is completely illegal, but if we don't get caught, I can get her treatment."

Stella slowly reached over and grasped my hand. "This is why I'm doing this. You're valiant. You're sweet and kind. I could tell from the first day I met you. Plus, it's a friggin' adventure that has huge consequences. So who doesn't want to make some lethal toxin?"

And with that, there was the real Stella I'd learned to like.

TEN

Stella held open the door to the old wing of the school, noise from the assembly floating through the hallways.

"I wish you could check to see if they've answered yet," she said quietly as we slipped into the empty hallway together.

"Yeah." But there was one thing I could do. "I need to check the library messages after school."

Stella stood in a doorway, her torn jeans hanging off her hips and not quite meeting the top of her boots. A hand rested on either side of the doorway, showing chipped neon-green nail polish. She leaned forward. "That journal is the most interesting thing that's happened to me since one of my stories went viral."

I stood behind her as she let go of the frame and stepped into the room. "We're gonna get caught back here at some point."

"Yeah." She nodded as she opened the first of a long row of cabinets. "But we both have good grades, so I think we're fine."

"Brock said you get into trouble." I hadn't meant to say it out loud, but I'd been thinking about it a lot with everything going on.

She turned and winked at me before letting the doors fall closed and moving to the next cabinet. "Then you'll get off easy. Just tell whoever catches us that you've been pressured into doing bad things by the reckless Stella Warner."

A laugh escaped before I remembered the list in my pocket. "I made a list of some of the things that Sam Miller used."

She snatched the paper from my hands and unfolded it. "Neat handwriting." She peered over the top. "Wonder what that says about you?"

"That I want to be able to read what I've written?" I offered with a smile. Her smile back was like a hit to the gut—the good kind.

The give and take with her always messed with my head.

She scanned the list. "Most of it's basic, but he has some kind of flask thing he made on his own. How are we gonna re-create that?"

I shrugged. "He made the toxin before without that— he added that later on."

"Hmm," she mused.

I started opening the other cabinets. "Nothing but old textbooks and paper."

"Next room!" she chanted in a military tone before marching out the door.

I followed—as was becoming the routine with Stella.

The second I stepped in the room, she gestured in dramatic fashion with two hands, bending her body toward the ground. "I present to you everything we need and then some."

Beakers, funnels, Bunsen burners, tubes, charts, and containers with sealable lids lined every shelf. "But . . ." And I couldn't believe this had just occurred to me. "How are we gonna get this to my place?"

Yeah, I'd considered how tricky it would be to bring

home what I needed in a backpack while walking, but this . . . this was a lot more work than I was thinking. Plus, were we just going to make botulism in the house where my mom was sick?

"I have therapy after dinner. Pretty sure the school will be shut down by then," Stella said. "You could meet me here about eight? Might be dark enough that we can hide."

I glanced at the window. "This doesn't face the street like the bathrooms. We could leave one of the windows unlocked, but also leave one of the bathroom windows unlocked just in case?"

Her eyes narrowed and she nodded in approval. "You got thinkin' skills, Chuck. I like it."

As I flipped the lock on the window farthest from the door, a twinge of uncertainty washed over me, lightening my head. Was I really planning on breaking into a school to steal glassware that I couldn't afford?

Okay, yes. But it was for a good cause, and it wasn't like I couldn't bring it all back if plans went well. Actually, I would definitely bring it all back once I was finished. Or whatever, maybe I'd even donate more supplies to the school as a thank you. With money, there was no end to what I could do.

"Okay," Stella mused as she started rearranging the supplies, putting everything on the list on the same shelf. "We need to be fast when we come back later. Cars by the school don't go unnoticed for long—though, most people wouldn't be suspicious of a BMW with a high-ranking officer's sticker in the window."

Her smirk said a million things. One, that she knew what I did—the world was easier when you could afford nice things—and two, along the lines of Brock's warning, I didn't think Stella would mind getting caught at all.

That could work to my benefit or to my detriment. Time would tell on that one.

* * *

No, I didn't want to make the walk to the library, but I did need to see if any of the universities had returned my inquiries. Creating something to be studied felt honorable, even. Like I'd be doing a good thing helping Mom and a good thing helping science.

Pinging in the back of my head as I stepped back into the building was the idea that any research institution should be able to do what a junior in high school had managed with a few textbooks, but maybe there were regulations against creating something like that. Or maybe Sam was right in that he'd found a way that created something fully new. No matter what, there had to be scientists out there who were researching how to counteract different toxins.

My homework weighted my bag. The stress of our nearly-empty house and Mom's illness waited for me at home. The end of the school year was in about two months, and all the normal end-of-year tests and projects would be due soon. Everything in my life was so boring and normal, but as I logged in to the email account belonging to Raymond Cartwright, a rush of finally being in control of something washed over me.

I'd reached out. I was moving forward. Stella and I would get the supplies we needed to create a toxin— something I'd have never even guessed I'd be doing even a month ago. But this . . . this one thing was giving me something to hold on to. To take control of.

And then, as my eyes rushed over the beginnings of

the responses, all my excitement dropped through the floor beneath my feet.

"*Who are you? I have reported this email to the authorities . . .*"

"*We do not deal with companies we have never heard of, nor can find records for . . .*"

"*. . . furthermore, it is highly illegal to create a deadly substance without specific government registration . . .*"

"*I cannot see any official seal of EPA approval attributed to your name, so I will have to pass . . .*"

"*. . . do not condone this creation and have contacted Homeland Security . . .*"

"*. . . have contacted the FBI and the EPA and OSHA . . .*"

I sat back and quickly deleted the emails with shaking fingers. Then deleted the sent emails in the Sent folder. With still trembling hands, I typed and asked how to delete a Gmail account permanently, then did each step one by one until the account was gone.

Someone had contacted federal agencies. The EPA? Environmental Protection Agency? Homeland Security? OSHA? Could they watch me here? Would they know who logged in to this computer to do this? Now I was afraid to leave the library, because how suspicious would that be? I had to walk around and make it seem like my work on the computer was done, but I wasn't terrified about what I'd found there.

Until now, no one had threatened me, or well, *Raymond Cartwright*, with federal government agencies. Every step toward following Sam now felt like a mountain—one that had to be climbed carefully.

Having a completely separate part of a computer now felt like an obvious choice. The botulism felt bigger than it ever had. The idea that Sam Miller had created this crystalline toxin felt a million times heavier than I'd have ever realized before getting those email responses. Professionals were threatening Homeland Security with the results of a Boy Scout project.

But there was no way I was going to do any online searches on my phone, or any more at this library. Maybe Stella would want to add this research to her recklessness. Of course, I'd read the warnings and seen the safety measures in the textbooks, but nothing could top a solid Google search. Those books had all been printed years ago. But I had no intention of creating a digital trail for them to follow back to my mom.

Every step home felt heavier than the last. And it was a long freaking walk. My feet ached, and my legs burned by the time I made it to the front door. It further confirmed walking to town for work wasn't going to be an option. But how was I going to save up for a bike if work wasn't on the table? Toxin? More videos? Mom's car sat in the driveway. I checked my phone—almost six. It had taken me ages to get here.

I stood at the shabby door and stared at the peeling paint. I glanced behind me at the car, which still worked by some miracle. We couldn't catch up. Couldn't get ahead. With a sigh, I pushed open the door. The entry was empty aside from Mom's granny-looking work shoes.

The light in the kitchen and dining area was off. Faint noise from the TV carried past the stairway, so I moved for the living room. *CSI* was on, almost whisper-soft. A sure sign that Mom had a migraine, which happened when her body wasn't getting enough oxygen.

She slept, her dark hair falling over her face, her breaths ragged and rough, curled up on the couch. She probably hadn't eaten. Just came home from work and fell asleep. She looked paler than usual, and I pulled my vision away from the red stain pooling below her mouth. This wasn't entirely new. She'd gotten the occasional bloody nose or coughed up blood. But she'd never had it simply *oozing* out of her mouth while she slept.

Everything had an expiration, and it was becoming clear Mom's would be soon if I couldn't do anything. Get her the right doctors. It always came down to money.

My fists clenched. I was so frickin' helpless. I moved into the kitchen, pulled two meals from the freezer, and stared at the directions, which were now blurring in front of me.

I followed each step. *Poke holes. Remove plastic from one part of the tray. On high for three minutes. Pull plastic. Stir. On low for two more minutes. Serve. Enjoy.*

I served us both, but I didn't enjoy the rubberized texture of the oversalted meal. Mom didn't wake until I'd nudged her at least four times. She didn't even sit, just propped herself up on her elbow and slipped a bite of chicken fried steak into her mouth.

This couldn't go on. Couldn't.

I thought of the messages on the computer upstairs. The one I hadn't checked since coming home.

Yes, I was dealing with something dangerous—maybe even more dangerous than I knew—but I had an in on the dark web. The dark web was real. If I couldn't make a decent amount of money by going to reputable research institutions, maybe I could make it there. MPG wouldn't turn me in, would they? According to Sam, they were some sort of foreign university. To sell to them wasn't illegal, was it?

ELEVEN

Back in my room, I turned on the old computer and waited for what felt like an hour for the thing to boot up.

My last message still sat there unanswered.

When I set my phone on the table, the time stared at me—8:00 p.m.

Mom coughed downstairs.

There was no way I could meet Stella.

I opened my texts.

> *Chuck: Can't tonight. Family stuff.*
>
> *Stella: Your mom okay?*
>
> *Chuck: Yeah. I don't know.*
>
> *Stella: I don't know if I want to waste all our prep.*
>
> *Chuck: Please don't do it without me.*
>
> *Stella: Fine.*

She could get into as much trouble as she wanted, but not for me.

I stared at the computer message again. Maybe this was like that "watched pot never boils" thing, but seriously, I just sat and stared at the last message I'd sent, hoping a new one would pop up.

But they hadn't responded, whoever "they" were.

I could do this. At this point, it almost felt like I had to.

I opened Sam's journal and went through his instructions again. Step by step. Honestly, creating the toxin was a little tricky because of timing, but nothing was terribly difficult. Well, not with his instructions. I'm not sure if I could figure it out on my own. Next grocery trip had to involve a dented and bulging can of Big Boy Beans.

> *Stella: I'm coming to pick you up. I have the car. Meet me at the sign by your neighborhood in an hour. Won't take us long.*

For a moment, I thought about asking her if she was going to get in trouble, or how she was working this with her parents, but maybe some things were better left alone. And how could I move forward if I didn't take risks? The truth was that I couldn't.

Chuck: Okay.

* * *

Goose bumps ran up my arms, but I'd just moved here from Arizona. I didn't have a coat. I'd need to figure that out before next fall.

Mom was asleep. Stella's parents were who even knew where or what they thought. But if Mom couldn't stay awake to watch TV, she certainly wasn't going to wake up as I moved in and out of the house.

The deep blue of the horizon disappeared into darkness just as Stella stopped her mom's car in front of me.

She waved frantically, and I sprinted to the passenger's side and jumped in.

"Sorry. I was freezing and couldn't find the right hoodie," I lied, "and it was a whole thing." The car tires screeched as she hit the gas, slamming my head against the butter-soft leather.

Her nails were bright pink tonight. Black thumbs. Freshly painted. That had to be tedious work. Mom never bothered. The smell got to her. Maybe Stella hadn't been able to sleep either.

The school was quiet when we pulled into the parking lot. The overnight lights were on inside, spilling more light around the school than I'd expected. They were also on in the parking lot. Stella pulled into the bus turnaround, putting us off to the side of the school, where I could just make out the courtyard between the new school and the old wing.

I opened my mouth to tell her we couldn't park there, but the moment I had the thought, it felt stupid. We were here to steal things from the school. If someone came to give us a parking ticket, we'd be arrested. Where we parked didn't matter. I pushed out a breath. Yeah, I'd snuck into buildings before, but I never created new graffiti or anything.

"Oh." She inched forward. "I'm gonna park behind the shed there."

"Too obvious to anyone driving by."

She sighed. "Suck."

Though it was so dark that I doubted anyone would see a car back there, if they did . . . definitely suspicious. Better to look like we were a teacher or something, swinging in to get something we forgot.

But . . . I squinted in the near darkness. We could use

the back side of the shed to get us to our open window. If it hadn't been locked.

Stella looked at me with maybe the biggest smile I'd ever seen on her. "Ready?"

I hated this, but it was necessary. As she bounded from the car, it seemed like she might love it.

Headlights shined on the road near the school, and I crouched low in the car, staring as it drove by without slowing.

"Come *on*!" Stella gestured toward the school. "Get out, or we'll never get this done!"

Three . . . two . . . one . . . I got out of the car, trying to let my arms swing and my body relax like I wasn't about to steal from our school. But was it even stealing if no one was using the stuff?

Okay, yeah. I knew it was stealing even if no one was using anything, but wouldn't the school donate it if they knew it would save a life?

Maybe.

Nah, I was going with definitely yeah. They'd donate that whole wing of the school to save someone's life, and all I was asking for were a few beakers and supplies.

Stella stared at the window we'd left open. We were cast in shadow in the corner where the old wing met the new. I scanned the side of the school and the newer doors for any sign of a camera, which I totally should have done earlier that day, but whatever. We were here now, and besides, I didn't see anything.

"I just did my nails." Her face twisted up. "You wanna do the honors?"

Yeah, she was a puzzle. I reached forward and shoved my fingertips under the old wooden sill. This was a slider window, which probably weighed a million pounds. But once I got both hands underneath the old wood and jerked upward, the window squeaked up a few inches.

Stella's hand was immediately under where I held the window open, and together we shoved the screeching thing up.

"Ladies first!" she chirped before slipping inside. "Actually," she called back as she hit the floor, "I'm gonna just hand the stuff out to you."

At which point I realized I had no bags or boxes or anything to get the large shelf-worth of stuff from the school to the car.

"Maybe put it in a trash bin or something?" I stuck my head in the window, but in the dark I could barely see her standing in front of the open cupboard.

She peered around the cabinet door. "Smart."

I wasn't sure any of this could be considered "smart," but I let the comment slide. All I had to do was make sure I didn't get caught. Mom didn't need the stress. My head wouldn't stop swiveling from side to side, looking for lights, or people, or anything moving. Any ways we could get caught.

The sill sat at about chest height, and I pressed my hands to the solid surface, just ready to hop up and squeeze in, when a small trash can jingling with glass was placed in front of me.

"I have one or two more loads. Drop that in the trunk and then come back."

When I checked the car, it felt so naked and exposed— in full view of the road, the parking lot lit up like a Christmas tree, and me with a bin full of stuff.

My mouth dried out as I walked along the wall of the building, where I was still hidden from the road. I stopped at the corner. Peered to my left to see if any headlights were headed this way. No way was I gonna take the time to figure out where to look on a car with a dashboard of mysterious switches and controls to find the button that opened the trunk. Instead, I took a deep breath in, grasped the bin more tightly, and sprinted to the side of the car not facing the road. The second I opened the back door, the interior light came on.

So much for looking like an empty parked car. I couldn't afford to break anything, so I quickly pulled each item from the tiny trash basket before closing the door and releasing a long breath.

"What's taking you so long?" Stella whisper-yelled from the school.

I peered through the windows of the car just in time to see headlights on the road.

Please don't see us . . . please don't see us . . . please don't see us . . .

The car's turn signal came on, and I held my breath. Were they turning into the parking lot? Should I run away? Hide under the car?

Blink. Blink. Blink. Blink. And then they turned on the street on the other side of the school. The one with the big, thick fence. My head grew light for a moment.

But I had to remember why I was here. That my purpose was far bigger than stealing a few bits of unused science stuff.

I sprinted back to the school and handed the small trash can back to Stella.

"That took an age—it's almost like you want to get caught." She cackled in a fake-witch laugh.

I should have told her to please be quiet, but we were almost done.

"I think I can get everything in," she said from the dark room.

I squinted, but could barely make out her form half-covered by the cabinet door.

More clinking of glassware. A clack of the cabinet door closing, and Stella set the same small bin in front of me. "That's everything we set aside, and that was way too easy."

I grabbed the can, and she slipped out of the school, dropping to the ground with a thud.

Without a word, I helped her pull the window back down. "I'm fine with easy."

Stella winked and laughed as she sauntered toward the car. No pause at the corner to check for cars. She moved as if she owned this place and had just swung in to check on it. Not like me, cradling the supplies to my chest, praying with everything in me that I could both make this happen and also find a buyer.

She already had the car on, headlights brightening the side of the school, at which point I ran for the passenger's side door.

"See?" she said as I closed the door behind me. "If anyone came over, we could just say we were looking for a quiet place to make out."

I glanced in the back seat, strewn with beakers and tubes and a few other things from Sam's list that didn't fit in the trunk. Then I looked at Stella, her features glowing from the dash lights. And then I glanced at my face in the sideview mirror—looking pale from the fear of getting caught.

Yeah. No one with half a brain would buy the make-out story.

"There's a house just past yours—I go there some-times." She tapped the steering wheel a few times. "We can set up there. I'm guessing you don't want to use your house?"

I guess I'd been blinded by the prospect of money fixing everything and hadn't thought that far, but she was right. Probably best that I not use the place where I lived. "Yeah, smart. We better not create a toxin in the house where my mom is clinging to her life."

"I just need you to not tell anyone about it." Her tone was more serious than I'd ever heard from her. "The house, I mean."

"Who would I tell?"

She glanced at me, her face reflecting the blue and green lights on the dash. "Promise me."

I was about to be let into another part of Stella's world. The fear and excitement from our night washed away, replaced with something new. "I promise."

Stella turned up the radio until my cheeks felt as if they vibrated with the sound, but honestly, it also helped fuzz my thoughts and wash away the adrenaline from our theft. The night passed me in a blur through the window as I rested my forehead against the glass. And then we were slowing as the music notched down.

"Don't need anyone noticing us this last little bit," she explained.

Logically, I knew the music was still loud, but after the ear-piercing sound, it felt like a whisper in the car.

When Stella stopped, her headlights bounced off the front of a townhome, which looked just like all the other spec houses. She'd picked the third in a row of four attached homes.

"This is a good spot, because it's close to the base so no one our age wants to come here to party or anything. Someone left the front door unlocked at one point, so I replaced the doorknob with one that I have the key for."

"Won't they notice?" I asked.

Stella snorted. "There isn't a single tenant on this

whole loop. What are the odds of them picking this place? One they don't have a key to? Especially when there are so many others here? *And* people want the end ones. They always do."

Solid point.

All the excitement pouring off Stella at the school had disappeared somewhere. We silently moved our things from her mom's car into the house, setting up a line of beakers, gloves, eye protection, and our few other pieces of equipment.

Once we were back in the car, I checked the clock. Just after five in the morning.

Our trip to the school felt as if it had taken days rather than hours.

"Are you gonna get in trouble?" I asked.

She shrugged with one shoulder. "Are you?"

There was no way Mom had any idea I'd left the house. "Mom's asleep."

Her head bounced to the music, maybe in a slow nod, maybe not.

"Thanks again."

"Yeah," she answered. "Now we just gotta make the stuff, huh?"

"Oh." The words from the emails came back to me in a rush. "I was threatened with a handful of government organizations in response to the emails I sent to universities and research institutions."

"Oh?" Stella perked up, a corner of her mouth lifting. "You emailed? Which ones?"

"Is that the point?" I asked as she crept through the neighborhood using only her parking lights.

"So a dead end there."

"A dead end."

She pulled in a long breath through her nose and

released it between her lips. "So we gotta find a way to get those MPG people to respond?"

Something like that.

I thanked Stella again, but her jaw was set, and her eyelids had lowered. Just as I stepped through the front door, I realized that a Bunsen burner was part of the extra steps that Sam had taken, and after setting the supplies on the counter, I knew we'd forgotten to grab one.

We were off to a rough start.

TWELVE

Before the hallways filled up, I slipped into the old wing of the high school. First thing I did was relock the windows we'd left unlocked. But then I stood there. What if we needed something else? It wasn't like people were through here that often. I cautiously leaned forward and slipped the lock again.

Mom's obsession with *CSI* meant that I spent the next ten minutes with paper towels and the bottom end of my T-shirt, wiping down every surface I thought we might have touched. After moving what was left in the cupboards around, not a single shelf was left bare. I couldn't imagine a scenario where Stella would think to do this.

The problem was that we didn't just need a Bunsen burner, but the gas it burned as well. I hadn't paid much attention to that when we used them at my old school. Whatever. The burner was the most important thing for now. No bells had rung, so my biggest issue was hoping that the janitorial staff didn't end up over here. Or a teacher looking for supplies.

In a quick move, I opened my pack, knelt down to the floor, and snatched a burner from the bottom shelf. Once it was safely tucked inside, a shuffle came from just outside the door.

"What do you think you're doing?"

My heart leapt into my throat, my stomach dropped through the floor, and I spun to see a flash of blonde and Stella's frame filling the doorway.

"Suck, you scared me!"

She snorted before breaking into laughter. "You should have seen your face!"

"Yeah, well . . ." I gestured to the cabinet and then my bag. "You're good at disguising your voice."

"What'd I forget?" she asked. "I assume we forgot something since you're stocking up again."

"It was me." I shrugged as I stepped around her, ready to be away from the room with the missing school property.

"So . . .?"

"A Bunsen burner," I whispered.

"Ooohhh," she whispered back conspiratorially, though it felt more in jest than anything else.

What kinds of things did Stella take seriously?

"Let's ditch, load up on Taco Bell, and get this thing started," she suggested.

Honestly, that was maybe the best thing I'd ever heard her say.

We walked right back out the front door of the school and headed for her mom's car.

"She's in the field." Stella grabbed the door handle, which immediately unlocked the car. "I'm telling you this because you seem preoccupied with me getting in trouble or whatever."

I crossed the front of the car and fell into the passenger's seat, breathing in without conscious thought. Maybe I'd get one of these someday.

"Food, then your house," she said. "Dad's working from home today, and besides, I don't wanna do all the paperwork to get you on base, plus all the stuff we need is on the backside of your neighborhood."

"Yeah. Okay." Home alone at my house. My gaze flipped toward Stella again as I thought about her lips on my cheek. My lips on hers.

Focus, Chuck.

I had to get this chemical process figured out, find a buyer, and then I could work on other parts of my life, but I had to keep that priority straight.

"What are you going to do about the emails and threats?" Stella asked.

"I deleted the account," I explained. "I didn't know what else to do. And now, nothing. I wait and hope no one can tie it to me."

"Now are you gonna tell me the agencies you were threatened with?"

Her nail polish was already chipped on her right hand, and I thought about how she'd asked me to lift the window the night before. Did she chew on them or something?

"Earth to Chuck." She waved her hand so close to my face, I could smell her fruity lotion.

"Oh, yeah. EPA. FBI. Homeland Security. And OSHA."

"Nice." We slipped into the drive-through, and Stella rattled off a long list of items while I attempted to do the mental math in my head. Who could eat thirty bucks worth of Taco Bell? But I wasn't gonna tell her she had to order less.

"And for you?" she asked.

"That was all for you?"

Stella peered at me over her sunglasses. "I'm not one of those girls who doesn't eat."

"Just a couple of bean burritos."

She snorted before pulling open the center console of her mom's car, where a stack of twenties and fives sat folded. "Mom's always got money in here, and she doesn't keep track of it."

This just felt weird, but I also couldn't remember the last time I'd felt completely full.

Three bags and two large drinks rested on my lap as we made our way back to my house, and in what felt like minutes, we were once again in my room, eating and staring at the last message I'd sent.

"We need to send them something else. Something that puts us on the line rather than them." Stella took another bite of her quesadilla and then said through a mouthful, "I think we need to be bold."

Of course she thought we had to be bold. She was always bold.

"How about this?" She reached over me, her arm nearly touching my cheek and typed:

Buy toxin?

Thankfully, she didn't hit Send, but sat back.

It was bold. We would be the ones taking the first step into naming what we spoke of.

Before I could fully think about it, I hit Enter, sending the message off to whoever sat at the other end.

"Let's get this toxin stuff started," Stella said. "And then I'll take you to a cool building for another one of your LegendCityVids videos."

"Yeah, I think it's too late for that now." That moment, my YouTube channel, felt like it had passed. I'd lost my audience. They'd moved on to other creators. I was a nothing now.

"You never know when one of those is gonna hit."

I shrugged—it felt so futile. Though at the moment, so did my plan of following in Sam's footsteps.

We moved for the door, but I stopped. "I'm gonna call you and leave my phone here, is that okay? That way if the computer beeps, we'll know?"

"If you want to be without your phone, that's fine by me."

I didn't want to leave this room after sending that note, but I also wanted to get started.

With a few quick taps of my phone, Stella had a call to my phone on the line. We left her car at my house and walked on the backside of the houses toward the last loop of townhomes.

"How goes the writing?" I asked her as we shuffled next to each other on the sidewalk. I almost reached for her hand after the cheek-kiss thing, but I still wasn't sure where we stood. And yeah . . . priorities.

"I got ten thousand reads so far on my latest."

"Bonnie and Clyde?" I asked.

"Yup. A pretty basic fictionalization, but people loved it."

"Cool."

"One day I'm gonna write my own story, and millions of people are gonna buy it." There was no sense of hesitation in her voice, and of all my friends, I guessed she was the most likely to make a big dream come true.

We stepped inside the abandoned house, and I immediately set Sam's journal down in front of me before thumbing to the instructions as to how he set up his chemistry set.

Stand with ~~steal~~ steel rod for holding the glassware. Heavy metal base with attachments. Clamps and such. Makes life much easier.

Magnetic stirrer. Magnet under with stir bar and stir. Various sizes of magnetic stir bars.

Heating plate/hot plate.

Round bottom ~~beaker~~ flask. Really useful. Reacting stuff, one neck or two neck. Or three neck. Use a stopper and stop off any of the mouths you're not using. 1000ml/2000ml two neck.

Tubing to release gasses. Teflon tubing doesn't react with anything.

500ml and 1000ml beaker.

Volumetric flasks. Measuring out stuff ~~good~~ really accurately. And glass stopper.

~~Separate~~ Separatory funnel 1000ml.

Reflux condenser—two tubes water goes in one and goes down and steam comes in and liquid comes out the tip.

Connectors. Glass stoppers and stopper with rubber tip for thermometers. And you can put wires in also for electrolysis.

"So, where's your dad?" Stella slipped up onto the counter, letting her legs hang. "Can I ask?"

I stopped with my hands hovering over the journal. "Florida."

"You talk to him?"

"Not if I can help it."

"Don't want to talk about him, I take it?"

A smile tugged at a corner of my mouth as I turned around. "Not if I can help it." I felt more comfortable opening up to Stella after the last convo in the back of the car. "My dad is, let's just say, mentally abusive. Not so much with me, but with Mom. I would get enough backlash from him, though, that it's not worth having any sort of relationship with him."

"Oh, Chuck," Stella said, "I'm so sorry."

"It's okay. I just don't talk a lot about it."

Enough opening up. I changed the subject. "Where are we going to get all this stuff?" I asked, pressing my finger into the page with the list of items.

"I think we can get most of it at the school."

Before I could agree or disagree with taking more things from the school, her phone beeped. Like, my computer beeped on the other end of the line we had open.

We both froze and stared at each other.

They'd messaged back.

"Last one to your room has to snort an infected pinto bean!" And Stella was out the door, her boots clomping on the pavement. I sprinted behind her, knowing we'd have to walk back to lock the place up, but it all meant more time double-checking Sam's notes with our work and . . . and more time with Stella.

When we reached my room, we were shoulder to shoulder, so I paused for a half breath, letting her get in before me.

"I caught that. I hate to win because of chivalry," she said without looking at me as she sat in front of the computer.

The words blared possibility.

MPG: Let's talk details.

I couldn't take my eyes from the screen, but I felt Stella shift her attention toward me. When I directed my attention at her, our eyes locked. Hers were bright. I couldn't begin to guess what my expression looked like.

"This is it, *Sam*."

"What do you want your cut to be?" I asked, only now realizing that she was nearly as invested as I was.

Stella laughed. "A thousand bucks for fun, and your permission to write about it."

"As fiction?"

"Whatever you want," she responded.

"You have it." A less desperate guy may have forced her to take fifty percent, but I needed whatever I could get for Mom. So I wouldn't lie in bed at night listening to her cough and feeling helpless.

I wrote them back.

> **SAM: Time frame?**

> **MPG: 2 weeks.**

"Can we do this in two weeks?" Stella asked. "Like, we've never even made this stuff before. What if Sam's formula and process doesn't work?"

"It'll work," I said as I stared at the last message.

> **SAM: 2 weeks sounds good.**

"What if it doesn't?" Her voice shook a little—this was maybe the first bit of uncertainty I'd ever heard from her. "This is some iteration of the darknet, Chuck. This is for real."

But my mind had already moved on, calculating the numbers that Sam had in his journal. And really, what choice did I have? How could I back out now? No, no way. Not when I was this close to getting a payout that could actually help Mom.

> **SAM: I can make 1.5 grams in that time.**

> **MPG: We'd prefer 3.**

> **SAM: With a little more time.**

> **MPG: 50K for 1.5.**

The emails threatening government involvement rang through my head. The years that had gone by since they'd last talked to Sam. What I actually needed out of this if we were going to move forward. Fifty thousand was a blink of medical expenses.

SAM: 500K—there are a lot of agencies who would not be okay with this exchange.

MPG: 300K.

SAM: Deal.

My hands shook as I sat back from the chair. Three *hundred thousand* dollars. That was enough to change our lives. The back and forth had felt almost automatic. As if by sending that first message, I knew I'd go through with this.

Stella released a long whisper of curse words before sitting on my bed and falling against the wall.

We were doing this. We were really doing this. I was finally taking control of something I could control and moving forward in a way that could change Mom's life forever. My life forever.

"This has to be a university," I said, "doesn't it? I mean, they have grants and can award that much money, can't they?"

The computer pinged with another message, and both Stella and I leapt back toward the screen.

MPG: We'll be in touch on drop spot.

The drop. Crap. Of course. We'd have to exchange money for goods at some point. *With who? Where? What if it all goes wrong? What if they need you to meet them somewhere you can't manage on your budget?*

Stella's smile lit her face. She turned toward me, her breath mixing with mine. "This is legit the coolest thing that's ever happened to me."

Stella was maybe the coolest thing that had ever happened to me. Well, until we made this exchange, and I finally had the funds to get Mom the treatment she needed.

"Aaahhh!" She threw her arms around me, and I wrapped my arms around her, breathing her in. Letting myself settle into this moment. I had to push back the fear, or I'd never get this done. We had a plan. We had a buyer. Now we just had to figure out how to make it happen.

We had a lot of work to do in a short amount of time, but I was finally regaining some sense of control.

THIRTEEN

"What do we need, again?" Stella asked as we pulled into the empty school parking lot. In the dark. As we once again went a night without sleep.

At some point I could rest, but not now. Not with a deadline and a number so big, my head felt as if it would explode. The messaging between Sam and MPG still thrummed through my brain, causing a low hum that blocked out so much else.

"Chuck?"

"Oh yeah. Glassware, tubes, corks, et cetera. I'll bring the list. It's so we can get multiple samples moving forward at once, and another Bunsen burner for the same reason."

"Oh, so just . . ." She trailed off with a wry smile. "Just another full load?"

I swallowed. "Something like that."

As we moved toward the school together just as we had the first time, the muscles in my body weren't as taut. Now there was an end goal—no, more than an end goal. A plan with an ending I needed more than I'd ever needed anything in my life.

I kept my breaths slow and even as we pushed open the window together, as a garbage can was handed out to me with supplies, as we whispered back and forth about what else I might need. The little voice in the back of my head—yeah that's what I'd diminished it to—was quieter this time about the ethics of stealing supplies from the school. First, I'd return them. Second, the school wasn't using them. Third, *three hundred thousand dollars*!

Within a few minutes, we were leaving the parking lot. My mind spun. Well, I sat silent, but Stella was an endless supply of words and what-ifs and who was on the other end of the chat and would we really get to hold that much money when this was all over and wondering if Sam's formula was maybe different and if we could replicate what he'd done as we moved forward. I had no answers, only a quiet determination to get set up and get started.

We finally pulled onto the street of "Stella's house." This was the point where I should have panicked again. When the reality of the dark web and who knows who was on the other end of that chat set in. But just having *some* control over *something* outweighed everything else.

"You with me?" Stella asked.

I just nodded as we moved the rest of the supplies inside.

"I think we should at least start. You don't have much time," she said as she began spreading the supplies over the counter.

I pulled Sam Miller's journal out of the inside pocket of my light coat and dropped it on the counter. "I have the page dog-eared."

I arranged the glassware in the best way I could tell how. A weighted stand off to the left, the steel rod with a couple of clamps facing right. I attached a three-neck round-bottom flask to one of the clamps, and placed a glass stopper that had a silicone grommet to hold a pipette or thermometer. I set a solid glass stopper in one of the open neck holes, and left the other one open.

"This is where we will put the infected beans." I tapped the open neck of the round bottom flask. "It looks like we need to place another stand with a round-bottom flask over here too."

Stella held a bulbous two-thousand-milliliter round-bottom flask upside down. "What if this were a huge lightbulb?" She held the round bottom to her face and smashed her nose and lips into the other side.

"Gimme that thing," I said, smiling.

Stella held it out, then lowered her hand quick, pretending to drop the piece of chemistry glassware.

My reaction was fast, and I reached for the falling flask. Both of our hands touched as I lightly slid it from Stella's grasp, raising one eyebrow. We finished unboxing two five-hundred-milliliter beakers and set them to the side. I carefully set two bottles of liquid containing sulfuric acid and ammonium sulfate next to the beakers.

"There," I proclaimed, thumbing the journal. "I think we're close to being able to start this sucker."

"All this work for a few grams?" Stella asked as she squinted at Sam's words.

"Yep." But that was the deal when something had to be reduced down to the most basic, and most deadly, form. Something else I'd learned from Sam.

I began with opening the can. An audible hiss emerged from the can of Big Boy Beans, found in the storage closet of the gas station down the road. They didn't even charge, and they were wondering why we would want to purchase a dented and defected can of beans. If they only knew what we planned to do with it. And the idea that something so simple as a bloated can of beans could get some serious cash rolling in.

"Just this can here?" Stella asked as she poured a few beans in the large three-neck round-bottom flask.

I nodded.

"This stuff stinks," she said.

"Tell me about it! I've been breathing through my mouth since I opened the can."

We followed Sam's hazmat suit instructions to a T.

Bandanna with N95 mask over it: Check.

Goggles: Check.

Duct-taped jackets to rubber gloves: Check.

Ziploc bags over our shoes, taped to the ankles of our jeans: Check.

And for good measure, we taped the collars closed around our necks. This had to be as sealed as possible.

Once we were done, I looked at Stella and she looked at how ridiculous I looked, and we both busted up laughing. I had to get myself under control because it was hard to breathe through all that material.

"I think the ankle-tight pants with Ziploc bags over our shoes got me the most," Stella said.

I had to resist responding like Darth Vader. We did look stupid. But hey, all in the name of science, right?

We had more than we needed, but . . . "We need to start a few samples because of the time limit."

We worked in silence for a few minutes, setting up four starts. The first part was a lot of checking Sam's notes, and setting up the chemistry glassware and the beakers and the other pieces we'd need to purify the bacteria. I wanted this to be as simple as possible.

I was also looking at the cans of beans. Sam had created an odd sort of holding beaker on his own, and he didn't have any drawings of the thing, but he'd done it our way first—using typical and easy-to-find tools. Never in my life did I think I'd be this into chemistry.

"Why?" Stella asked as she used another one of the old cans of beans.

"Why what?" The counter now felt like a living, breathing thing. Four identical setups that looked somewhat, but not wholly, the same.

"Why do this?" she asked. "Super risky reaching out to some randos online to make an exchange of something we don't really understand. And you don't exactly seem like a risk-taker."

Every reason led back to the same person. "Mom." We locked eyes for a moment. "Why you?"

A corner of her mouth lifted, just enough that my brain flashed back to our brief almost-kiss. "Because you said I could write about it."

A low chuckle erupted from my mouth. Another night's sleep ruined. More things stolen. A venture into the unknown.

"Okay, Mr. Nye," she said.

"Nye?"

"Are you not online?" she teased. *Bill Nye the Science Guy.*"

"Okay. Whatever." I shook my head, the name now sounding slightly familiar. "I need a nap before school."

She nodded. "I'm gonna nap here. I told Mom I'd stay at Cheyenne's house tonight."

I hadn't had to tell my mom anything. All she could do was work and sleep. As I looked over what we'd accomplished again, my head grew heavy, my arms sagged. The past day and this night were catching up to me fast.

Stella grasped my shoulders and turned me toward the door. "Go. Sleep. I'll pick you up for school in the morning."

"But won't people talk?" I teased as we reached the door.

She pulled it open, and I turned to face her, putting our bodies dangerously close together. She peered up at me through thick lashes. "You afraid of people talking about you?"

"You thrive on it," I said instead of answering. When people were talking, it generally wasn't good.

"I do."

I leaned down and pressed my lips to her cheek. "Thank you again."

"Night, Chuck."

And then I was out the door, the warmth of Stella dissipating in the cool night air. The paved path seemed to grow more weeds each day, but I just shuffled over them to find my way home. The draw back to that place, back to our experiment, and back to what I hoped would change my future . . . leaving it all behind felt so wrong, but I had to get home. Had to get sleep. Had to check on Mom.

Before I was aware, I was through the front door, still in a haze of exhaustion. Mom's snoring carried down from upstairs. I trudged up and paused outside her closed door for a moment. She pulled in another long breath, ragged and almost juicy-sounding. Released another long breath. At least it was rhythmic. It was when her breathing wasn't rhythmic that she was really tilting downhill.

This could be over in a few days.

Mom and I could live off three hundred thousand for a long time.

A very long time. Even with her medical bills. We'd lived off less than forty thousand a year many years. We could make this money last a long time.

I had to make this work.

My leg wouldn't stop bouncing. Stella was the only person who knew what I was up to, and I couldn't get the last few days out of my head.

What was I thinking making a deal with an entity I didn't know for a deadly toxin I wasn't sure I could make? How had I gone from doing my best to get good grades and fly under the radar to stealing school property and fabricating a deadly toxin in a makeshift lab? What was I thinking?

Mom.

I knew it was for Mom. For us. For our future. But with the events of the day before pinging around in my brain, and my teachers' words only making that pinging louder and stronger . . . I didn't know what to do.

What if I couldn't make the toxin?

What if the people I was selling the toxin to were criminals? Or one of a million other things? All I had to go on was that it was some university out there somewhere. I buried the fact that we had accessed them through some darknet device on an ancient computer. They were a reputable university, and that was what I told myself over and over.

What if I can't deliver and they come after me? Do universities send thugs after people? How illegal is this? It wasn't like I was making drugs.

Stella didn't show until halfway through period three. She had to help the nurse with something during lunch, and the pit in my stomach over the seriousness of what we'd stepped into had grown every minute I was awake.

As I moved through the hall toward bio, the most obvious thing hit me. Those people thought they were dealing with Sam Miller. Not me. Sam. They wouldn't come after me since they didn't know I existed.

But even with that assurance, it wouldn't take a genius to trace the computer back to my room. The feeling of having *some* control was a hard thing to ignore, and it overcame my concerns. If I could do this—and I'd know in a couple of days—if I could do this . . . life changing. Maybe that needed to be my new mantra. Just get through the next few days. Change my life.

Mrs. Lawler stood at the front of the class, her face somber.

I rubbed the sleep from my eyes and took my seat. My partner, Leo, gave me a quick side glance, but we generally didn't talk.

Stella breezed in just as the bell rang. "Sorry, Lawler. There was a line in the ladies'. That lunch, man . . ." She patted her stomach and collapsed into her chair.

A few kids chuckled. I couldn't stop myself from throwing her a smile.

Her smile back hit me like a train—but in a good way. She stepped into a room and took it over. I stepped into the room and disappeared. She had an indescribable *thing* that I couldn't quite pinpoint.

Our eyes were still locked when Leo leaned forward, blocking my view. "You and her . . ." He waggled his brows, shoving his thumb over to Stella.

"What does that mean?" I asked, mimicking his ridiculous gesture.

"You know." This time an eye roll. Full of generic gestures, this one. "Are you . . ."

"Are we, what?" Of course I knew what he meant, but why did people have to act like children instead of just *asking*?

"You kno—"

"I need to talk to you all about a very serious matter," Mrs. Lawler started.

My attention moved from Leo to the front of the room. Her arms were crossed across her chest as she stared at the class through her chunky glass frames. "We've had some things stolen from the unused wing of the school. Things that were needed for our experiments this week."

Don't look at Stella. Don't look at Stella. Don't look at Stella.

My head grew light. The school's air-conditioning clicked on and roared in my head.

"If any of you return these items, we will take them back, no questions asked."

All of the unknown of our success or failure would be over. The pressure of delivering to the unknown would be over.

I could return everything. I could get money another way.

I shook my head.

Stella leaned forward and raised a brow at me.

"I'm good," I mouthed back at her.

"Do you two have something to share?" Mrs. Lawler asked.

"Oh . . . no . . ." I stammered. "No, ma'am. It's okay. Fine. Okay."

Stella snorted, her hand in a loose fist in front of her mouth as if holding in a laugh. "We usually chat over lunch, but I was helping at the nurse's office."

I shrugged.

Leo waggled his brows again. "Chatting, huh?"

Lawler looked between us a few times and then continued. "Instead of actually doing this experiment, we'll be watching a series of YouTube videos."

Stella sat forward. "From that cool site—"

"No, not from the *ducking love science* people," Mrs. Lawler said as her eyes narrowed at Stella.

Why did Stella have to antagonize her in this moment?

"Obviously," Mrs. Lawler continued. "But if any of you have information that leads to us finding the stolen items, there will be a hundred-and-fifty-dollar reward."

A hundred and fifty dollars.

That used to seem like a lot of money. But I was aiming a *lot* higher than that.

A lot higher.

There was nothing linking Stella and me to the things from that wing of the school. We'd checked for cameras. We were good. Besides, if they had cameras, they'd have just come to Stella since it was her mom's car.

At the end of class, she looped her arm through mine.

"Nice to see you," I said, letting my irritation at hardly seeing her all day seep into my words.

"Don't be weird," she shot back. "I was exhausted and then I called my therapist this morning."

"You have an on-call therapist?"

"Yup," she answered without hesitation.

"Wait." I stopped in the hallway and leaned in close enough to feel her warmth on my face. "Do they know . . . I mean . . . what we're doing?"

Stella laughed. "Stop panicking, Science Guy. Of course not." She started up the hall, and I had to jog to catch up.

"But it means I need to check in at home before I can help you this afternoon," she said. "Think you can get Brock to give you a ride home?"

"Yeah." Though I wondered if he'd try to give me another lecture about Stella.

"What do you have a therapist for?" The second the words were out, I cringed. Bad form. "Crap. Sorry."

"Yeah. Nosy much?" She peered up at me, but didn't seem too annoyed at least. "Everyone should have a therapist. Trust me. I'm definitely not anywhere near the top of the list of kids in this school you should be worried about."

Huh.

"Anyway, I'll be there as soon as I can."

"Yeah. It's fine," I said. And it was. At times, I almost wished she'd back out because I wouldn't need to worry about her, and at other times . . . at all the other times, I didn't want to leave her side. Didn't want her to not be a part of this.

"I like you," jumped out of my mouth.

"I'd have never guessed," she said dryly before shaking her head. "You're so formal, Chuck. Relax. I like you too. I just . . . I like this . . . the kisses and the hanging out and the bit about playing on the darknet and making stories."

Was that what this was to her? Making stories?

I'd take it, but it made me realize again that her parents worked to take care of her—whether she wanted them to or not. My mom wanted to take care of me, but it had never been in the cards for her. She had started my life at a disadvantage. It wasn't her fault, but Stella didn't know what it was like to have someone need you.

I did.

"Take your time," I told her. "It's all good. I'll see you when I see you."

FOURTEEN

Brock pulled to a stop in front of my house. My body ached from my day at school. From my mind racing. From my body tensing over nothing. Well, not nothing, but over future stuff that I couldn't change.

"Thanks again." I reached for the door.

He cocked his head to the side. "You okay?"

"Tired. Didn't sleep much last night."

He stared at me a moment longer before nodding.

"See you tomorrow," I told him, jumping out of the car before he could ask again. At least he hadn't started that conversation when we'd first left the school.

I glanced up at the house. Mom's car sat in the driveway. But it was a workday.

My stomach twisted. Had she already come home early again? I knew employers couldn't fire someone because of their disability—but if they wanted her gone, they'd find a way. Missing too much work was a sure way to get them wondering if they'd made a mistake.

I reached for the door. Unlocked. As soon as I stepped inside, Mom's voice carried from the living room.

"Yes, I know, but I've been on this medication for three years."

I'd heard this conversation a million times. She was talking to the insurance company.

"It's genetic," Mom explained. "This should be in the notes from my last conversation with you. Before I took this job, I called this office."

I closed the door quietly behind me, slipping the deadbolt into place.

"But the out-of-pocket expense for this is half of what I make in a month."

As my gut continued to twist, my resolve began to solidify. Yeah, I was still facing a lot of unknowns, but if I pulled this off—*when* I pulled this off—Mom wouldn't have to have these hours-long conversations to fight for her right to live.

Not wanting to bother her with a text, I scribbled out a note for the table telling her I was studying with friends. I grabbed a soda and some almost-expired pieces of lunch meat from the fridge and started toward the house with Sam Miller's journal tucked under my arm and my phone in my pocket.

My timeline for getting this stuff ready was ticking down fast.

I should have asked for more time.

Too late now.

The key was under the mailbox like Stella had showed me, and I let myself in.

The bits of beans we had put in the beakers and sealed off was growing nothing that I could see, so that was terrible. I needed to hurry the process. Because this condo was in the middle of the row, the house felt cool. This was one of the reasons for wanting a Bunsen burner. Sam had used one a few times to speed up the process. Just a little warmth, not a ton. Just enough to help the bacteria grow faster. And then cool moments to allow the stuff to breathe or something.

I glanced at my phone to check the time and also look for a text from Stella.

Nothing.

As soon as I picked up a Bunsen burner, my gut dropped. I stared at the attachment for a hose that hooked up to the gas used to create a fire. But of course, we didn't have fuel for one of these things. The power, gas, and water to these townhome-condo things probably hadn't been on for years. No way was I bringing any of this to my house.

And these guys didn't want ordinary stuff. Anyone could do that. They needed what Sam had made.

I read over his instructions again. He had some special airtight something he'd made.

Squinting at how we'd put together the beakers and the bulging can of Big Boy Beans that Sam recommended, I hoped we'd re-created his idea well enough.

Yeah, I'd rushed offering this up for money.

But maybe this would all still work out.

"Okay, Chuck. Think."

My fingers tapped a frantic rhythm on the counter. I could move one of the beakers next to a window for more heat. But the deal was we had to keep this in a room at a specific temperature, and it wasn't warm enough. Then we were supposed to add a *little* more heat.

I flipped the drawers open until I came to one filled with plasticware, ketchup packets, mini containers of barbecue sauce, chopsticks, and napkins.

Napkins.

I grabbed a handful, crumpled them up next to a beaker with a bit of beans, and then pulled a lighter from my pocket. That would add a little warmth.

I flicked my thumb over the lighter, and the napkins

caught in a ball of fire just as Stella stepped inside. "What the heck are you doing?"

When I jerked, the beaker, ball of fire, and the dead Bunsen burner crashed to the floor.

I stared at the ball of fire as the napkins twisted around each other and burned, before stamping them out with my foot so the house didn't catch fire.

Stella snorted. "Again. What the heck, Chuck?"

"I was trying to warm it up a little." Now that the words were out, it felt stupid. I shook my head. "I need to get serious about this."

Her gaze floated over the counter.

"We need more gas for the burner, to get the stuff at the right temperature," I explained.

"Trip to the hardware store?" She took a step back toward the door.

"Yeah." We had thermometers, but I needed gas and a tube for the burners. A few steps forward and then a step back. Even though we'd stolen most of our supplies, the few things we did need were draining my account fast.

"At least we did four samples," she said as she held the door open.

At least there was that.

Each part of our trip to town felt as if it took an age.

The drive.

Getting out.

Finding a small camping tank.

A hose that matched.

Promising the people who worked there that we really just needed a new one for our mini grill—the whole time wondering what we were doing this for. Who was on the other end of that chat? *Who were we doing this for?*

I read Sam's journal the whole way back. The part where his process veered away from the easy method of creating this toxin, of the basic forms like what was used for Botox. That was what set this apart. That was what would make this worth so much.

There was no going halfway.

By the time we'd made it back to the house, my focus was prepared and ready.

Stella must have sensed that I needed to be without distraction. She sat on the counter, scrolling through her phone for a while.

I unwrapped our propane and tube—new purchases that added to the suffering of my bank account.

Just a few more days and then I'd be set.

This process just had to go the way Sam said it would.

I grabbed another bulging can of Big Boy Beans that had a compromised seal. We had to assume it had some cultures of clostridium botulinum cells growing slightly in it. I dumped the whole can into a slurry mix of milk protein, brewer's yeast, and corn sugar. From my studies, it seemed like since the bacteria wouldn't be competing with any other microorganisms, they could multiply quickly, within eighteen to twenty-four hours.

We kept the temperature above fifty degrees. The flask was sealed off, absent of oxygen.

"It'll grow into a rod-shaped bacterium," I said, "then when all that sugar and yeast gets eaten up by the bacteria and nutrients become limited, the whole thing goes into a mass cell suicide."

I felt dumb for narrating while I worked, but couldn't seem to stop myself. "That's when the toxin is released from the cell. Then the whole thing should turn clear according to Sam's notes. You'll be able to see right through it."

I checked temperatures on the three remaining samples and fired up the Bunsen burner to bring the temperature up. Not too high—just enough for the process. Moving the samples closer together, I kept the burner on, warming the area. "According to Sam, it takes about three days to grow the culture of bacteria and produce the clear toxic liquid."

"Hey," Stella whispered. "I gotta go soon."

I nodded once.

She stepped up next to me and wrapped her arm around my back, tucking her thumb in the belt loop of my pants.

My attention snapped from the temperature gauges to her.

"You're cute when you're concentrating."

I felt a corner of my mouth lift. "Are you objectifying me? Admiring me for my beauty instead of my brains?"

"Maybe a little," she teased back before planting a kiss on my shoulder. My arm burned as I stared at her.

Purple bags rested under her eyes, and there was a tiredness in the focus of her eyes that I'd never seen before. "You okay?"

"Yeah. Gonna go home and sleep for two days. Or at least until my mom drags me out of bed to go to school."

"I'll see you there," I told her. "Thanks again for finding this house."

She released a breath and her chin rested on my shoulder as she looked at me. "You need sleep too, Mr. Science Guy."

Yeah. I did. "I'm gonna watch these for a few more hours."

"Your mom won't worry?"

"I left a note." And I'd break something if I had to listen to her argue with insurance companies.

Her brows twitched upward. "You need a ride tomorrow?"

I leaned closer, drawn in by her, always. "Mom's got me."

In another quick move, her lips touched my shoulder again and she left in a blink.

Once the door closed behind her, my attention moved back toward the beakers, the temperatures, and Sam's journal. Okay, and the place on my shoulder where she'd kissed me—twice.

For two hours, I stared at the temps, adjusting the burner again and again. But how to keep them at a consistent temperature all night?

I spun in the kitchen a few times and my attention fell to the oven. There was no power here, but . . . I set up the Bunsen burner in the oven, turned it on high, and closed the door. One by one, I moved the three sealed beakers next to the oven.

The homemade hazmat suit was becoming less cumbersome. I had to teach myself how to walk with baggies on my feet without slipping and spilling the whole toxin experiment on me. I got pretty good at steadying my breath too, so I didn't feel like I was going to suffocate.

After forty-five minutes of me tweaking a video I would never upload to YouTube, I still couldn't bring myself to the idea that my channel was dead. Plus, I still liked editing videos more than playing some game.

Enough time had passed that the oven temperature was just above a hundred. That temp was a little higher, but as soon as I opened the door and set my materials inside, it would lose heat.

Okay . . . I stood in front of the oven. The faster I moved, the less heat would be lost. The closer I'd be to fixing Mom.

"Okay, Chuck, you got this." I jerked open the door,

quickly—and gently—set each beaker in the oven, and flipped the lid closed.

According to my thermometer, I'd only lost a few degrees. Not perfect, but I wasn't sleeping here, and I wasn't bringing this stuff home. Hopefully that warm air would really make the bacteria produce more spores.

"Okay. Okay," I said, still staring at the oven, now wondering if I could leave this behind.

No. Staying was dumb. The temp should remain steady enough in the oven until I turned on the Bunsen burner again.

I flipped my phone over. Almost midnight.

Every step toward home felt like a step away from my goal. Like I was betraying this thing that I needed to do. The house was dark and quiet when I arrived. Mom had added to my note.

Going old school, huh? Sorry I missed you. I was on the phone. See you in the morning before school. Love you, Mom

* * *

There was no sleep. Just shifting one way and then another. Wondering how cold the oven was. How the samples were doing. If I was going to make my deadline, or if I'd have to ask for more time. If I had to take time, would they not give me as much money? So many unknowns.

Just as my body found some measure of relaxation, my phone buzzed to wake me up. I rolled onto my stomach and hit the alarm. My body was wood. There was no way I was going to school.

"Chuck?" Mom called down the hallway. "Did I hear your alarm?"

"Mmph," I replied, my mouth thick and dry.

Two knocks were followed by her cracking my door.

"I can't," I croaked. "Too tired."

One of Mom's brows rose a bit and a half smile lit her face. I hadn't seen her well enough to tease in a while. "So you studied so hard that you can't make it to school? Am I understanding this correctly?"

Not at all. "Yup."

"Get some sleep." She shook her head but was still smiling. I was off the hook.

I could nap. She'd leave.

I could watch the samples all day.

Sometimes, not-so-great things worked out for the best.

FIFTEEN

Turned out that watching temperatures on beakers wasn't riveting.

I knew I was following Sam's instructions, and in about ten hours, I'd need to start the next part of the process, but I'd already laid out my gloves, goggles, and mask.

There would be no sleep again tonight, but then I'd be another step closer. For now . . . sit and watch.

When I had to pee, I went in the backyard to make sure that I wasn't seen. The weeds wouldn't care. Honestly, in this dry place, they'd probably be grateful for the moisture.

Twenty minutes after the last bell rang at school, Stella came in the door. "How's it going?"

The room shifted with her presence. All the boring sitting and waiting became more of a sit and wait *with Stella*. An excitement that was missing before she arrived hummed in the air. Stella just knew we'd make this work, so we'd make this work. Simple. At least, that was how it all felt when she was with me.

"So?" She leaned forward again, staring at me. Probably because I still hadn't answered her question.

"Good, I think. Almost to the part where I actually get to work with my hands."

"Aside from the setup?" she asked.

I shrugged in agreement.

"What have you been up to all day?"

"Uh . . ." What had I been doing? "Playing on my phone, watering the weeds . . ."

Her brows furrowed.

"Watching rod-shaped bacteria grow in cheap beans."

A smile lit her face then. Her eyes were brighter than they'd been, less darkness rimming the underside.

"You look rested."

"Took something to help me sleep last night." She shrugged. "I needed it."

"I didn't sleep."

"Which is why you missed school, huh?"

"I guess," I answered.

"So, how's it going?"

I leaned over the counter and pointed at temperatures that matched Sam's perfectly.

Stella wiggled her brows and rested her elbows on the counter next to mine. "Well done, sir."

"Thank you, madam." I grinned. Who knew I'd be good at chemistry?

Though the stakes were pretty high, so . . .

I released a long sigh, almost as if the whole day had been spent waiting to see Stella again and show off my work. We both paused when a car engine sounded outside, pulling into the complex. We stilled as if it would make a difference in someone looking at this place or not.

Two knocks were followed by, "Police!"

We both startled back, staring at one another. *Police? How? How were police here? Why?*

"The car," she whispered as her eyes fell closed. "Damn it. I didn't think to park it somewhere else. You know, somewhere people live."

Yeah, I hadn't thought of that either. But, like, no one ever came back here.

"Don't suppose we could pretend no one's home?" I whispered as the slamming of my heart drowned out everything else.

Police. Either the school supplies or the chat on the darknet had brought them here. Suddenly, I hoped it was for the school supplies. There was no good explanation for the chat.

She shook her head. "Don't think so."

Two more knocks. "Police! Please answer the door."

What could I do . . . where . . . I had no time. There was no time. I grabbed one of the sealed-off beakers, opened the cool oven, and set it inside. Then the next, then the last.

The door opened just as the oven door closed and I stood up tall. "Afternoon," I squeaked. That wasn't gonna help our case.

The uniformed cop's eyes narrowed slightly as he took in the mess of equipment we'd taken from the school littering the counter behind us.

"Hey, Officer Mass," Stella chirped.

"Hello, Stella."

I glanced between them. "You two know each other?"

"We've met a few times," the officer said dryly. "You two wanna explain what's going on here?" He stepped around me and into the kitchen.

No, no, I did not want to explain. At all.

"We needed dishes?" Stella offered.

He pulled open the oven.

Because I hadn't fully closed it before he'd opened the door.

"Don't you need a warrant or something?" I asked.

His gaze slowly moved from my precious botulism starts to me.

Right. Of course. This wasn't my house. Sometimes, I was an idiot.

"What . . ." He leaned sideways and peered in the oven. "What is this?"

"Uh . . ." I stammered. I glanced at Stella for help, but she leaned against the wall of the house with her arms crossed, still chewing her gum.

How could she chew gum at a time like this?

"Moonshine," I blurted.

The officer cocked his head to the side. "That looks a lot more like the manufacturing of drugs than alcohol." He stepped back as if the concoction was going to attack him.

"No, really." Stella picked up a can of beans. "See, like, people ferment grapes to make wine. We thought we'd try to ferment beans. Bean booze. A new invention in adult beverages!"

"You better hope that's what this is, or you two are looking at hard time in juvie."

Stella's brows shot up. We stared at one another for a moment before she shrugged in a gesture that felt like, *okay, this seems okay.*

I took what felt like my first real breath. "I'm . . . I'm . . . We're . . ." I stammered. "We're sorry about the stuff. We planned on giving it all back. We didn't realize it was being used."

"Uh-huh," he grunted. "Well, we're gonna have you two and your parents come to the station so we can ask a few questions."

I swear all the blood drained from my body. All of it. The room spun around me. No, no, no . . . this was supposed to HELP Mom, not make her life harder.

138

I released a long sigh. "Our parents are both on base. It may take a while."

"That'll give you two some time to turn over whatever that is to us." He gestured loosely toward the jars in the oven. "And time to get the rest of this stuff loaded into the trunk of my car."

"No problem," Stella chirped, as if the officer had asked if she wanted to help with cookies or something.

Nothing bothered her. I was convinced of that now. Nothing. Brock's warning may have held some weight. Was Stella bad news? Too late. I liked her too much.

Her parents were going to totally lose their minds over this.

As Officer Mass loaded up most of the glassware in a tattered cardboard box, Stella leaned close to me. "Isn't he going to get sick? I mean, without all those masks and Ziplocs on his feet?"

"I hope not," I replied. "Honestly at this stage of growth, the only way to get sick was to eat it . . . I think." I grimaced at the idea that I truly didn't know. All I knew as of now was that we weren't getting sick, and it wasn't like this old house had air locks we entered first. Everything I had read about botulism, you had to eat it, and I didn't see Officer Mass dipping his finger into the culture to taste it.

My mom would just be so . . . disappointed. Honestly, that was the worst. Anger was something I knew how to deal with—I'd dealt with that in Dad for years. But disappointment?

The. Worst.

And this was the last thing Mom needed. Me screwing up and causing more for her to deal with.

Please let this not cost money.

* * *

I rubbed my dry eyes, the noise of the police station rattling around me, Mom's sadness and disapproval wafting toward me in waves. We sat in a strange waiting place—not outside, but not really inside either.

"Well," she said in a tired voice. "Let's go."

I gave Stella a small wave—her parents hadn't arrived yet. I guess I got off easy on that one, because they'd probably have words for me too.

"I suppose we're lucky that they just want you to replace the broken and ruined glassware," Mom said as we neared the receptionist's desk.

Only, beakers were freaking expensive. Way more money than I would have guessed. Fortunately for me, the school had purchased the Pyrex ones, but still . . . That was a hundred and fifty bucks down the drain. I was basically down to a few dollars in my checking account. No way would Stella be paying for this.

It physically hurt to hand my bank card to the receptionist at the station. The money would somehow magically make its way back to the school after all the paperwork I'd just signed.

"At least you're not getting charged," Mom said softly.

Yeah, at least there was that.

A sharp woman with Stella's eyes strode into the waiting area. I kept my attention on the counter like a coward. Now was not the time to introduce myself.

With a quick signature casting away my life savings, Mom and I were back outside. Walking in silence.

"Sorry," I mumbled.

She didn't speak until we were both in the car. "I just don't understand."

"It was dumb. We didn't think anyone was using all that stuff, and we thought . . ." We thought we could do something big and change our lives. Give Stella something else to write about.

"Moonshine, though? Out of beans? After watching your father, you swore that wasn't even . . ." She trailed off again. "You've always promised me that drinking wasn't something I had to worry about with you."

Of course she was at a loss for words. I generally stayed out of trouble and under the radar, and now this. It was only because of our stellar GPAs, and my clean record, that we hadn't been charged. And even though Stella had been picked up before, her priors were just because she'd been out after curfew.

I mean, we could be going to jail. I had to find some relief, but we were almost out of time, definitely out of supplies, and everything I'd been working toward was slipping away at an alarming rate.

The car bumped over the pavement on our way home. My gut twisted with the loss of money. I was in this awful position of knowing that getting a job was the smart way to get money, but I could get so much more, so much faster, if I could redo Sam's process.

Slipping down in the car seat, I stared out the window, the houses blurring around me.

What had happened to Sam? To his stuff? To the special beaker he created to make the toxin? I'd found his other things—even his computer. What if his custom chemistry glassware was just . . . in a different house or something?

Maybe I could do some online searches for him, or there had to be another way to learn more. To do more. I was out of cash to buy supplies, but there had to be a way to make this thing work. I couldn't imagine giving up after getting so close.

When we pulled up to the house, Mom just stopped the car and didn't move.

Right.

"Was this move a bad one?" she asked in the smallest voice I'd heard from her since Dad left.

"No." I shook my head. "It was a dumb thing, I just . . ."

"And Stella seemed so nice."

"She *is*," I insisted. "This isn't her. I just . . . I had all those chemistry books, and I was curious. Looking for something to do. That's all it was. I swear."

Mom didn't need the kind of stress she'd had when Dad was around. I was not going to cause her more stress.

"So, what do I do with you?" She turned to face me.

Stella would probably lose driving privileges. She might end up grounded or without her phone or something.

"Can we chalk this one up to my one act of teenage rebellion?" I asked hopefully.

We looked at one another for a moment, Mom seeming to study me. She nodded once, a corner of her mouth lifting. "Yeah, we can do that."

As soon as we got out of the car, coughs wracked her body until she was doubled over.

I ran around the front of the car, stopping only when I reached her. "Okay?"

She nodded slightly as we started for the front door. "Just been off my medication for a day or two, but it looks like it'll get straightened out soon."

That wasn't going to be enough time.

That was something, but I still needed a way forward, and Sam Miller was gonna lead me. First thing was heading upstairs to start doing some real research on Sam Miller—who he was, and where he might have stashed his equipment.

Mom needed help now.

But first . . . first I'd need to figure out a way to message MPG to ask for an extension on time. And then I'd have to take whatever they offered.

SIXTEEN

All I'd managed to do last night was mention on the chat that I'd run into trouble and had to move labs, and that there would be a delay. I hadn't heard back, and all I could wonder was what if they backed out? What if they thought I wasn't trustworthy and took away their support? There were too many unknowns.

There was no avoiding school the following day. Sam's journal was tucked in my pocket as I moved through the hallways. With the long stares that darted away when I turned my head, I guessed that word had gotten out. The cops would probably be dropping off the stolen stuff sometime today, so that could be awkward and horrible.

I peered through the crowd for Stella, but didn't see her before first period, during first period, or between first and second. Brock caught up to me after US government.

"Hey, so . . ." He trailed off.

"I've heard whispers," I said. "You don't have to tiptoe around the fact that I got caught for taking the stuff from the school."

Brock rubbed his forehead. "Stella's tricky, man, I warned you."

"It was my idea," I said flatly. "It was stupid. I was just . . . looking for something to fill the time."

"Sorry, I . . ." He shook his head. "I wasn't trying

to get in your business or whatever, but man, it just didn't seem like you. Stella? Nothing would surprise me, but . . ."

"What *is* her background?" I did everything I could to keep moving. Pretend like knowing more about her didn't suddenly feel like the most important thing.

Brock snorted as we rounded the corner and walked into English. "You've spent more time with her than I ever have."

"But what's the scoop or rumors or whatever?"

"The rumors are wild and unfounded," Brock said, shrugging. "We all know she's been picked up for being out past curfew, maybe for minor in consumption or something, but her parents are, like, important on the base here. A lot of people think she knows military stuff she shouldn't, or that she hates her parents. Some have talked about her dad being an abusive jerk, but we've all only ever seen him once for a choir concert last year. That's it."

"Huh."

The familiar smell of coconut and something sweet wafted over me. I looked up to see Stella staring at me, her arms crossed over her chest. "Don't you know it's rude to gossip?"

Brock jumped back across the aisle and into his seat.

I swallowed.

"If you want information, it's best to go to the source. Though Brock is right about one thing—most of what's talked about is totally unfounded. My dad's fine. He's just hyper-focused on his job. He's nicer than Mom. Mom's fine. She's doing her best. There's nothing wrong with my parents." Her face twisted up into a smile that sent goose bumps up my arms. "Just me."

And then she sat. And I knew I'd messed up something else.

Because of course.

* * *

At that point, I basically had Sam's journal memorized. The most important pages were bookmarked. The ones that laid out the steps for the purified toxin. The book sat in my backpack as I headed for the downtown library. No way would I do this search from the high school—their search engines stopped everything. But why search anyway? Getting caught again would be more than restitution and a slap on the wrist.

But the money. If it was a university, then no harm done to deliver. And of course I could help Mom. I had clues as to Sam's life, but maybe if I had a few more, I'd know where to look for whatever supplies he might have still had whenever he left this area.

When I sat down, there was no way around the fact that I had to use my student card at the library, but searching for a person wasn't new. People did it all the time. If I ended up with his books, it would make sense that I'd be curious.

I started with the basics: "Sam Miller, Twin Falls, Idaho."

The top article was from the local newspaper. "Local Teen Dies of Alcohol Poisoning, Heightening Awareness of Teen Drinking."

An unexpected pang of loss dragged a trail through the center of my body. Sam wasn't quite eighteen when this happened. Just older than me. I pulled the journal out of my bag, wanting to see his writing again.

This was the property of a dead kid.

Maybe he could tell me how to handle the people on the other end of the chat. How to manage what he'd done. Or what he maybe intended to do before he died.

Had he worked out a meeting with the people on that chat? Had he died before it happened? After? *During*? So many questions. And frankly, it seemed too convenient for him to just die like that. I needed to do a more thorough investigation.

I went back to my original search, and quickly added "toxin" to the list of search words.

The top result this time was a site called Conspiracies R Us.

Well that was unexpected. Though it could be any Sam Miller—it wasn't like the name was super unusual.

But the second the browser jumped to the article, I knew I was in the right place.

WHEN THE CASE RUNS COLD:

WE PUT OUT THE INFO, AND HOPE YOU CAN HELP SOLVE IT.

Like every week, we have a good one for you.

COLD CASE FILE #B35—The "Death" of Sam Miller

Sam Miller, a teen in Twin Falls, ID, supposedly died of alcohol poisoning, but the inside scoop from a Boy Scout friend is that Sam had created a crystal form of botulism toxin, planned to sell it, and was killed in the exchange. The EPA took most of the items involved in this case.

This has been only somewhat verified, though it follows the pattern of government involvement in interesting things regular people do that the government doesn't want them doing. Sam Miller was working on a merit badge for his Boy Scout troop and then didn't stop work-

ing on botulism. He had a gift, and time, and developed something incredible.

His friend, the one who agreed to speak to us if we kept their name out of the record, was a genius in IT, and that's how Sam found himself set up on the dark web. It exists, people. It exists.

So, what do you think?

Government cover-up of a young genius who must have contacted an enemy of the state, or another kid who drank too much? Did the government kill him? Did the people he met on the dark web? Or did he get too close to his creation?

We may never know . . .

A chill ran down my spine as I finished reading, and in that second, it hit me why Stella was ready to jump into this thing with me. One day someone might talk about the two of us this way—not dead, hopefully, but still . . . she wanted to write about what we accomplished. Would people wonder if it was real or fake? Would they guess as to the outcome of what we did?

Now I had another word to add to my list of search items: "Conspiracy."

The page filled with random websites talking about the legendary Sam Miller. I started at the top. My stomach growled, reminding me of home, and I sent Mom a text to tell her I was studying at the library. One after another, the sites talked about a young kid who had somehow figured out a formula to create a new toxin from botulism, but no one had cracked the formula, and the amateurs who thought they might have were too scared to use the toxin.

On one hand, I wasn't surprised at all. According to the journal, that is what Sam had done, but to see other people in on his secret—my secret—felt exposing. And another part of me wondered how anyone had found out if he'd simply died of alcohol poisoning. There was a chance I'd never get the full story.

I had only a few more ideas on Sam—not really fully fleshed-out ones. But I did wonder how much I might be able to get for his journal among the people on these conspiracy sites. With this amount of investigation, I couldn't believe that his science texts and journal hadn't been confiscated. Though maybe he'd done what Stella and I were doing—used a different house.

I went to YouTube to see what else I could dig up. Conspiracy blogs were one thing, but videos? A lot of it wouldn't be true, but right now, I just needed more information on someone who died at my age, whose footsteps I was walking in.

Opinions varied, but very few people believed that Sam died of alcohol poisoning like the media said. His girlfriend wasn't named anywhere, but she had come forward a year or two after he died. My search was getting more solid, and I figured that if I could find the same piece of information in several places, it held more weight. I also disregarded looking for old yearbook photos from ten or so years ago, and I didn't want to start snooping around for his past girlfriend. I had to keep things secret.

Some sources even wondered if Sam were still alive somewhere, working deep underground for the government. Though if that were the case, he'd have known where to come get his experiment things.

Once I knew to check federal agency sites, or use federal agencies in my search, and spent a couple hours on YouTube, I learned a few more details:

Sam died too young—my age. Unless his death was faked—conspiracy.

Sam had contacted foreign agents from somewhere,

and the FBI's investigation didn't go over well with the military base's security.

The EPA had come to the military base and confiscated some of Sam's things.

Right around Sam's death, the EPA, the CDC, and Homeland Security were all in town for one thing or another. So if the EPA had taken Sam's stuff, they must have done something with it.

Some "authorities" on Sam's death said that the EPA had taken his stuff to try and re-create what he'd done, but he was dead, and they had equipment, no notes. This was something. Apparently, the EPA buried things in a grid to ensure that they had room for more things, and so they'd know what section held which items. This meant they'd dig up a place, and for the next chunk of time, that place would be the section used. Or as in the case with the EPA site closest to Twin Falls, they kept less hazardous materials in a field of CONEX boxes.

Now that I had a year of "death" and an idea of where to look for Sam's original supplies, things were looking up. What I did not want to think about was the possibility that he'd died in the exchange. Though if that were the case, why would MPG think that I was Sam? No, they hadn't been the ones to kill him, or they wouldn't be talking to me. They'd be far too suspicious about who I was.

Google Earth was about to be my best friend. I glanced around me, only now noticing that the after-work crowd had arrived at the library. Families, maybe people here looking for better jobs after leaving their current one.

A sense of anonymity helped me relax—the librarians would be busy helping people who wanted help rather than looking over my shoulder. I found the large EPA site—a spot in Utah—but as soon as I used Google Earth, the image blurred out.

Seriously? The EPA was being this secretive? All the stuff was behind a fence. And in CONEX boxes, from what I could tell.

With a sigh, I stood and stared at the books behind me. Something, somewhere, had to have information about the EPA and where and how they buried stuff. I logged off the browser and went to the library's search tool: "EPA, Utah, Idaho."

Most of what they had was for some test that the EPA did, but there was a book called *Strange Modern History in the State of Utah*. That seemed as good a place as any to start. Most of the conspiracy sites said that the Utah burial place was far larger and more used than anywhere else except Nevada. I could believe it.

I made note of the section of the library where the book sat, logged out, glanced around to see if anyone was watching, and started for the reference section. The book was dusty, resting on the second shelf from the floor.

The pictures on the front were grainy and weird. I couldn't conceive of a publisher using this type of cover image, but whatever. If this book had what I needed, I was set. The title hadn't lied. It was full of random facts. In March of 1968, about six thousand sheep died inexplicably—though later it was very obvious that military tests had caused the deaths. There was a town that made its residents say whether or not they supported the United Nations. *What?* In the middle of Utah? And the dude who some thought was the infamous D.B. Cooper went to BYU? Some guy had started his own country within Utah—so weird. And then . . .

EPA in UTAH—grid schedule and burial site of some of the western US's biggest threats.

YES. This was basically spot-on for what I needed.

I said a silent thank you to the two authors of the book, who were very likely as disturbed as its contents. I marked the pages, complete with black-and-white photos, and headed to make copies. And then stopped and stared at the sign: "FIFTEEN CENTS A COPY"

I sighed. I had two pennies crammed in my wallet. That wasn't gonna be enough. I walked with the book back to its shelf. But I needed this information. If I could pinpoint the area where Sam's stuff might be buried, I might be able to find a way forward. No buying science equipment I couldn't afford, and no more second-guessing on this final piece that Sam had created to help make the toxin.

Oh yeah. I could just check out the book. I walked to the main counter, and the woman frowned. "This is a reference book."

"Yes," I responded. "I . . . need it for school." I was not at all convincing, because who would look at that book and think that it was necessary for school?

"We don't check out reference books." She frowned in apology. "If you need to make copies of the pages, you can use the copy machine."

Yeah, for fifteen cents a page, and I needed three pages.

She reached for the book. "I can put it away for you."

I clutched it to my chest. "No thank you. I'll just . . . take some notes. You know, for school." All those conspiracy videos and articles online had clearly fried my brain.

I walked back upstairs and to the reference section. I needed those pages.

Before allowing myself too much time to think, I knelt down, opened the book, and ripped out the two pages I needed. I folded them immediately, stuck them in my backpack, and then allowed myself to peer up to see if I'd been caught.

No one in this aisle.

I released a breath, replaced the book, and stood. Time to make the long walk home. As much as I didn't want to bug Mom, I did want to crash in my bed and let my brain sort through everything I'd learned.

I walked back down the stairs and headed for the front door, the pages in my backpack feeling like lead weights.

"Young man?" the librarian called.

My body washed cold in an instant. Someone had seen me. They had turned me in. I wouldn't get my pages. I slowly turned. "Yeah?"

"Your backpack's coming unzipped." She gave me a warm smile before turning to the two kids waiting in line to check out books.

"Uh, thank you." I carefully swung my pack down and closed the zipper.

Once I was outside, I pulled out my phone to text Mom. The second my fingers connected with it, I shook my head.

You idiot, you could have taken a stupid picture of the pages with your phone.

Too late now.

SEVENTEEN

Mom coughed all the way back to the house. The deep, underlying rasp said that her assurances were lies. The last time she'd sounded this bad, she'd ended up in the hospital for a month. We were still paying off those bills and would be for a while—unless I could do something about it.

"You sound terrible," I said quietly as we pulled into the driveway.

Mom shrugged. "I think it's just getting used to a new climate and a new schedule. It'll settle."

But she didn't look at me as she stopped the car and got out, leaving the familiar pit of helplessness in my stomach. Every cough, every labored breath, every bill—it all pushed me forward to just deal with MPG. I would rather save her life than my own at this point. I was tired of seeing her suffer. I had to be honest with myself—if she went to the hospital, there was a good probability she wasn't coming home. At least I had the pages from the book. I had a destination. I wasn't completely helpless.

As I got out of the car, Mom was watching me. "Are you okay? I keep thinking about the police . . . and the . . ."

I waved her away. "It was a one-time thing. I'm

good." *And I'm sorry.* The main thing was that I could not afford to get caught again.

Mom wheezed her way upstairs, and I rolled a couple mystery-meat hot dogs in a moist paper towel and tossed them in the microwave. I stared at the food rotating, thinking about how microwave technology was "discovered" accidentally. Spencer had taught himself using textbooks—like Sam and like me. He was working on something totally separate and melted a snack. Then he followed that trail instead of calling his true experiment a failure, and now I had dinner in less than a minute.

The microwave beeped. I grabbed my dinner and a couple buns and jogged up the stairs for my room. As soon as I sat, I set Sam's journal on my desk next to my dogs. I flipped to the back page and stared at the badge he'd earned for his experiment.

Another pang hit me, knowing he died in a way that shouldn't have happened. People who said he was still alive just wanted him to be. And after reading his journal, I didn't believe for a second he'd died of alcohol poisoning. I did believe that if he'd lived, he would have been an incredible scientist. I was just following his plan. He was the one who'd come up with the map to the specialized version of the toxin. I was gonna see this through for me, and most importantly, for Mom.

I pulled the badge from the book and set it on my desk. This thing would be my good luck charm. No more mistakes. No more getting caught. I flipped on the ancient computer.

Our last few message exchanges stared back at me.

As I took a bite of the mystery meat, I took the stolen pages from my backpack and flattened them on the desk.

Funny that someone from the government thought to blur out Google Earth, but never realized how much information was in this obscure book about Utah. Sam's stuff was taken about seven years ago. He died about seven years ago. That would mean that if the EPA buried his stuff, it would be in this section.

My cheeks ached before I realized I was still just sitting there and smiling. The area was far too big for me to dig up, but now that I knew about the time Sam died, and I also knew that there had to be records of tax money spent, and to whom, for anything not considered for the safety of national security, I'd just need to look up any contractors who maybe transported or buried Sam's stuff.

I popped in the last bite, which was mostly bun, and pushed my plate aside. Mom's coughing came from the bathroom now, only driving me farther back into my room and onto my phone.

And yeah, I knew that digging up the records wasn't going to be easy, but three hours and two sodas later, my head ached, and my eyesight was so blurry, I could barely make out my phone's screen.

I had the dates. I had the location. But with the base beginning to close down at that time, and the US Army using a lot of outside contractors, there was a ton to sort through. Okay, I had to regroup. There had to be a way to make this work better. Maybe instead of looking here, I should look more specifically at the EPA site in Utah. And not wanting to go to the library again, I decided to use Sam's computer for the quick search.

Thirty minutes later, I was staring at a picture copy of a receipt for a drop-off and transport. I took that date back to the stolen pages. Back to how the EPA used their grid to aid in them knowing what was buried where.

The grid square for the year his stuff was buried was near one of the light posts placed in the yard. The chances of exposure were terrible for me, but it would mean a greater chance of finding *Sam's things*. I picked up the small merit badge again.

After promising myself I wouldn't get in any more trouble, I was considering trying to find a way to dig up Sam's stuff from a government site a whole state away. I was determined to use his equipment. According to his journal, he had devised a couple of specialized chemistry flasks to make sure the toxin's purity was off the charts. And that was what I wanted to provide to MPG since I had already blown my deadline with them. If I used Sam's chemistry set, it'd make up for me being late on delivery.

But there had to be a way to make this work. There had to be. Google Earth was blurred out, but not everywhere and not completely. Now to plan a road trip that would definitely require an overnight alibi . . .

I sent another message to MPG explaining the shift in timeline again and hoped we could still make it all work out.

✳ ✳ ✳

Exhaustion tugged at my coherent thoughts, but I still stood at the front door of the school waiting for Stella. She hadn't reached out since her mom had come to the police station. Well, and since I'd been caught talking about her with Brock. I glanced at the clock again. The first bell would ring in just a few minutes. Where was she?

I refolded my arms across my chest. Shoved my hands in my pockets. Refolded my arms again. Students passed by in a blur. My eyes ached, they were so dry. I leaned forward and rubbed them with both hands. There had to be a way to wake myself up before classes started.

"Rough night?" Amusement ran over every syllable of Stella's words.

When I dropped my hands, she stood in front of me, hands tucked into pockets of another pair of destroyed jeans and a smirk on her face. "Uh . . ."

"You here? Or should we take you to the nurse?"

"I've been worried," I said before thinking of all that might imply.

"Had my phone taken. I have it back during school, or basically anytime my parents give me the okay to be outside of their immediate presence." She sighed and then gave me another wry smile. "It's super fun."

"Sounds terrible."

The bell rang, and she slipped her hand in mine, dragging me into the school. My mind fuzzed further with her palm pressed against mine. Lack of sleep. New information. The thought of *breaking into a government facility.* But now I was on Sam's path, and I at least had an idea that he'd messed up and gotten himself killed and how I had to be careful. Or I knew I needed to be careful. I also knew that I needed the things he had used. Not just to help me get his formula right, but to actually finish what we had started. I knew Sam's chemistry set could whip up a batch in no time, and we were back in business.

"We don't need a tardy on top of all that getting detained," Stella said over her shoulder as we rounded the corner on our way to math.

Despite the lack of sleep, and the plans swirling in my brain, I found myself smiling as she led me to our first class. And then it was all I could do to keep my eyes open for the first half of the day. Another day where I retained nothing wasn't going to help my grades.

Once we finished IT and left the classroom for lunch, I stopped in the middle of the hallway.

Stella turned to face me, students wandering around the block we created. "You okay?"

I shook my head. "Totally forgot I needed to eat today. Long night. And I feel bad about asking Brock about you the other day."

Stella shrugged. "Honestly, if someone were willing to create a toxin with me, I might ask around about them too." She shrugged again, more loosely this time. "I need to hear about this long night."

That was definitely true. "Yeah. I did a ton of research on Sam yesterday. It was wild."

Her brows danced upward. "Is that so?"

I blinked, my lids still heavy.

In a quick move, Stella popped up on her tiptoes and planted her lips on mine. Soft. Coconut. Warm. So close. She fell back down to being flat-footed in her boots. "I thought you could use a little waking up."

Waking up wasn't quite the expression I'd use.

"Maybe try again?" I offered with a smile.

She snorted and swatted my chest before turning away from me. "Let's use my lunch credit, find a corner of the caf, and then you can spill."

I was still in a haze, but more from the shock of feeling her lips on mine. So casual. So easy. Like it was nothing, but it wasn't nothing. It was—

"Pizza? One or two slices?" she asked.

"Uh, I . . ."

She rolled her eyes before flopping three slices onto her tray.

"Wait, you can't pay for my lunch."

"My *parents* are paying for the lunch." She didn't slow in adding food to the overflowing tray. "You're just eating my leftovers."

And she was gathering way more food than what she could eat—that I was sure of. I was also sure there would be no arguing with her. I didn't have the energy anyway.

Right now, I just wanted to tell her what I'd learned about Sam and to see if she had any ideas of how and when we could get to Utah.

"Okay," she said as we sat in a far corner of the cafeteria.

Brock caught my eyes between students, and I gave him a nod, which he returned as he cocked a brow upward. I shrugged in response. We could talk if he was giving me a ride home. And anyway, I still had no idea where I actually stood with Stella—only that she was all in when it came to Sam Miller.

"Okay," I responded. "Just pull up a search on your phone and type in 'Sam Miller, conspiracy theory.'"

"Oh-kay." But she did as I asked. I watched her head tilt to the side in curiosity, and then her body got straighter as she scrolled down the long list of sites that had heard of Sam Miller.

I should have waited until she'd at least started eating, but my stomach protested, and I took a large bite of pizza.

"This *is* wild," she finally said. "I wish we knew where they took his stuff, huh? Or what really happened to him."

"I figured that out," I said as I took the folded pages out of my pack and set them on the table. "I did a ton of research. The people who bury things for the EPA are contracted by them, so there are at least *some* records online. I had to set up an account to see them, but whatever . . . anyway . . ."

"You know about where his stuff is?" she asked.

"The dates match up," I explained. "To when Sam died. His death certificate says alcohol poisoning. Because of the conspiracies floating around, his parents gave permission for his death certificate to be online. It didn't help, obviously."

"Well, his parents were or are part of the US government anyway, so who even knows."

"Exactly." I pointed at the square on the map. "They had just put in this light when a contract was paid for to bury more things. When the EPA buries stuff, it has to be carefully marked because of the hazardous measure, right? They don't want things to break underground. I saw the tubs, barrels, and almost coffin-like things that they put materials in before burying them. But stuff like Sam's? That's usually kept in CONEX boxes. You know, those big things that are on the freight shipments and on the semis on the highway."

"You think there's a chance we could get Sam's stuff." Her eyes were on mine now. Solid. Unwavering. Excited. "We have to do it."

"It's in Utah," I explained. "Like, way out in the desert west of Salt Lake City."

Stella nodded slowly. "We'll need some kind of car, but your mom needs yours, and there is no way my parents would let me borrow theirs. This is gonna be an all-nighter."

"Yeah." And we were both still a bit in trouble from the whole stealing thing. I was already dreading going to bio again. The teacher knew what we'd done, and I hated that. If I knew that stuff was actually used by the school, maybe I'd have found a different way.

"What if we found a piece-of-crap car close to the site? But not too close? We could buy a POS car, dig up the stuff, and run back home?"

"And get there how?" I asked. "And pay for the car how?"

"Bus. That's how we get there."

"Okay." Taking the bus made solid sense, and buying

a car in Utah rather than here also made sense. "But I'm down to, like, forty bucks in my checking account."

Stella picked at the cinnamon roll on the tray. "I skim from my parents *all* the time. I have a few hundred bucks. I can get a little more. I'm already in so much trouble, it won't even matter at this point."

This was another piece I should have felt guilty about, but I tucked my fingers into my pocket, feeling the edges of the merit badge that rested there.

"How are we gonna do it?" I asked her. "Ideas?"

"Mom's got another trip to Fort Bragg. Dad never knows what to do with me, so I'll just tell him me and Cheyenne have a project and I'd love to crash at her house. She's right next to the school, so he won't have to drive me the next day. We're set."

But I had to come up with something too. "I feel weird, you using your money."

"You that old school, Mr. Science Guy?" She nudged my arm as she plucked a piece of pepperoni from a pizza slice.

This felt like a question with no safe answer. "I don't know." All I knew was that it all felt backward. "I'll pay you back once we make the exchange."

"Sounds solid."

The bell rang, and we both sighed.

"I like Mrs. Lawler," Stella said as she folded a slice of pizza and took a bite out of the end. "Not thrilled that what we did affected her."

I stared at Stella for a moment. She'd been so casual about taking all the stuff, but here . . . maybe she and I weren't as different as I thought. And yeah, Mrs. Lawler. I needed to have a sit-down with her and apologize or going to bio was gonna continue to be torture.

"I'm gonna take a tardy," she said. "I wanna eat

more and think about all that Sam stuff we found. Maybe my next bit of fiction will be about him."

"Or us," I suggested, half teasing.

"Oh, I'll write about us," she said, "but I'm gonna wait until we're past the best part."

"What's the best part?"

Stella stood. "The breaking into a government facility, of course."

So, maybe not as alike as I'd thought a moment ago. Still, I started out of the caf and looked over my shoulder to see her watching me. No, *studying* me with a serious expression. If someone told me she was reading my thoughts in that moment, from the look on her face, I'd have believed it.

As I walked down the hallway, running over Stella's plan in my head, promising myself the whole time that I was gonna pay her back as soon as I had cash, I realized that this was just as much about recovering Sam's actual tools as anything else.

So yeah, I was looking forward to having his specialized homemade chemistry set—not looking forward to the steps required to get it.

EIGHTEEN

Stella didn't show up in bio.

"You're so gone for her," Brock said with a smile as my attention moved around the room again.

I was on the bench, the bar in my hands, and no desire to do bench presses. None.

"She's . . ." I let myself smile a little because maybe Brock wouldn't push me if he was getting something good to talk about. "She's different, and I like different. And yeah, I like her."

"I bet more than half the guys in this school fantasize about her a little, you know?" he said softly. "But I also think most of them have either been rejected by her or are scared of her."

Yeah, I could see both of those things being true.

"So, how'd you get her to spend time with you?" Brock asked as he stood over me as my spotter, waiting for me to do *something*. "Don't get me wrong, I still think it's a bad idea, but I am curious."

"I'm interesting because I'm the new guy." And maybe that's all it was at first, but now we had Sam, and we had this thing we were doing and planning, and if we did go through with it—if we did go to Utah and buy a truck and steal the chem stuff—we were both trusting the other with our freedom. Our ability to stay quiet and stay out of trouble.

There was a lot on the line.

"You just got pale," Brock teased.

"I'm thinking about lifting this giant bar," I lied.

But surely, Stella's book or story or whatever would work out a lot better if the main characters got away with it, wouldn't it?

I lifted the bar and began my circuit, trying to focus on form and intention rather than how to break through a fence around government property.

"You want a ride home?" Brock asked.

My body was swimming in heat with the workout. The thought of walking home after this felt like a special kind of torture. "I'd love it."

Just as I stepped into the quiet house, a text from Stella pinged on my phone.

> *Stella: Look at this beauty. I told him we'd pick it up on Tuesday. So we have less than a week to figure out how to make this work without just running away.*

I was surprised Stella cared about running away. Though that could involve police, and that was the last thing we needed. There was no way I'd do that to Mom.

Just as I went to answer her, another message popped up on my screen.

> *Dad: How's things?*

A message from Dad? I stared at the short text. The only thing I'd gotten from him in months. Did I answer? Not answer? Mom must have put him in the phone, because I definitely hadn't.

No. I wasn't going to answer. At least not now.

Instead, I followed the link to the truck. An old clunker of a GMC with a single cab and a short bed. Too-big tires, but no lift package. A weird pale yellow and brown with two snakes painted on the hood. Not just snakes. Cobras. Gold ones. Who in their right mind painted gold cobras on their truck? Looked like I was gonna find out.

> *Stella: We can call him Two Snakes. The guy posted a video of it running and it's only 250. I told him I was a college student, and I PayPal'd him fifty bucks to hold it.*
>
> *Chuck: I'll pay you back. Promise.*
>
> *Stella: JUST CHILL ALREADY.*

But too much was happening for me to do that. Right now, I was completely unable to move forward. We couldn't work on the toxin without supplies, and I was going to at least TRY to get Sam's glassware and supplies before trying to find other glassware that would let me do it on my own. Plus, Sam had the homemade custom flasks I was after. And our attempt to retrieve the stuff wasn't happening for days. So what now?

Then it hit me—what I could be doing with my time.

Sam Miller was one of a thousand urban legends— bits of truth were sewn up with bits of make-believe. But I had his journal. I was living in his house, or in a house near his. I could play this up on YouTube big time and try to give new life to my channel again. Even if we weren't able to create the toxin, which after the lure of three hundred thousand dollars, I wasn't willing to consider . . . but even if we couldn't do that, I had information conspiracy theorists on the internet wanted. Unlike my dashes into old buildings, I was gonna do better with this.

Because trying to tell what I knew of Sam's story . . . that was gonna take some time, and Sam's experience was so close, I could hold it in my hands. Literally. I felt the round Scout badge in my pocket.

I set up my small tripod in my window for good light. Left the closet door open behind me, showcasing the place where I'd found his books to begin with. Kept my face out of the frame of the video. Shoulders to the floor.

"I had no idea Sam Miller was a legend. I knew only that I found a box of books in the closet behind me, and with them was this." I held up the journal. "I don't have all the pieces of Sam Miller's last year on Earth, but I have a lot of them . . ."

* * *

During the middle of my recording, a memory popped into my head. The backpack. It was still in the shed, and I hadn't bothered with it because I'd been focused on getting the computer. Then I'd been preoccupied with making the toxin. I really needed to start sleeping more. My brain wasn't usually this scattered.

I headed outside. The door of the shed in the back-yard sat slightly ajar, and I stared at it from the house for a moment. If I remembered right, the bag was way in the back. One that wasn't linked to me. One that wasn't my school pack. One that held far more than my school pack could hold.

Now, it was also in a spider-infested shed, and had who even knew what inside of it. Still, I wanted that pack. It might even be a clue as to if this was Sam's house or not. That was the last straw that pushed me across the weedy backyard and toward the shed.

Once I got the backpack, I'd clean up the backyard—

give Mom something nice to look at when she came home from work. This was what I forced through my head as I neared the shed, opened the door, and guessed it would take three steps, or two big steps, to get to the pack. Probably three, because it was on a pretty deep hook.

"Okay, wuss. Just get in there," I said to myself.

Don't look up. Don't look down. Keep eyes on the backpack. I took the few steps in, slipped the dusty pack off the hook, spun around, and sucked in a lungful of air when I was back in the yard.

I shook off the pack, jerking it from left to right. Then my whole body went into a severe shiver. It was all I could do to not run around the yard spastically, completely freaked out by the invisible spiders I had convinced myself were crawling down the inside of my shirt. I didn't look at the ground to see if my shaking had any effect, just took the pack closer to the house.

Just as I started to unzip it, I glanced back at the yard.

This was the worst job, but the yard wasn't big. Even doing the whole thing with the weed whacker wouldn't take too long. I picked it up from where I'd left it on the porch, plugged it in, and methodically swung it from side to side as I went back and forth across the yard. Then I had to rake all the weed tops into piles. They'd dry out in a day or two and would be far easier to bag up. I left the piles and took the pack into the house.

It was an army pack, but one of the smaller ones. The strip of fabric with the soldier's name had been taken off, leaving a darker spot where it had been. But even that was hardly noticeable through the dust.

One pocket after another I opened to find empty. With each empty pocket, I felt the weight of what I'd hoped for—more of Sam.

When I unzipped the main pocket and pulled it as

wide as possible, the name *Kayla Smith* was written in black marker, and a space blanket and old water bottle sat at the bottom.

So, not Sam. She could be anyone. Someone the pack was stolen from. Someone who used to live here. A soldier. Someone who bought this at a surplus shop. So many possibilities.

Still, it was bigger than my school pack. And the space blanket and water bottle would be useful for the trip to Utah. That was something. But knowing that I maybe had all of Sam's stuff I was going to get felt . . . off, and added another level of determination to find the speck of a space where his stuff had been stored in the EPA burial ground in Utah.

My phone buzzed again.

Dad: You there?

Chuck: I'm here.

I'd answered before really thinking.

Chuck: Idaho's fine. School almost done.

Dad: Mom said you'd gotten in a little bit of trouble, and I wondered if you'd want to spend the summer in South Carolina? I know how you love the ocean.

Mom had told him? Why? How? I didn't even know they talked.

Chuck: I'd rather stick around. Mom's sick, remember?

Dad: How could I forget?

And that was it. I could even hear the words in his sarcastic tone whenever Mom's health interrupted what he wanted to do. I turned my phone off. Just as I started up the stairs, the front door opened.

"Chuck?" Mom called.

I turned and stopped at the bottom of the stairs. "I heard from Dad. Was it necessary to tell him?"

She sighed. "He emailed me to ask about you and it had just happened, and I was still . . . in a bit of shock."

Well, now there was no way I could be mad. "Yeah. Okay. But please . . ."

"At least he cares enough to reach out."

No, he reached out to do what he thought was his "dad" duty, forgetting that Mom needed help—help he'd rarely been willing to give.

"Yeah," I said as I started to turn. "Oh." I had to let her know now. "Brock and I are working on a project together . . . for school . . . weight lifting. I mean, it's not a huge deal, but he has a decent gym setup at his house, and he can also get me into his gym as a guest before school, but that's early, and I don't want to wake you, so . . ."

"So?" Mom urged as she set her bag down on the small kitchen table.

"So I was thinking I could crash at his house? It's a school night, so I know you might not love that, but it just felt like something that I could do, just to help us get it all done at once, you know? Rather than dragging it out."

"You can't do it over the weekend?" Mom asked.

Which was a good and valid question that I didn't fully have the answer for. "Well, it's this guy . . ." My brain was coming up with a story, just not fast enough. "There's a particular guy, former military, at the gym who Brock wants us to work out with, and Tuesday morning is his next shift."

Mom's brows tugged down, but then she coughed. And then again. And then a trickle of blood slipped from her nose.

"Bloody nose," I said as I turned to get a washcloth.

And I knew that I was going to use her illness against her. She'd remember us having this conversation, but she might not remember how it ended, and I was going to tell her that it was all set up because she'd told me yes. And I felt like a jerk knowing I was going to do it, but it was going to happen. And in the end, it was mostly for her anyway.

"I cut the weeds down in the backyard," I told her. "I'll bag them up tomorrow."

She coughed again, sputtering blood around her washcloth. She mumbled something incoherent, and I offered to make mac and cheese and some frozen vegetables.

Once I had her set up on the couch, I turned my phone back on. Ignored the three texts Dad had sent and opened up my conversation with Stella.

> *Chuck: Talked to Mom. All good for Two Snakes.*
>
> *Stella: You're cool with my name for the truck?*
>
> *Chuck: I mean, of course.*
>
> *Stella: You're weird. I like it.*

I like you is what I wanted to say back. I typed it. Deleted it. Typed it. And then sent it. Held my breath. Waited.

A few moments later:

> *Stella: You too.*

And then I let myself smile and think about traveling with her, searching with her, finding Sam's stuff, making this drop, and earning the money I needed to change my life.

We had to get this right.

NINETEEN

I stepped into bio before first period and stood in the doorway until Mrs. Lawler looked up from her desk. "Can I help you?"

"I just wanted to apologize," I said.

She waved me in, and I walked to her desk, standing just a few feet away, the guilt still weighing me down far more than my pack. "I'm new here, and I was bored, and it looked like none of that stuff was being used."

Tapping a pencil on her desk, she took me in for a moment. "You seem like a smart and good kid."

I never liked being called a kid, but I wasn't going to correct her.

"If you take a moment to think before you act, you'll save yourself a lot more conversations as awkward and terrible as this one."

My shoe squeaked on the floor as I took a step back. Right now, I couldn't afford to think first. Not with Mom's degrading health. Not with me being so close. Not with people on the other end of a chat with money that would change our lives. "Yeah. Thanks."

"And thank you, Chuck," she said earnestly. "I appreciate the apology and that you made it right."

There was really nothing else to say, so I turned and walked out of the classroom, hoping no one would see me in here and ask what I'd been doing. Fortunately, the hallways were still mostly clear—benefit of waking up stupid early and walking.

Stella and I sat close enough that our shoulders touched once we were turned over to do our homework in math. We didn't hold hands between classes, but she never left my side.

We were leaving on Tuesday. It was Thursday. Impossibly close. Impossibly far.

Just as I sat down in English, Cheyenne whispered to Stella, and they were absorbed in seconds.

"Chuck?" Ms. Lincoln held a phone up, the one that sat behind her desk for talking with the office.

I stood, moved to the desk, and picked up her phone. "Uh, hello?"

"Chuck. This is the nurse."

"Okay." Why on earth would the nurse be contacting me?

"I got a message that your mom was taken to the hospital after passing out at work. She's okay," she added hurriedly, "but she won't be home when the day is finished."

My head lifted from my body. I swallowed. No way was I going to sit in class while Mom sat in the hospital. "Thank you." I hung up the phone.

"Everything okay?" Ms. Lincoln asked, her elderly face wrinkled in worry.

I shook my head. "I gotta go. My mom's . . . sick . . . hospital." But I wasn't dumb. Mom was dying. A person couldn't live like she did without their life shortening. They couldn't.

Stella met my eyes. "Okay?" she mouthed.

I shook my head and left the classroom.

"Chuck!" Stella ran up behind me in the hallway,

grabbed my arm, and turned me around. "What's going on?"

"Mom passed out at work." I put as much calm in my voice as I could, but my throat had closed up, and the words came out sort of warbled. "That happens . . ." I cleared my throat. "That happens when she has a hard time breathing . . . doesn't get enough oxygen."

"Hey." Stella took my hand. "It'll be okay."

It might be okay. Might be. I just nodded.

She squeezed her fingers around my hand. "I'd drive you if I could, but . . ."

"It's okay." I turned and dropped the warmth of Stella's hand.

"Text me, okay?" she called as I walked down the hall.

I gave her a half wave in return, my body numb, my thoughts numb, but my determination to change this situation on fire.

* * *

"But school!" Mom protested through the mask she wore.

She always looked so tiny in a hospital gown, in a large bed, machines attached to her. "It's fine." I shook my head. "Stella will get my stuff."

She coughed a couple times before whispering, "I don't know what to think of her. Part of me adores her, and part of me worries because you two got into trouble together, and that's not like you, and then part of me is sad for her because there's something missing there . . . something she needs . . ."

I glanced up at the nurse. Mom wasn't really making sense.

"Morphine." The nurse shrugged. "She was tense, and her blood pressure was really high due to the pain of her lungs when she got here."

Pain. I mean, I partially recognized there was discomfort, but I'd always thought of it as more of a—she had a cough that she couldn't quite satisfy. Not that Mom's lungs or chest or whatever were in *pain.* "Is there a specialist here for that kind of thing?"

The nurse tapped on the computer next to Mom's bed. "This is a bit rare, you do know that, right?"

Of course I knew that. I just gave her a look that must have conveyed my sentiments.

"Be nice," Mom whispered, but her eyes were fluttering closed.

The nurse turned her attention more fully toward me. "We all had to look up her condition, that's how rare it is."

"Right."

"There are two specialists in the *world*," she said, her gaze more fully on me, "and only one is in this country, but they're in LA."

Of course.

"We've asked for a treatment plan from the doctor in LA, and we're waiting to hear back."

I took the first full breath since picking up the phone in Ms. Lincoln's classroom. That was something. Not perfect, but something. Finally, I grabbed my phone and messaged Stella.

> *Chuck: Mom okay. They have questions sent to a specialist in LA. More medical bills.*
>
> *Stella: Sorry, Chuck. More bills until . . .*
>
> *Chuck: Yeah, until . . .*

Mom had fallen back asleep, but I couldn't bring myself to move. It wasn't like we had any animals to take care of. I wasn't needed anywhere but in her room. When the nurse brought her lunch, she had stacked extra food in each section of the tray and gave me a wink as she left.

I ate a stale roll as I looked back over the footage I'd taken of myself, of Sam's stack of books. I'd re-created my discovery in a series of short videos, and now I had to come up with some good voice-over to go with the introduction that I'd done and still liked.

Taking the pen and little pad of paper with the hospital's navy-blue logo on it, I began to write up what I wanted to say over the videos of the books, of the shed, but not the computer. I'd almost shown the computer and taken it apart, but the messaging was too much. The computer itself might even be too much—and who knew what would happen to it when or if I posted this video publicly.

Mom kept sleeping. I kept merging clips together to make something coherent. I didn't want one video—I wanted a series. My life. Sam's life. I took videos of the inside of his journal in the harsh light of the hospital, blurring out the edges of things I didn't want people to see. Not venturing to the sections with his specific formula, but rather the sections where he said he'd found something new.

The one piece of information I allowed to slip in was the Big Boy Beans—but only because it was nice comedic relief from the rest of Sam's notes. Each half second was carefully planned; each fade from one shot to the next was done with precision.

The window darkened. Nurses came and went. Mom woke only long enough to take a few nibbles of food. All

I could think was that if she had to take too much time off, she could lose her job, and then what?

Getting disability when you had something so rare that no one was quite sure what to do with you wasn't as easy as it seemed. And Mom had been trying for more than three years. Since Dad left the military, and us, and our support system had disappeared.

At about nine, my phone vibrated in my hands.

Stella: You still at the hospital? Just finished with my head doc. Thought I'd swing by?

Chuck: Here. Room 308.

Stella: See you soon.

Mom's comment about not being sure what to think of Stella pinged for a moment, but she was asleep anyway.

Another nurse stepped into the room. "I'm Angie. I'm just on shift and have been updated. The doc says that once she's able to maintain a good oxygen level on her own, we can send you home."

"Okay, thanks." But this wasn't really new news.

"I'm going to see if I can swing some grant money to send you home with oxygen, okay?" she said.

I just nodded in response.

"The doc thinks that may help your mom in the evenings after work, or maybe even during her workday." Angie's attention was on the computer screen, making notes, checking blood pressure, oxygen—all the same things nurses had been checking since I'd arrived hours ago.

"She has a small . . . inhaler thing," I mentioned, but they probably already knew that.

The nurse nodded once. "It's a nice shot of help, but

it's not the same as that ongoing oxygen for your brain and body."

Brain and body. Brain and body. Because Mom's brain and body weren't getting what they needed. That wasn't something I could fix. But what if Mom was able to take months off work? Months off with oxygen and a few specialist visits. Life-changing.

Now I was itching to get home, just to read over my messages again with MPG. Just for reassurance that I was headed in a good direction.

The nurse left, and two seconds later, Stella peered into the room.

"You were given the car?"

She shrugged.

Mom shifted in bed, but immediately went still again, her breathing rasping even with the equipment there to help her.

"This normal for you?" Stella asked.

I'd shifted the chairs around to sit more comfortably, and I kicked one of the three in her direction. "A little."

She sat, her attention drifting toward Mom for a few moments. "How often does she end up in the hospital?"

"I don't know. Like, when I was a kid, I know that it hardly ever happened, but as I get older"—*as she gets older*—"it happens more."

Stella seemed to mull this information over for a few minutes. "Rough."

I had no response. Yeah, it was rough on me, but not nearly as rough as it was on Mom.

"So, what have you been doing with your hours?" she asked.

I glanced down at my phone, plugged in now from working so hard. "A YouTube project."

"Been exploring abandoned parts of the hospital?" she teased.

"Are there—"

Her head fell to the side. "I was teasing, Chuck."

"Right. Yeah." I shook my head. "Long day."

She pulled her feet onto the chair and sat cross-legged. "So, what kind of YouTube thing?"

I pulled up the first video. "It's missing the voice-over, but you get the idea. I've been working on the script."

Stella took the phone from my grasp, and it felt almost as if I were giving her a look inside my brain. Inside what finding this journal had meant to me since we moved. Being in a new place. Finding a guy my age, someone who'd died too young, someone who was desperate to make a mark on the world. And he had, in a strange sort of way. In circles of people who were devoted to learning what happened to him. The real story. I suspected they would want the story I had.

But even then . . . even then he'd made a mark. Had created something new, and it had all started from being shoved into Boy Scouts by parents who were probably desperate to give him something to do.

"Chuck?" Stella peered at me over my phone. "I can't wait to see this with the voice-over. This is . . . you've leveled up, and the conspiracy peeps will love this."

"It's definitely a new direction. I made it personal." But personal was a stupid word for how exposed I felt.

"Leveled up." She handed my phone back to me. "I'm impressed."

"Are you gonna get in trouble for being here?" I asked.

Stella shook her head. "I explained that your mom was in the hospital, and Mom said I should drop by. She's still unsure of you, after the whole stealing-stuff-from-the-school thing, but I keep assuring her that it was just an adjustment period. Mom loves terms like that. It means that your behavior is temporary."

"It is temporary." Stealing wasn't in my nature. Neither was creating a toxin to sell to . . . a foreign university?

In a quick move, Stella gave me a playful slug to my shoulder. "You're way too good for all of this, Chuck Yarrow. We both know that."

So are you, was what I wanted to say. And while I knew Stella wasn't a thief, I also knew that she loved this process for similar reasons that I didn't like it. Maybe this all did feel like a work of fiction to her. A game. Maybe that's what Brock had meant when he told me to be cautious.

"I gotta head." She stood. "Don't need the parents liking you less."

Oh, that was great.

"Will you be at school tomorrow?" she asked slowly.

I shook my head. "Even if they let Mom go home tomorrow, it won't be until later."

"Need a ride?"

"Staying here."

Her forehead wrinkled. "In the chairs?"

"In the chairs," I confirmed. "I have practice."

"You're a good guy, Chuck." She stood in the doorway. "And consider doing the voice-overs here. The weird background noises may even help with the ambiance and help disguise your voice a little."

The crazy thing was that Stella was right. The background noise did add a cool effect to my voice-over. The strange suck-hiss that barely came through, the occasional beep. There was an air of being somewhere just off normal.

Three in the morning, and I had four videos uploaded and ready to be published on YouTube. I wasn't gonna do them yet. Not until we'd made the exchange. Or until the exchange failed, or I'd failed at the toxin. I wasn't even sure yet.

But now I wasn't just moving forward in one direction to help us, I was moving forward in two.

Mom blinked at me. "Can you see if *CSI* is on?" she asked in a whisper.

I gave her a nod, found the remote, and brought the TV to life.

Someday soon, I'd be able to do a lot more for her than finding a stupid TV show.

TWENTY

My whole life, I'd hated waiting. When I was little and still liked my dad, I had to wait until he came home from wherever the military had taken him. Then the wait for a move had always been torture. Once we learned we were going somewhere, it was so hard to just sit and stay and wait until the movers came to pack us up.

Mom had come home from the hospital. We were four episodes into some cop show with subtitles on Netflix, and I couldn't stop fidgeting. It was Sunday afternoon. Stella and I weren't leaving until Tuesday morning.

The bus tickets had been purchased. She'd checked in with the guy about picking up Two Snakes, and now . . . waiting.

A plastic mask was attached to Mom's face, a can of oxygen sitting next to her on the floor as she rested on the couch. Her eyes looked brighter than they had since our move, and her rasping was less noticeable.

The hospital had definitely helped.

But what about a week after she worked again?

I thought about Dad for a moment. As much as I'd learned to hate his shifting moods and inability to be happy no matter his present circumstances, if he were here now, Mom wouldn't be alone while I left for two days.

She just seemed so fragile.

I flipped through Sam's book again. Wondered where Stella and I would be able to start making the toxin—the house she'd had a key made for was out. That lock had been changed by the owner, I'm sure, the day after we were detained and nearly arrested.

I shook my head. When I thought about possibly dealing with the cops, it was always when thinking about being caught inside a building. Not stealing.

There were a lot of empty houses here, but the cops might start watching them more closely after finding me and Stella. There was no way to know.

"What will you do when you grow up?" Mom asked me with a faint smile.

"Be a doctor," I said. "To help people like you." This wasn't true. I couldn't imagine that much school. But maybe I could. "Or keep making YouTube videos."

She snorted a small laugh. "You're smart. I'm sure you'll find something that suits your talents."

"I'm sure I will," I told her.

Her blinks grew slower as she drifted off to sleep.

The weekend passed in a blur of getting more electrolyte water for Mom and watching one crime show after another after another.

School on Monday morning felt like a slap back to reality. Mom wasn't set to go back to work until Thursday, which gave her more resting time.

"I talked to Cheyenne," Stella said by way of greeting in the hallway.

"Okay?"

"She said that if your mom has any issues or whatever, she can sort of be on call."

"Oh." Well, that was something. Mom didn't know Cheyenne, but at least I knew someone here could go over if it was needed.

Leaving this week felt almost criminal.

Criminal.

I laughed a little to myself. We were leaving for the sole purpose of breaking into what was basically a government-sanctioned EPA burial ground.

"What's funny?" Stella asked.

I just shook my head. "That was thoughtful. Thank you."

"Couldn't have the good guy backing out on me—even for his mom," she teased.

The one thing I hadn't done yet was ask Brock if he could cover for me. Asking him would be a calculated risk because he might be tempted to say something to somebody, which would leave us dead in the water, or forced to just run away, which would add another layer of complication. I was still undecided.

All day, Stella and I moved from class to class in silence. Still walking together but not talking. We had a sub in bio, so I pulled out the grid again and rechecked positions. How I'd find the CONEX at night. Wondered if the locks could be cut open so we could get inside. And then I hoped that Sam's stuff wasn't dangerous enough for them to bury it instead of putting it in a CONEX. They did put things in containers for a reason—they didn't want stuff leaking into the soil. But they wouldn't have kept Sam's materials in the ground. Not at this site. And not at this time. I was sure of it.

Stella and I sat with Brock and Cheyenne and a few other people at lunch. I picked at my sandwich and texted Mom to make sure all was well. She messaged back right away to say that she was feeling much better and that a neighbor had brought by a giant lasagna and a bunch of cookies.

The group at the table in the caf continued to chatter around me, but I couldn't think of a thing to contribute. How could I talk about the newest video from some TikTok creator I hadn't heard of when I was trying to save my mom's life? It all just felt so trivial.

Now I understood more why Stella had wanted in. I could see the bored look on her face as the conversation continued—this wasn't nearly enough stimulation for someone like her. Not even close.

I reached for her hand under the table and her fingers immediately laced with mine. This was us telling each other that we were part of something so much bigger than debates over whose prank had come off better.

Her hand felt so small in mine. But she gave me a squeeze, reminding me of her strength. Kind of amazing that I'd found someone like her in Twin Falls, Idaho.

By the time last period came, I knew I wouldn't ask Brock for any favors. I'd just have to hope that I was always in a position to answer Mom if she called or texted. And to make sure that she wasn't tracking my phone's position.

Stella followed me out of weight lifting. "My dad'll drop me off super early," she said, "and then I'm gonna get an Uber in the morning from the school and go to the bus station, okay?"

"Okay." Because it was happening tomorrow. The waiting was finally over.

"Can you get to school?"

I'd walk. There was nothing else to do. It's not like I was gonna sleep anyway. "Of course."

Stella just nodded. Half of me expected her to jump up and yell or squeal or . . . something. But maybe at this point, the seriousness of what we were about to do was starting to settle in.

TWENTY-ONE

Since I didn't have any money to contribute to our trip, the least I could do was pack a bag. I sealed up some cookies from the neighbor—chocolate chip, the best cookie. I took four sodas, packed some sandwiches—though they'd be soggy soon—two cold packs, the space blanket, two water bottles, a deck of cards, and a bulging can of Big Boy Beans just in case.

There was just enough money in my account for bolt cutters, depending on where we went.

I left Mom another written note, reminding her that I'd be home tomorrow night because of the project with Brock. The guilt I felt at lying would be worth it once the exchange of botulism was made. This was just another necessary step.

Just as the school came into view, so did Stella's dad's car. There was really nowhere to hide in the desert, so I just kept walking. Walking as if Stella and I had to be here early for the same school project.

Breathe normal. Walk normal. Breathe normal. Walk normal.

But my worry was for nothing, because Stella's dad

just pulled right back out of the parking lot, leaving her in front of the school, and continued back to the base, not giving me a second glance as he drove by.

Once the headlights disappeared behind me, I raised my hand in a wave, but Stella was on her phone.

I reached her just as another car pulled into the parking lot. "Who the heck . . ." I started.

"That's our Uber to the bus station," she explained. "I gave her a heads-up last night. I've used her before."

How did Stella always seem to be a step ahead? Actually, she was probably a step ahead because she was looking at this whole venture like a story. Like a work of fiction. And she was planning ahead in our story, just as if she were planning ahead in the piece she was writing. She grinned. "Finally, something interesting is happening again, eh?"

And with that remark, she jumped into the car, and I jumped in after her.

The ride to the bus station was quick. Stella was in charge of the tickets, which she pulled from her tight back pocket. We took our seats and settled in for the ride to Ogden, Utah.

I slumped low, letting my hood come up over my head.

"You can't be tired yet," Stella said. "We're just getting started."

"I'm resting," I explained. "For later."

She tapped on her phone a few times, and I decided she was too spritely this early in the morning. "Are you so curious about Kenny?"

I peered at her sideways. "Kenny?"

"Like, who paints two gold snakes on the front of their truck?"

"Oh, the truck guy." I'd been thinking ahead to

where exactly the EPA fence line was in relation to where we needed to dig. How far we'd have to haul Sam's stuff if we found it.

"Yeah, the truck guy."

"What if we don't find it?" I asked her. "Sam's stuff, I mean."

Stella scooted lower in her seat, matching my posture, resting her leg against mine. "Then we figure something else out. We can't let it go."

"Oh, I'm not letting it go." Once the seed of that much money had been planted, I didn't know how to back away—especially not after seeing Mom in the hospital again.

"Good." Stella peered at me then, and for a moment, the outside became a blur. "I'm glad we're doing this."

I wasn't sure *glad* was the right word, but even still . . . "Me too."

We sat in silence for a moment, the brown landscape flying by.

"Cookie?" I asked. "Breakfast of champions."

"Oh. Definitely."

I handed her a cookie, and she showed me a video she'd found the other night, and we slouched in our seats.

And suddenly, this venture felt so normal. The two of us on a bus, eating cookies, and swapping favorite YouTube videos.

It could have been almost any day. Could have been.

* * *

As our Greyhound for the day grew closer to Ogden, Stella got another Uber so we could get to our Two Snakes pickup place. I shifted lower in my seat. Fortunately, the bus wasn't full at all. In fact, no one sat directly in front of or behind us.

The Uber was waiting when we got to the curb, and we were off for the third leg of our trip. Small homes grew farther apart, older, and shabbier.

Ripped tarps were strapped over what was left of detached carports, the ends flapping in the desert wind. We'd lived in a lot of crappy places, but this sort of sprawling desert quasi-neighborhood was something altogether new. We passed a few orchards that looked as if they hadn't been taken care of, weeds climbing around tidy rows of unpruned trees.

I released a sigh and rubbed my forehead. What had we gotten into?

"It's North Ogden," Stella whispered in the back seat of the worn-out Prius. "What did you expect?"

I widened my eyes, hoping the driver wasn't catching our conversation. "I'm not *from here,* remember?"

Stella's familiar crooked smirk twisted her smooth lips. "Oh, I remember."

The pavement under the car's whirring tires turned to gravel—loose and scattered, making a sort of hailing sound on the bottom side of the car.

"Okay," the driver said, stopping in front of two trailers that looked sort of smooshed together—like a terrible version of a double-wide.

We were supposed to get *out* here.

Stella hopped out of the car with excitement, as if we'd just been dropped off at a movie theater, or Target, or a mall or something.

"Okay," the driver said again. "Thank you." Which was probably his polite way of telling me to get out of the car already.

I grabbed the door handle and pushed my body out of the car, backpack in tow.

Stella and I stood next to one another as the Prius, our last chance of escape, pulled out of the driveway and disappeared back down the dirt road.

This house also had a weedy orchard creeping against the tired trailer to the right. "Well." Stella released a breath as we stared at the trailer. Her eyes darted over the facade of the place, and she chewed on the inside of her cheek.

Excitement faded, and this was maybe the first time I'd seen any measure of uncertainty on her face.

"Yeah."

The rickety front door swung open to reveal a bulging stomach, a bald head, and a gray and reddish beard that nearly reached the man's chest.

He shrugged inside a camo-print coat as he lurched down the wooden steps. "Truck's this way," he said by greeting. "I'm guessing by your stares that you're here for it."

"Uh, yeah," I responded.

He glanced up at us, just briefly, before walking around the side of the house.

Stella and I exchanged another look. "Chances of us being murdered behind that house?" I asked.

Her head wobbled slightly, as if mulling over the information. "I think less than twenty percent."

I snorted. "Terrible odds."

"We want Sam's stuff or not?" she asked.

I took a step forward. And then another one. We waded through overgrown . . . lawn? When we turned the corner of the house, the bearded guy was tugging on a half-shredded tarp, his belly bulging out from underneath his stained T-shirt.

Stella and I were about to buy a truck. A whole truck. And then a million scenarios began to spin through my mind.

What if it didn't start?

What if he wanted more money?

What if he hit us over the head with a shovel and used the truck to transport our bodies to the desert?

What if everything went terribly wrong?

"What?" Stella yelped, excitement in her voice as she jogged for the front of the old truck. "So cool!" She ran her hands over the painted snakes. Cobras.

The man chuckled. "Did those myself."

I wanted to tell the guy we'd only buy it if it ran, but if the truck didn't start, we were a long way down a crappy road, and even if we called another Uber, it could take someone a while to get out this far.

"She's rough, but she runs," he said, as if reading my mind.

The guy climbed into the driver's seat, pumped the gas pedal a few times, and after a few slow turnovers, the engine rattled to life. Didn't roar. Rattled. The entire truck shook back and forth a little with the motion.

Stella and I exchanged a look.

She shrugged.

I shrugged.

"Two-fifty?" she asked.

"Cash," he said as he crawled back out of the driver's seat.

I was gonna have to sit there. Right where that guy had sat his filthy, dirty self. I shuddered.

He reached up and patted the hood, which revealed a sliver of a revolver tucked into his jeans.

My heart sped. I stepped back once. Stella raised a brow.

The guy turned sideways, showcasing the wooden handle of his revolver. "That a problem?"

I quickly shook my head, attempting to swallow the lump in my throat.

"Smith and Wesson, three-fifty-seven?" Stella's eyes narrowed as her head cocked to the side. "Am I right?"

Of course she'd know guns—after her Bonnie and Clyde thing.

He chuckled a little, making his belly jiggle. "Well, aren't you something." And then his eyes didn't leave Stella's face.

I mean, I couldn't blame the guy, but I was also getting her out of here.

"You can drive it around the side of the house on the trail there," he said.

Stella handed the man the cash, and they both signed some random bill of sale that he'd printed off the internet.

She jumped into the driver's seat, and her face fell. "Standard. I forgot."

"I can drive it," I offered, side-stepping around the bearded gun guy.

She scooted over on the vinyl seat, and I climbed in, the truck still wiggling a bit from side to side.

If we get Sam's stuff and if it gets us back to Idaho, it will be worth it.

I shifted the truck into gear and slowly let off the clutch as it lurched forward and wobbled over the trail that ran between the house and the orchard.

This was supposed to be the easy part of our trip, not the terrible part.

Stella waved at the guy as we drove around the house.

I didn't realize I was holding my breath until I eased the car into second once we hit the road.

"Look at this radio!" Stella squeaked, pushing in the

buttons that jerked the tuner from side to side. "I've never seen one like this outside of boomer memes!" She pushed her finger into the cassette slot.

I pressed down on the stiff clutch again, wobbling the gear shift around until I found third. Or fifth. Whatever. The truck kept moving away from the guy's house.

"And the snakes look even cooler from in here. Can you believe we got a truck that RUNS for so little?"

"Actually . . ." I teased as we reached the stop sign.

"Don't be rude to my truck. I think she's beautiful."

"So, sure it's a she?" My heart was almost starting to feel normal again.

"Oh, definitely. Only a she could still be kicking after the abuse this thing has seen." Stella ran her hands over the dash, where several cigarette burn marks were scattered. Someone had put out the butt on it for sure. The plastic was blackened and smooth.

"Something to add to the story, yeah?" I was just so glad to not be at that guy's house anymore.

Stella grew quiet, drawing her knees up to her chest. "Isn't there always more to the story?"

Yeah, there really always was. My thoughts went back to Sam Miller. To what could have killed him. Alcohol? His own experiments? Something else? Or was he alive somewhere, still working on what he'd started at my age?

"I don't think we should go to the EPA site until like . . . three in the morning?" Stella said. "You think?"

It was still only early afternoon. "What do you suggest we do until then?"

"You ever been out to the Great Salt Lake? Like, the actual lake?"

I shifted down as we neared the freeway. "Never."

Stella sat back and let her legs cross, looking more

relaxed now. "We used to go when I was little, and my parents were stationed at Hill."

"But that's air force, right?"

"They do weird work," she responded. "You game?"

"Yeah. Why not." We had to do something to pass the time, and I didn't want to use much more of the money she'd been sneaking from her parents.

I mean, I kept telling myself that I'd pay her back, but it didn't make any money spent feel easier as it was happening. Though . . . we still had supplies to get. "We need a hardware store."

"Bolt cutters. Gloves. Something to make the fence look not broken?" Stella stared at her phone. "What can make the fence look not broken?"

"Uh . . . zip ties?" I asked.

"Right." A few more taps on her phone and we took the highway south.

My foot was nearly to the floor, and we were going about sixty miles an hour. Car horns blared as they jerked around us, but it wasn't like I was *choosing* to go this slow on the freeway. Following the map on her phone, Stella gave me directions over the rattle of the engine.

Please let this truck get us where we need to go.

We pulled into a feed store. Like, for livestock.

"Less noticeable at a place like this, yeah?" she asked.

I'd just assumed we'd go for a hardware store. "I guess?"

"Less noticeable," she assured me as she got out of the car, the truck door rattling as she shut it behind her.

We wandered through rows of farm tools and buckets and special feed, slowly picking up the bolt cutters, shovels, and black zip ties. I stopped at a large bucket—one big enough to have a handle on each side. I didn't want to be the one to suggest we spend more money, but . . .

"You think?" I asked.

She bumped her hip to mine. "Smart. Because last time we got supplies, we needed a wastebasket, so this seems better. Also less suspicious."

And then I spotted some of the fake log things. "Campfire?"

She reached over and dropped a small package of them in the bucket. "Good cover."

We wandered up to the register, where a man stood in overalls and a camo-print baseball hat with cow horns embroidered on the front. It did not feel as if he were wearing either of those things ironically.

"Where you two from?" the guy asked.

"Mountains," I said before thinking.

He didn't pause, just adjusted the bulge under his lip before casually spitting on the floor behind him.

Okay, then.

"One-thirty-three."

Stella handed over the cash while my stomach once again clenched up. We were *buying* this stuff, and I still felt as if I were stealing.

The shovels were for unburying something the government had buried. The bolt cutters were for getting through a government-built fence. And we'd been worried about some weirdo with a gun and snake truck.

"You all right, son?" the man asked.

"Good. Yeah." I nodded.

"My brother's spacey," Stella said as she gathered the bucket and bolt cutters. "Don't mind him."

Brother?

I picked up the two shovels and followed her out of the store. We set the stuff in the back of the truck, as close to the cab as we could manage. I used a piece of bailing wire attached to the bed of the truck to secure the bucket.

As soon as we were both seated in the car again, I peered over at her. "Brother? Really?"

"Don't worry, Science Guy, I don't see you as a brother." She kissed her fingers in a playful gesture and then smooshed them into my cheek.

"Nice. Thank you." I shoved my foot down on the clutch, said a silent prayer that Two Snakes would roar to life, and she did—rattle, that is.

"Let's get food and hang at the lake." Once again Stella brought her knees up to her chest. "In-N-Out okay?"

"Fine."

This day was a weird thing followed by a normal thing that felt weird because of the weird things, one after another. Suddenly, I couldn't wait for Stella to write this story. To see all of these steps through her eyes rather than through my own.

If her fan fiction was any indication, she was going to nail this story. Our story. Well, maybe really the end of Sam's story.

TWENTY-TWO

A stiff breeze came off the Great Salt Lake, spreading goose bumps up my arms. Even with the breeze, the air felt thick, salty, and stale—like nothing I'd really ever smelled outside of the tidal flats in the southern US.

Stella grasped another fingerful of fries, dipped them in the top of her chocolate shake, and shoved the whole wad in her mouth.

"Honestly, I thought people only did that with Frostys?" I nudged her leg with my knee.

"I'm an equal opportunity dipper of fries in shakes," she replied seriously before grasping another fingerful and doing the same thing again. "Want some?"

While the thought of my lips against her fingers was appealing, soggy chocolate fries wasn't.

"Your face, Chuck." She snorted in laughter. "I'm gonna take a wild guess your answer is a no."

"Correct." I stretched my legs out, my stomach already full.

"I can't believe we're here." She pulled her knees up and rested her arms there for a moment. "This is, like, the best thing I've ever done."

I patted my chest in mock arrogance. "I am pretty spectacular."

Her gaze snapped toward me almost immediately before she shoved her hand against my shoulder. "Boys are the worst."

But her words lacked any sort of conviction, and we sat and stared at one another for a few moments. The urge to wrap my arms around her and tug her closer, kiss her, feel her against me, nearly overwhelmed me for a moment. But I didn't move.

Of course, Stella was the one to break the moment. She turned back toward the water, but shifted until our shoulders and legs touched, resting against one another in the salty sand.

"I feel like I hardly know you," I said just above a whisper.

She looped her arm through mine and rested her cheek on my shoulder. "I don't talk about myself because my real life is boring."

"How boring?"

"I'm an only child with workaholic parents who love the military and can't understand why I don't. There's not a whole lot to talk about."

But that was something.

"I sometimes wonder if we'll even be talking ten years from now, you know?" she said. "Like, when I'm an adult and they're still adults, we'd never cross paths if they weren't my parents."

A stab of loss jammed sideways through my chest. "I hope my mom is alive in ten years."

Neither of us spoke for a moment. Then Stella shifted, tilting her face toward mine, and our lips touched again. Just briefly. Just enough to make my heart feel like it could explode.

"We'll finish this, Science Guy," she said with a smile, her lips moving from mine. "We'll figure out Sam's stuff. We'll do it well. You'll get the money and run."

"And what will you do?" I asked.

She sat back, pushing her hands into the sand behind her for support. "Count the minutes until high school ends and I can leave. Write all of this up in a work of 'fiction' that people can't put down." She put her hands in air quotes.

"Good," I told her. "I hope it makes you millions."

In a swift move, Stella stood and brushed the sand off her pants. "Let's get a little closer to this EPA site, scope it out, and then find somewhere to park."

"Park?" Visions of fifties movies and people making out in cars flashed through my brain until Stella snapped her fingers in front of my face a few times.

"Rest until we break in?" Her brows danced upward. "Because I bet neither of us slept last night."

There was a lot of truth in that. I fumbled with the keys in my pocket as we moved back toward Two Snakes. This felt like driving up to the school that first time to steal supplies. Only . . . only this was so much bigger.

* * *

When the EPA site came into view, we slowed. The fence was just a fence with "Hazard" and "No Trespassing" signs. Four lines of barbed wire sat at the top, but the rest of it was just . . . just a basic chain-link fence. Okay, two rows of chain-link fence. Yeah, I'd already sort of known this, but seeing it felt so much different.

"There weren't nearly as many box things in the book," Stella said on a release of breath. "How are we gonna find the right one?"

A giant field of "box things" in tidy offset rows spread out into the desert, the main EPA storage office building resting somewhere south of center. "CONEX," I said. "Or a CONEX box. The box things. That's what they're called."

"Okay, thanks," Stella said, though I could hear the sarcasm in her voice.

My gaze couldn't stop scanning the field of these things. I had to get higher if I wanted to see where the light was. And even then . . . I tried to reorient myself with the pictures from the book. The approximate area where Sam's things would be stored. We might have to break into more than one to find his stuff.

Blood pounded in my ears just considering racing through this maze, using our newly purchased bolt cutters to get through the locks. We should have bought a more boring car. Some old silver Toyota Corolla or something with less identifying markings than two golden cobras.

"I'm just sayin' that I'd rather not call them box thingies when we're searching in the dark." Still, my attention was on the field of CONEX boxes. On how much we'd have to navigate, how far we'd have to walk with the way they were staggered. Walking there, attempting to break into one—or several—of the CONEX boxes, and then coming back, hopefully with a load of fragile chemistry supplies.

"We're gonna need to park a ways away and walk," Stella said. "With our bolt cutters and plastic bucket."

I rubbed my forehead. Anyone coming by—anyone—would be suspicious of that kind of thing. "We could say our truck broke down?" I suggested.

Stella released a long breath—her attention was also still focused on the EPA site. "I say we still shoot for close to three in the morning. No one's gonna be driving way out here. It doesn't coincide with any standard government-schedule shift changes or anything. We should have until six or so before there's any real traffic."

I nodded, even though I sat on the opposite side of the direction Stella faced. "So we have a few more hours to kill."

Finally, she turned to look at me. "Did you say you brought cards?"

I couldn't imagine being able to focus on anything until this was done, but if I could keep my mind busy, maybe my heart would find some chill. "Yeah."

"That's something."

"We could use that shredded old tarp in the bed of the truck to cover the front a bit?" I suggested. "If we can find a house to park at?" Though that would also be a walk.

"Why don't we just head out to one of those random trails we saw leading off this road into the desert?" Stella pointed. "Come at this from the backside."

"Pretend we're out here camping."

She waggled her brows. "Surely, we won't be the first couple who came out here to escape parents and 'camp.'" She used air quotes around "camp."

My neck flushed hot. I'd moved too much for any kind of actual relationship with anyone. And if anybody had told me someone like Stella would be within my reach, I'd have said they had no idea what they were talking about.

"Awww." Stella pinched my cheeks. "I made you speechless."

"You do that," I teased.

She pulled her knees up to her chest and grinned. "Let's go find our *camping* spot."

We picked a trail off the backside of the EPA site, and for the first time, I was grateful for the POS truck, its large tires, and my lack of worry over scratching it or anything. We bounced along the trail, and aside from my concern about how long it would take us to drive back out with our stolen stuff—assuming we found Sam's things—the plan felt more and more solid.

Honestly, we had our age going for us. If we were caught, we could say we just wanted to camp and then we got curious, and . . .

No. This was a government facility, and consequences would be serious, no matter our age. If I got caught, I couldn't help Mom. Getting caught wasn't an option.

"How's here?" I asked Stella as we settled into a shallow valley between rolling desert mounds.

"You're happy, I'm happy." She batted her lashes in mock jest, and I wondered how often she let down her facade. I'd only seen it happen a small handful of times.

"Ready to camp, Science Guy?" she teased as she slipped out of the truck.

No, no I wasn't ready at all. I wasn't ready for any of this, but I also wasn't going to let Mom die because we didn't have money for treatment. This was the last-ditch effort to get some money.

TWENTY-THREE

Stella and I sat in the desert, staring at the quiet grounds of the EPA storage site. I'd expected patrols or something, but only one Jeep had made one circuit of the grounds—just after two a.m., when we'd first hiked over from the truck. And I had to remind myself that this wasn't a research facility, just a place where things were buried underground or stored in CONEX boxes.

My phone cast a strange blue light over our faces as I triple-checked where we were going through the fence and the direction we needed to go once inside. I was now so grateful for the light pole near the CONEX we needed. It wasn't bright this far away, but it still gave us a point to follow. Coming back, we'd be going blind. As soon as I slipped my phone in my pocket, we were enveloped in darkness, the few lights near the EPA offices not reaching nearly this far.

Bolt cutters in my hand, my attention drifted upward to the dark sky and the scattering of stars. I stood next to the fence of a government installation, and all I could think was that the stars out here were incredible. We'd spent hours in the car playing Go Fish and poker and blackjack and Speed and War and every other card game we could think of. We'd both texted our parents. The whole time, I kept expecting to feel groggy or tired, but all I could do was attempt to not stare at the clock. And now that the moment was here, I was staring at the stars.

"If all you wanted to do was look at the stars, we could have done that in Idaho," Stella said on a breathless laugh. "My nerves are kicking into high gear. Let's get this over with."

I positioned the bolt cutters around the lowest section of chain-link fence. "You have nerves?" I teased.

"Ha. Ha." Stella crouched next to me. "Getting the local cops ruffled is one thing, but this . . . this is something else. I can't imagine the hell my parents would put me through if I were caught here. Not with their jobs."

I clipped two more links and paused to face her. "You can stay out here. Go back to the truck and pretend like you didn't know anything about this."

She scoffed. "I'm not scared enough to do that."

"Fair enough." After clipping two more links, I crouched down and wiggled through, Stella right behind me.

"I'm gonna just put one zip tie here, yeah?" she asked.

I pointed near the bottom of our hole. "Just so that it's not obvious there are holes if they drive past here again. I don't want them to see our way out."

"Smart," she said as she took a black tie and quickly hid the hole.

We now stood in the space between fences. One block down, several more to go. Another fence. A maze of CONEX boxes. Finding the right one. Finding the right stuff in the right CONEX. And then getting out through all the same obstacles. In a facility designed to store dangerous things.

For Mom. This is for Mom and all the chances she should have. For a way into a new life. For the treatment. It's a few pieces of danger, for a big payoff. A very big payoff.

We were through the second part of the fence and running in what felt like both seconds and hours. I glanced behind us just before turning a corner, and unless someone were looking closely, the fence looked pretty okay.

"If we're in a hurry on our way back," Stella said as she panted, "we can just push through. I think the zip tie would break."

We rounded a corner until we had our backs to a large box, out of sight of the outer perimeter. Now, whoever was in the vehicle that had come through here before might also drive between. There were certainly the tracks under our feet for that kind of thing.

"Let's hope we don't have to run," I said as I leaned against the metal. "I think I need to jump on top of one so I can see where we need to go."

Stella spun around a couple of times, the large bucket spinning with her. "We should have marked the fence."

"But we didn't—"

"Want anyone else to see the mark," she finished.

We should have gotten a giant spool of black string or something—though I wasn't sure if I'd have the guts to use something so obvious. At the very least, we needed to get back to this side so we could get Two Snakes and head back to Idaho. "We need to count the rights and lefts?"

But it was going to be a matter of seeking our way back through this maze in the dark. There was no way around that. If we found our spot, great. If we didn't, I might have to be cutting the fence a lot faster than I had on our way in.

"Let's just think about next steps," I said. "Going forward. We'll worry about getting out when we get that far."

Stella took a deep breath in, paused, and then started forward. We zigzagged, left, right, left, right, until we finally caught a spot of light.

I'd still need to orient myself. Figure out which side of that light the offices were so I'd know to look in a CONEX on the other side of the light. "Should be."

"I can't wait to write this," she whispered as we continued forward and then fully stopped just as the light post came into view.

The vehicle that had tracked around the outside—a green Jeep now that we were closer—was parked next to the small shack near the light.

"What are the freakin' odds," Stella whispered.

We leaned our backs against the nearest metal side, the large bucket resting between us. "Guess we wait. Again."

"How long can we afford to wait before we have to worry about morning?" Stella asked.

Not long enough. A few hours. But if we were going to be cautious, we had to be patient.

Our shoulders touched as we stood side by side, in a field of government storage containers. *Please don't let this all be for nothing.*

"I can't even tell if we've been here for an hour or, like, three minutes," she whispered softly. "Why do our brains do that to us?"

"Maybe you'll figure it out as you're writing the story," I whispered back, feeling an actual smile tug at the corners of my mouth.

"Maybe I will."

And then a door closed and a car door opened and shut, and the Jeep finally left. As scared as I had been of them doing rounds of the area earlier, I was so grateful now.

"It can't take them long," I said as I rolled off the side of the CONEX and glanced around the edge.

The alleyway here was just wide enough that I could see the top of the actual building to my right. That meant . . . I calculated off to the north of the small shed. Two to three CONEX boxes in that direction should be the right one.

Squinting at the small shack, I could just make out a light through a window, but no bodies inside. At least none that I could see. We had to move. Now and fast.

I ran toward the first CONEX where I thought Sam's things might be. A thought in the back of my mind wondered again if this was worth it, but I pushed forward. We were way past the turnaround point. We were a bus ticket past it, a purchased truck past it, and a break-in past it.

We moved to the back of the first container we planned on checking.

"Master Lock? Are they kidding?" Stella scoffed. "I've been picking these since I was ten."

"Picking?" But a half second later my question was answered when Stella pulled a few tools from her coat, crouched, and slipped two slim pieces of metal into the bottom of the lock.

"This came with a magician set I got for Christmas one year." Her eyes narrowed as she stared at the lock. "For years I'd go and unlock all my neighbors' storage sheds behind their houses on base. Just unlock the lock and then let it sit there, the lock in place, just not locked."

"Scandalous," I teased. And just as I wondered if she was lying, the lock popped open.

Even in the faint light from the light post, I could see her grin as she undid it and slowly opened the large door.

Inside were thick plastic boxes—labeled and stacked against each side.

We slipped on rubber gloves.

"Wow. Whoever did this must hate their job." Stella laughed as she flicked her phone light over the labels.

I gently pulled the door closed behind us, leaving a crack to listen for the Jeep. The walkway in the center was so narrow that reading the labels on the bottom containers took some maneuvering. Dust filled my nose and dulled the labels.

"I think we're close," Stella whispered. "But I don't think his stuff is in this one."

I let my eyes fall closed for a moment in the near dark. We were so close. And of course, I knew that we'd be very lucky to find the stuff on our first try but still . . . we didn't have endless time. At least the boxes were only one deep.

"Why keep all this?" I asked quietly.

"Who knows what'll end up useful at some point?" Stella shrugged. "I have no clue. Most of what the military does makes no sense, and these organizations have the same boss. So . . ."

So.

We left the CONEX and were able to lock it behind us—basically erasing any evidence we were here.

Silently, we stood for a moment, but I heard no sign of the Jeep. They'd be back at some point, and I'd far rather be gone. "Any lucky guesses?" I asked. "I think those three"—I pointed to them in turn— "are our best bet."

Instead of answering, Stella bit her lip.

We were close, but . . . "Let's do that one." I pointed to one two boxes away.

"You're the boss." She stepped around me, jogged for the door, and once again crouched in front of the lock.

All I could do while she worked was keep watch and focus on continuing to breathe.

I heard the click when the lock opened, and then I swear I felt Stella's smugness at getting us in without needing the bolt cutters. No one knowing we were here was far better. It hadn't taken the local cops long to find the supplies we'd taken from the school, so yeah . . . a broken lock would be a dead giveaway that they needed to be looking for someone. How long would it take for them to figure out that Sam Miller's stuff was the stuff taken? With the labels on these, probably not long.

But honestly, if I could at least make the trade of the money for cash and hide it for Mom, that would be enough. I slipped in through the crack in the door and Stella followed. I scanned one side with the light on my phone and she scanned the other.

"I know the door is closed," she whispered. "We gotta hurry."

My flashlight went over names I didn't recognize. Items with labels so foreign, I couldn't even guess what they were, and then . . . *Sam Miller.* At the freaking bottom of the stack.

"Here," I said. "I got it."

I got it.

We were about to recover Sam's actual things. All the research and hoping and moving forward . . . all of that had brought us here. My fingers trembled as I started at the top, the center aisle having *just* enough space for us to turn the boxes and start stacking.

My elbows hit each side—the weight of the bins making the restacking even harder.

"Hurry, hurry, hurry," Stella whispered.

There was nothing to say because of course I was moving as fast as I could. It just wasn't fast enough. When I had shoved the last box over Sam's stuff as far out of the way as possible, I half climbed on them for Stella to pull his out.

A commercial-grade plastic bin. But I had never in my life wanted to open a present or a box or a package as much as I wanted to open this one.

"Okay. Shift them back," she said. "At least that way it might take longer for them to figure out what we took."

Of course she was right, but each move to shift things back rather than running felt like a marathon. Like the slow walk from school to home. Three miles in the wind for every box stacked.

"Okay. Go," she whispered as she once again pushed open the door.

We both held our breath, listening.

"Clear?" I whispered.

She nodded once.

As soon as we stepped out, the hum of the Jeep sounded from . . . somewhere.

"The sound is bouncing off the containers," Stella whispered. "I don't know which way to go."

We each grabbed one side of the bin—who knew we'd get Sam's stuff in a convenient carrying case—and sprinted from behind one container to the other. I grabbed our bucket on the way, but now it was just an inconvenience.

If we didn't hear the Jeep, I'd have Stella open another container and put the bucket in it, but we didn't have time for that. Did we?

The bolt cutters jangled in the bucket as I dragged it behind me, and the arm holding Sam's stuff began to ache with exhaustion. Stella held her side with two hands.

There was more than just glass beakers in here.

The Jeep grew louder.

"This is not good," she breathed out. "I can't tell where they're coming from. Every aisle is wide enough for that thing. We need to hide!"

"Where?"

"In one of these." Stella held out another Master Lock in her hand.

I grabbed the bolt cutters, and checked behind us to see that the CONEX we'd left was about five behind us. I squeezed the jaws of the bolt cutters around the lock shackle, and it broke with a snap and clattered to the ground.

"Let's just climb inside until we don't hear the Jeep anymore. We're far enough away from the light now."

I could just make out her pointing to the slightly lightening sky. We'd been here way longer than I thought. Stella was right, the complete darkness was messing with us.

"Ten minutes," I said. "If it takes longer, we run for it."

We shoved Sam's box inside, followed by the bolt cutters and our empty bucket.

"This thing felt like such a good idea at the time." Stella shoved it on top of a stack. "Let's hope no one finds it."

But they would find it because I'd broken this lock, and I definitely wasn't going to take the time to have Stella remove a lock from somewhere else to put here. Though maybe it would take days for someone to notice a single lock missing on one of maybe two hundred containers? Even a hundred. It would still take forever. I hoped.

I stared at my phone, unable to do anything but count seconds and press my ear to the metal, hoping to hear the

Jeep or the lack of the Jeep, but my pulse was too loud in my ears.

"We can't just sit here," Stella whispered. "We can't. Not with a broken lock on the ground outside."

Surely, I'd earned some good karma in my life. Surely.

We pushed open the CONEX door slowly, and the air was quiet. Suddenly, each footstep felt like thunder. The door squeaked a bit as we pushed it shut, the bucket inside, the bolt cutters in my hands in case we couldn't find our hole in the fence.

"Let's just make a break for it," I said. Because tiptoeing around was probably just as likely to get us caught as sprinting for the fence.

Stella held one side of the crate with Sam's stuff with two hands, and I still held with one, the bolt cutters in my other hand.

Left, right, left, right . . . I knew we were a few CONEX boxes up from where we'd come in, but I couldn't think about that. I just wanted out. I wanted out with Sam's stuff.

Grasping the corner of the box, Stella stopped, her breaths raspy. "PE makes a little more sense now."

"I'm sure this isn't one of the goals," I tried to joke, but my wheezing made my words fall flat. Well, the wheezing and the light-headed fear that we'd be caught before I even had a chance to see Sam's things.

The engine was faint but growing louder.

"I think it's from the left?" Stella offered.

All there was to do was run. My lungs burned. My arm ached. My vision blurred as we moved. *Left, right, left, right* . . .

"Fence!" Stella said, her voice far too loud.

We sprinted to the last CONEX and then stopped. Headlights bounced along the chain link.

The world froze for a moment before I jerked backward, bringing Stella with me. We rounded the back side of the CONEX just as the Jeep drove by. Our jagged breaths cut through the early morning air.

She dropped her end of Sam's box, and I jerked upward, trying to lessen the impact. The box hit and jangled a bit, but I slowly set it down.

A laugh burst out of Stella's mouth. "Way too close, Science Guy. Way too close. But can you imagine reading this scene? Epic."

The edges of the sky were lightening, fading the stars above us. "Let's get out of here."

We hit the inner fence line and sprinted back south until Stella stopped. "Here."

In one quick move, I snipped the zip tie with the bolt cutters. We shoved the container through before following. Stella used another black zip tie to help hold the fence. The longer it was before they knew someone had broken in, the better. Better yet would be some solid wind or rain to cover our tracks.

Once we'd shoved the large bin through the second fence, and Stella had once again mended the hole slightly, we paused. I looked back the way we'd come, the smudges and marks in the dirt making it look as if we'd dug a trail.

It wouldn't take a very observant person to see the marks we'd left in the otherwise untouched desert dirt. The race to get home wasn't over yet.

"Why didn't we park closer?" Stella's voice was tinged with both laughter and something lower, like exhaustion.

At some point the adrenaline would leave my system, and then I'd have a hard time staying awake, but I wouldn't feel safe until we were home. And even then . . . after being caught once, I might never feel safe. It was a risk I'd knowingly walked into.

I might not take a deep breath until this whole thing was behind us.

The half mile through the desert felt like ten. When we finally reached the truck, Stella rested against the side. "I'm dying to see what's in there, but . . ."

"Yeah," I agreed without her finishing. But we had to get as far away from the EPA as possible.

I found the strength to load the storage bin as Stella crawled into the passenger side of the truck. There was some kind of seal around the top of the bin. It might take us a while to figure out how to undo it, and we had the added issue of needing a new place to work.

But the fence line was behind us, the sky was lightening on top of us, and the world was about to open up around us. After a silent, pleading prayer, I pumped the gas and then started up Two Snakes. We slowly bumped and bounced back the way we'd come. Stella sat silent and almost dazed-looking in the passenger seat.

I reached down to turn on the headlights, but then stopped. Would that make us more noticeable? But then, if someone saw us without headlights, was it light enough for us to not look suspicious? "I'm second-guessing everything."

"Turn on the headlights," Stella said. "It's almost seven a.m., which isn't a totally unreasonable time to be driving out here—especially if we're headed home or to school or something."

I reached down and grabbed the pull handle that would turn on the lights, but paused. I wanted to be just a little closer to the road first. Make it look like we hadn't camped so far away. The logs sat unused in the back of the truck, but maybe they'd still make it look like we'd been camping. We inched along in the near dark for another few minutes before I realized we'd be out here forever without light.

Okay. I drew in a deep breath and pulled the knob, lighting the trail in front of us. We were just two teens. In love. Sneaking out for the night. In a truck that looked as if it belonged to a low-level drug dealer. Yeah. No big deal.

After twenty agonizing minutes, we were finally back on the road. As we headed back to the freeway, more and more cars joined us. The more cars on the road, the more it felt like we were actually going to drive home with *Sam Miller's* things in the back.

"We did it," I breathed as the freeway entrance came into view. "We did it."

But Stella's head had dropped back on the seat, her eyes were closed, and her breathing was soft and heavy. I still had a few hours of driving this crappy truck on a freeway it couldn't travel the speed limit on. We weren't fully out of the woods. Not yet. Maybe not ever. I wasn't stupid. What I'd gotten into was dangerous on a lot of levels. I just couldn't let go of the fact that I could change my life. My mom's life. I just had to get through the next few weeks. That was all.

After a few more miles, Stella slid down in the seat, her head resting against my shoulder. I tried and failed not to breathe in as she relaxed against me, her body falling deeper into sleep.

I paid attention to the road, mostly. I also paid attention to the slope of her small nose. The freckles scattered across her skin. Her lashes against her cheeks. The small puffs of air that sometimes burst from her lips as she dreamed.

Earning this place, this level of comfort from someone who I was sure put on a show for most people, helped me settle into my seat. Helped me think about things that weren't. *Are we really okay? Did we really just do that? What's in the storage bin?*

The miles rolled by underneath us, and when we were finally back in Idaho, another layer of tension slipped away. We'd done it. We were in the clear.

For now.

TWENTY-FOUR

The roar of the tires on the pavement grew quiet as we left the freeway for Twin Falls.

Stella blinked, her head just now leaving my shoulder. "Food," she mumbled. "I need food."

My stomach rumbled in response to her words. I couldn't remember eating. Burgers and fries by the lake, but that was a lifetime ago. A lifetime before we'd broken into a government facility and stolen items they'd confiscated. A smile tugged at the corner of my mouth.

Stella sat up and pressed a finger to my cheek. "What's that smile?"

"We did it." I regripped the steering wheel. "We did it."

"For sure we did!" She pointed. "I know that car. It's Mike's. Let's get McDonald's."

Because probably she had Mike wrapped around her finger and would get us some kind of deal. I jerked the wheel and we pulled into the parking lot. And then I did a super normal thing and just sat in the car while Stella went in and got us food. Just a guy skipping school in a crappy truck and getting breakfast sandwiches, *with Sam Miller's equipment* in the bed.

Stella bounced out a few minutes later with a giant drink and a brown bag. "I had an idea," she said as she slid into the car.

"Yeah?"

"Last time we tried to hide in one of the empty houses, but that backfired. What if . . ." She set the boxes between us, taking the passenger seat. "What if we hid in plain sight?"

"Like, one of the buildings that's almost full." I nodded.

"Exactly."

"What if someone moves in?"

"What if we use an empty building and are caught? What if we do it at your house and it gets you or your mom sick? What if we use someone's shed and they catch us? What if we—"

"Okay, okay," I said with a laugh. "There's no perfect place when you're doing something sketchy."

"I'm gonna use that line in my book." Stella unwrapped a breakfast sandwich. "And Mike gave me the deal of a lifetime."

"Brilliant."

She took a giant bite out of the sandwich, and my stomach growled. She handed me one. "Your reward, sir, for a job well done and a successful mission!"

I unwrapped the sandwich, and hot steam wafted into my nose. I took a bite of the soft bread and combo of salty cheese and egg with a greasy sausage patty. Delicious!

We drove through the neighborhood in silence. I stayed focused on the wonderful, warm food.

Stella sat back. "I was thinking. Did you see that last

neighborhood? We could just pull the truck in like we're the new neighbors?"

I didn't love the idea, but it wasn't like we had a huge number of choices, and with Sam's formula for heat and stuff, a place close to my house would definitely be best. It wasn't like I could suddenly be driving a truck I didn't pay for. There would be questions. "What if someone comes to offer cookies or something?"

Her brows raised, and her mouth twisted into a dubious expression. "Would you come knocking on a door with this POS truck parked outside?"

"Your turn to make a fair point."

We drove back toward my house, all the while me hoping the school hadn't called Mom to say I was gone, or that she hadn't gone online to check attendance, and hoping she wasn't home. That she felt good enough to go to work. But I kept glancing back into the bed of the truck, back to Sam's stuff. I'd gotten it hours ago, and finally, we were about to see what was inside.

The truck rumbled to a stop at a series of three buildings, six townhomes in each, only four of which were occupied. Four out of eighteen gave us pretty good odds to be left alone. We picked an end one, because like Stella had said, the end ones always went first, and it would look weird otherwise.

She picked the lock and promised to get us a new door handle that matched the others over the next day or two. Until then, we'd leave the back door unlocked.

We each took an end of Sam's box and hauled it into the house, leaving Two Snakes in the driveway. Finally, I was going to get to see his chemistry set.

The place was musty, the dust and smell tickling at my nose. There was just something stale about it. Though my townhouse hadn't felt much different when Mom and

I moved in. The same kind of mismatched old furniture dotted the space.

"My skills are lacking," I said as we set down the tub. "I gotta learn to pick locks."

"You start with the clear ones." Stella shrugged as she knelt next to the large bin. "This thing is super sealed. You think there's some toxin left in here and we'll die when we open it? In some epically cheesy scene like in *Raiders of the Lost Ark?*"

"Not you too." I crouched next to her. "My mom is obsessed with those movies."

Stella pulled a knife out and began picking at a waxy seal that sat like caulk between the lid and the body. "I'm not obsessed. I've just watched them a few times. Good storytelling, and they don't fully follow a traditional story structure. Like, they do, but they don't."

I paused at picking at the caulk using my pocketknife. Everything was a story to Stella. Her life. This adventure. And yes, movies were stories, but she didn't just watch them, she dissected them.

I continued to pick at the lower edge of the seal, which finally released a hiss.

"The first victory!" Stella grinned over the top of the box.

Tiredness began to prick along my skin, within the dryness of my eyes, and something obvious hit me. "We have school tomorrow."

"Ra, ra," Stella chanted.

I couldn't imagine leaving this stuff, but I couldn't imagine being in more trouble with Mom or the school or anyone either. "Let's just get set up. I can set alarms and check it tonight."

"You don't even know if we have what we need," Stella pointed out.

I was just so tired. We peeled at the sealing caulk from each end until I finally reached where she had started.

We put protective equipment on. Gloves and a mask.

Crouching on her side of the box, she waggled her brows. "You ready?"

Beyond ready. I dug my fingers under the lid and pried upward. With a weird *thwap* sound, the lid came free.

Each piece was wrapped in bubble wrap with some strange foam blanket-type thing around that. Someone had really wanted to preserve it all—Sam must have really been on to something.

I pulled up the first bundle and slowly unwrapped the beaker from the plastic. The glass had a strange yellowish-orange tinge to it. "What's that?" I mumbled.

"You're not actually asking me, are you?" Stella shifted. "I mean, I'm going to assume you're just sort of asking questions out loud to the universe or something."

I couldn't stop staring. "Why would it be discolored like this?" How would it get discolored? What had this thing been through? Maybe getting Sam's things had been the worst idea. It was old. Had been in storage. And had been fully used.

"Let's just keep going." Stella unwrapped another bit of glassware.

We silently unwrapped each piece of glassware, the rubber stoppers, the Bunsen burner with a strange attachment on the top, and a few beakers that had been altered with some kind of removeable waxy lid. Each piece was labeled in evidence bags. I didn't know if that lent weight to the theory that the government had either killed him or taken him. I studied the materials we had. Some strange crusty oxidation had grown on the Bunsen burner. The yellowing of the glassware wasn't at all consistent, and that had scenarios spinning through my head, but honestly, we had so few choices.

"Was this that thing he was talking about, you think?" Stella asked. "That he built?"

"And the flask." I pointed to the holder he'd created for it also—something to keep the flame the perfect distance away for the perfect temperature, I guessed.

"He was our age." Stella shook her head. "And I call *you* Science Guy."

She wrapped her long hair in a twist and pulled it over her shoulder. Her makeup was long gone. And I wasn't sure I'd ever seen her look so . . . *human*. Normal. Like maybe she could be within reach.

At the bottom were a few textbooks, Sam's highlights throughout. Steps and trials that he'd done. Two battered notebooks had scattered notes. Sam's attempts he'd scribbled out. What the EPA didn't have was his journal. The one where he wrote up what finally worked.

I had that missing piece.

"The wax seal feels a little soft," Stella said. "And this one rubber hose feels a bit dry, but overall, I think we're in good shape."

"Let's set up and then I gotta get some sleep." I rubbed my eyes a few times. Finding and using Sam's things felt like a near miracle, but exhaustion was leaving this whole experience fuzzy.

"Can you handle getting up to alarms?" Stella asked.

"You gotta get home."

She pulled out her phone. "I'm getting an Uber now to take me to the base entrance. I'm good."

"I could drive you," I offered. "In Two Snakes."

Stella jumped onto the counter, letting her legs dangle. "Probably best if no one sees us at this place or with that truck—not for a while anyway."

"Yeah. Okay."

I pulled out Sam's journal, the whole thing now feeling so *real*. I had his words. His materials. His contacts. He'd paved the way to create a whole new life for me and Mom. And maybe one day I'd figure out what had actually happened to him. If not, at least I had this.

"A neighbor just left," Stella said, peering out the blinds. "I'm gonna walk until I catch my Uber."

"Hey, thanks," I told her as I pulled another bulging can of the beans from my backpack. "Like, I don't know how I'd have done this on my own. Or *if* I would have."

"As long as you keep up your end of the deal, I'm happy." A corner of her mouth quirked into a half smile. She blew me a kiss and quickly slipped out the door.

I had no idea what we were. Friends? More? Partners who had kissed a couple times? From what I knew of Stella, probably the last one. I'd have time to figure out what she and I were after this was behind me.

Following each of Sam's steps, I got two sets of the toxin started. The initial bacteria sample would need the night to get started. There were a bunch of random test tubes with stoppers, and it took me way too long to realize that he had these set up for the final toxin. Ten. That should be more than enough. A couple grams was next to nothing.

I locked the front door, went out the back, and crouched behind the fence until I was sure everything was quiet. Which took a while because once again my pulse was drowning out all other noises except my breathing, which felt earth-shatteringly loud. I slipped out the back gate and sprinted for the sidewalk trail that connected all of the housing areas.

This sneaking around was going to give me a heart attack. Leaving Sam's things behind felt like a special kind of torture. I wanted to just sit and stare and absorb. Remember and realize and soak in that the exact beakers and tubes he'd used in his experiments, I was about to use in mine.

We had time for one trial, maybe two, before we'd need to make the toxin for the drop. This was right about the time I should be getting home from school, so that was something.

Mom's car wasn't in the drive, which meant she'd maybe last the whole workday. I never knew if that was good or bad. I rested my hand over Sam's patch in my pocket when I stepped in the front door.

I hadn't checked the messages on the computer in a while, so once that was behind me, I'd get some sleep. I started it so it could warm up, stripped, and stumbled into the shower. The grime and memories needed to be washed off my clothes. Well, my clothes and Sam's Atari T-shirt.

After my shower, I sat in front of the computer, the messages sitting on the top left as always. But now there was a new one.

MPG: We need a sample.

Well . . .

SAM: When?

MPG: Within the next day or two. We've given you the time you asked for. We need to make sure product is correct.

Yeah, so did I. But testing out the potency of something on . . . anyone . . . wasn't in my realm of possibility.

SAM: Give me four days.

MPG: We will give you details on the drop location tomorrow.

New worry began to settle, but I was too tired for it to actually stick. Not right now. I'd done my bit and started the stuff. Now to hope that Sam's formula was as potent as the EPA felt it must be if they'd confiscated and then stored his supplies.

I turned off the computer, rolled onto my bed, and let sleep take over.

TWENTY-FIVE

The Jeep crashed through the fence behind us as Stella and I ran, dragging a bin the size of Two Snakes. We needed the bin, but we also needed to escape. There was no way to make it in time. The Jeep grew closer. Mom and Brock were driving, each with a steering wheel. I didn't know if I should run faster, or if that meant escape.

I gasped awake, sucking in the dry air of my room. My fingers fumbled with the blankets as I tried to toss them off me. I swiped my sweaty hair off my forehead and inched out from under the covers.

Mom's subtle coughing carried from downstairs. Light still crept in around the blinds. I'd just taken a nap. A groan escaped as I rolled over, my body stiff from driving and running and hauling and stress.

Another cough from downstairs pushed me to my feet. I stumbled down the stairs and heard the familiar low hum of Mom's breathing machine. Oxygen. Because despite this move being one that was supposed to help her, it didn't look like that was the case.

I stood at the edge of the living room, staring at her with her mask on, watching more *CSI*. "Hey."

"Oh!" She rolled, holding her mask to her face. "I saw you were napping. I figured you and Brock wouldn't get much sleep."

Brock? Oh right. My fake alibi. "Yeah. We were up all night."

"Well, at least you're making friends." I could just make out her smile underneath her mask.

"Yeah. Friends," I agreed, because there was nothing else to say that was safe. "How are you?"

Mom shrugged. "Better with oxygen."

Forcing my gaze to not travel to her oxygen tank, I took a deep breath before responding. "Did the insurance come through?"

Mom's mouth twitched. "The medical supply company is letting me use this for what we hope is my copay."

Which wasn't definite. "I may have an in on a truck," I told her. "And then I can get a job. It's almost summer anyway." Which I had to add because she always worried about school. And Mom didn't know how little money I had in my account—maybe I did have enough to buy a random truck from a creepy dude with a gun in North Ogden. One with two golden snakes on the hood.

If she only knew what she should actually be worrying about right now.

"School first," Mom said. "Always."

Soon, with any luck, I could easily put school first—without sacrificing finances. I was so close. So close. "Of course."

"And I know I've seen Brock drop you off, but it would be nice to actually meet him."

I took a step back toward the kitchen. "I'm sure you will at some point. He's a nice guy. How about I make us some dinner?"

"Mac and cheese," Mom called. "If you're up to it!"

My body still wanted to be asleep. My mind wanted to be with Sam's stuff—just watching it or something. All the CONEX boxes, and with a little research and a crap-ton of luck, and we'd found it!

"It's silent in there," Mom said. "You okay?"

"I'm good," I said around the corner. "Mac and cheese sounds great."

At least we had some cream to make the cheesy powder bearable. I filled the pot. Started the stovetop. Set out the ingredients. So boring. So pointless. Just down the street was an experiment that would change our lives.

Going back and forth between my place and Sam's stuff when it wasn't necessary would mean that we were far more likely to get caught, and I'd come too far for that. Way too far. So I made our cheap dinner and sat with Mom and watched *CSI*, and then went to bed so I could get up and finish the school week, then have the weekend to finish a toxin sample, and a day or several trying not to puke while I waited to hear from MPG, whoever they were.

*　*　*

The day after one pulled off an incredible heist was not a day one wanted to find themselves in the principal's office.

"You've missed two days of school, and we've been unable to contact your mother." Principal Wills leaned forward across his desk, sliding his thin fingers together. "Where have you been?"

"Not, um . . ." I forced a cough. "Not feeling well."

"And it's just coincidence that Stella wasn't feeling well on the same days?"

"That makes perfect sense," I said with a straight

face. "We spend a lot of time together. It makes sense that we'd get sick at the same time."

"You and Brock also spend a lot of time together . . ." The principal trailed off.

This was so pathetically dumb. He was just the principal at a high school. After running from EPA guards, he was nothing. "Two things," I started. "First, Brock and I don't kiss."

Principal Wills frowned.

"And second." I even held up two fingers, leaning on his desk in nearly the same manner as he did. "Second, Brock is probably the healthiest human in this school. He probably never gets sick."

"Hmph." Principal Wills sat back in his chair, his eyes still focused in on me. "Don't miss school, Chuck. And when you do, make sure you have a note. At some point, we'll get in touch with your mother."

"Of course." Only they wouldn't. They'd only get "Mom's" voicemail. The one I'd set up in IT class.

At least it was the weekend, and this was all I'd have to suffer through this week.

Stella looped her arm through mine as we left IT for lunch. "This is terrible after the last two days, isn't it?"

"Completely," I agreed.

"You need help tonight?" she asked.

"Need is a strong word, but yeah, I gotta have a sample by Sunday. We got a drop point last night. Some old farmhouse about forty-five minutes from here."

"Yeah. Way better than school." Stella looped her arm through mine. "Kinda scary right?"

I shivered.

"Like, this is really *real*, you know? What we're doing is something that most people just watch movies about," she said.

"Or read books about." I nudged her with my hip.

And Stella beamed up at me, making my heart roll over in my chest. I was so sunk for her. I knew I was only getting half of her. I knew she had things going on in her life that I only had a hint of, but I was all in. I wanted to know all of it. All of her.

She stopped in the hallway, and I turned to face her. "I actually told Principal Wills that we were sick on the same day because we kiss."

"Ha." She grinned. "Wish I could have seen his face."

"I don't think he was impressed." I leaned closer. Close enough that I felt the warmth from her breath on my face.

"Guess we shouldn't make you a liar, huh?" And in a quick move, she stood on her tiptoes and pressed her lips to mine. "Now I need some crappy cafeteria pizza because I am so done with this school day."

Principal Wills stalked up to us in the hallway. "I called your mother at work, Chuck."

Well, crap.

"Come to the office with me, please." He glanced over his shoulder. "You too, Stella."

I knew we'd both be suspended, and honestly, that worked in my favor at this point because I had to get this toxin done. But Mom didn't need the stress, and I hated that this would add to her terrible health.

"You okay?" Stella squeezed my hand, and I squeezed hers back.

"Mom. That's all."

"I'm gonna get an amazing dinner sent to your house tonight as an apology. You can say it's from Brock. Maybe she'll hate him instead of me."

The gesture was so perfectly Stella. There was a problem, and she'd find some way to offset it.

I leaned over just before we stepped back into the office. "I like you, Stella."

"I like you too, Science Guy."

* * *

Tonight was the night when me and Stella needed to really set timers and follow Sam's plans. Mom's worry was palpable, in the way she picked at her delivered steak, and the way she peered up at me with a frown.

"The year's almost over," I argued. "I'm sorry. We didn't get into any trouble. I promise. We just . . . wanted some free time."

"For what?" she asked.

"Road trip. We drove . . ." No way could I tell her we'd gone all the way to Salt Lake. "We drove to Boise. It was . . . fine. Just another city. I won't do it again."

"Stolen stuff from the school and now this." She released a long sigh. Twisted her hair over her shoulder. "I thought that was your one act of rebellion?"

Oh yeah. I remembered saying that. "The year is almost over," I said again. "I have good grades."

"Which is the only reason I'm not panicking."

I hated that my plan for the phone thing didn't work. Principal must be bored to track her down at work. But better to be caught by the school and my mom than by the FBI or Homeland Security or whoever else had been after Sam.

Now I just had to make sure Mom got to bed sooner than normal so I could start the rapid-growth part of the process. I needed tomorrow to do the refining. I'd started the growth before, but to be doing the refining *just* before handing over a sample?

Yeah, I'd need all the luck I could get.

TWENTY-SIX

Something about setting alarms, rechecking Sam's notes, and standing over clear liquid, which was turning to a refined toxin, had hit centers of my brain I didn't know I had. The world quieted. My worries about the drop-off and Mom and money all quieted.

Turning. Changing. Warming. Cooling. Watching the bacterial solution become clear, just like Sam showed in his notes.

Stella sat in her favorite spot on the counter, her legs stretched over a portion of the kitchen I wasn't using, typing away on her phone.

"You writing about us?" I asked as I stared at the now boiling liquid.

"I already made those notes," she said in the distracted voice she used when her mind was somewhere else.

I could relate. I was only half here. It was just that the polite side of my brain couldn't shut off the fact that I was sharing the room with a girl I liked.

"A part of me wishes I could take pictures," Stella said. "But I know that would be a terrible idea."

Her eyes were still on her phone. My attention was still on my work. "Yep."

After a day and a half of monitoring, half sneaking out around Mom, and continually staring at the unchanging messages with MPG, my eyes were dry, my head felt weighted, and my stomach rumbled.

I flicked off the Bunsen burner and then fully stood and stretched my arms overhead. Now I had to isolate the toxin. I'd never gotten to this stage before. In fact, when the cop came and caught us before, I'd only barely witnessed the slurry starting to turn clear.

"I've got to precipitate the toxin out of this." I held up Sam's specialized flask full of clear liquid.

"How are we going to do that?"

"Hand me that bottle that has H2SO4 on it, por favor."

"Dang, Chuck, not only are you good at this science stuff, but now you're fluent in Spanish! I'm loving it."

I added sulfuric acid to the clear solution to increase the acidity, making the toxin insoluble.

"What's happening?" Stella asked.

"The acid is making the toxin settle out into a thick yellow mixture at the bottom."

"Oh nice, we created yellow mud."

"That stuff right there"—I pointed to the flask with the yellow mud in it—"has all the botulism in it, I think, or at least that's what Sam said. We need to keep purifying it." I turned back to the journal. "We have to dissolve the yellow mud in a saltwater bath."

Stella reached into a grocery bag.

"You had to get the Himalayan salt, didn't ya?"

"I mean it looked so fancy. And we want our botulism to be sophisticated, don't we?"

"I suppose." I laughed.

Stella dissolved some of the pink granules into a beaker. She stirred it until the salt was fully dissolved, all while I was pouring off the sulfuric acid, leaving the yellow mud at the bottom of the flask. Then I poured the sophisticated salt solution into the flask, and the yellow mud dissolved, creating a gold-colored liquid. I added more acid, and we waited. The yellow mud thickened at the bottom again, and we repeated the salt solution and acid precipitation five more times, six in total.

"Why are we doing it so many times?"

"It says that the more times you do it, the purer the toxin will get."

"Oh cool," Stella said. "So now we have a sophisticated, pure little virgin toxin."

She made me smile. "Sam says we need to cool the whole thing down to negative five degrees Celsius," I said.

"This is the hardest part. Converting Celsius to Fahrenheit." Stella rolled her eyes.

"Good news, we don't have to. Sam's thermometer is in Celsius."

"Oh good. I didn't want that nerdy conversion in my searches," Stella said. "I'd get hit up with chemistry-set ads or some stylish lab-goggle ads." "That's exactly what I want for Christmas."

I poured the acid salt solution down the drain, leaving the yellow mud at the bottom, then carefully scooped the moist mud and piled it on blotting paper. "See that jar of white powder labeled $(NH_4)_2SO_4$? Hand that to me, please."

"What's this for?"

"It's ammonium sulfate and should cause the botulism to dry out and crystallize into microscopic, clear needles that are the pure toxin."

"I see."

"Now we put it in the fridge and cool it down even more."

Even though Sam's notes were memorized, I still reviewed everything again. Every step. Every detail.

"You really get off on this, huh?" Stella's words were laced with low laughter.

I just shrugged as I stepped back, looking over all the pieces again. "I'm gonna start another batch. We'll need a lot more to make even a gram and a half."

Her laughter paused as she stared at me. "You love this."

"A little, yeah," I admitted. But really, a lot. I loved the method. I loved creating something new out of something boring. No, something *exceptional* out of some boring beans. I loved that Mom and I had somehow ended up in a crappy house with Sam Miller's stuff.

"You know a lot of people think he's still alive?" Stella asked. "That the government basically stole him, and he's working for them now?"

"People never want to think someone exceptional died," I said as I leaned against the counter. "But exceptional people die every day."

"That turned dark." And then Stella smirked. "But yeah, you're right. When I write this story, I'll slip in a twist or two."

"Good," I told her. "I want people guessing."

The idea of Stella putting this whole thing to words felt better every day. We'd accomplished a bizarre and incredible thing in a short amount of time—and I'd literally fallen into it. Now . . . now I couldn't imagine the boring life I had before this one. Tomorrow, I'd be doing a drop for an unknown identity I'd met on the dark web. Most people went their whole lives without doing something so big.

"Well, I got my therapist to make my parents go easy on me, but you'll be alone for the drop." Stella swung her legs over the side of the counter and slipped to the floor.

"I figured." I was actually surprised she'd been able to be around at all.

"I need you to note everything, okay?" she asked. "Like, sights or smells or cars, or anything I could use."

"Got it."

She breezed past me like I wasn't someone she'd kissed before and paused at the front door, pressing her ear to the metal. In a quick move, she slipped out and most likely sprinted toward wherever she'd stashed her mom's car.

I turned and stared at what I'd accomplished, the small bit of liquid already beginning to crystallize on the edges. Sam said to leave it. The liquid stuff was what he'd injected into the cat, but the crystals were safer to transport, and they'd liquify in any type of liquid later on.

There was a yellowish tinge that Sam hadn't noted, but there was nothing I could do about that now. And then I remembered the YouTube videos—some of which were totally finished, and others that needed some final details. Yeah, Stella was going to write this up, but I wanted to at least have the chance to tell my part of Sam's story for all the people out there poring over conspiracy sites, wondering what happened to the guy. Maybe someone would see something I posted, and it would spark some answers.

But there would be no posting until this was over. Not until I had the money—maybe not until long after. Knowing this might be a terrible move, I took a short video of Sam's journal pages, and how I'd used his own materials to set this up. Okay, some of it was ego—I could admit that. But some of it was just that I couldn't imagine not providing more information about Sam Miller to the people out there who were starving for it.

* * *

In every movie scenario and every book and every . . . everything spy-related, they did the drop at night. But MPG wanted to have it before dinner, and I had to be back home before Mom woke up from her nap.

Pale light stretched across the edges of the Sunday morning sky as I stepped out of the townhouse. The same light that Stella and I had sprinted under when we'd left the EPA grounds. I paused and stared at Two Snakes longingly as I tapped the vial in my pocket. I climbed into the driver's seat and started the old truck.

And then I did what I knew I was going to do when I first found out where the drop-off was. I drove—and drove—miles from my house to the outskirts of town. There wasn't a *lot* of traffic, but the road was winding enough that I had to pay attention. The farmhouse was sitting out in the middle of an unkempt field. The roof had caved in, and the white paint peeled off the outside, exposing weathered gray planks underneath.

Constantly looking over my shoulder would be way too obvious, so I forced my gaze forward. Forced myself to orient with north, south, east, west. The house looked tired—the whole thing sort of slumped around the boarded-up windows, weeds having eaten the grass. The yard was fenced off with a few warning signs, but there were enough holes in the fence that I guessed it had been like this for a while. I ducked under it, and then paused to just look at the house. As I got closer, I noticed that parts of the porch had fallen away from the main house.

Actually, this dilapidated place wouldn't be a bad

spot for LegendCityVids. I took a few shots of the outside, and then a few through the dusty windows. Mostly just broken up walls and a floor with as much empty air as floorboards. Not a place I'd venture into. But still, a lame video was maybe better than no video. Maybe.

I paused, shoving my hands in my pockets, feeling the vial. It was now or never. I glanced over my shoulder. They could be watching. They could have a sniper aiming at me. The movies taught me to look for any laser dot on myself. Phew, nothing—I was good. A chill ran down my spine and I shivered, sucking in a breath. Once I was satisfied that I was the only one out here, I followed the instructions to a T.

Twenty-seven steps from the northeast corner of the house, along the side. Two feet up was a loose board. The specific directions made me pause again—how did they know this area? I couldn't imagine an entity like MPG, whoever they were, hanging in Twin Falls, Idaho. Why would a university need a drop site? A chill ran up my spine when the realization came to me that maybe what I had worked up in my mind wasn't a university. Someone from there, or them, must be here now.

I pried on the old siding and a rusty nail squeaked while I worked. With a little effort I got the board off the house. A small, exposed hole with a metal box sitting inside confirmed to me I was on the right track. I removed the box, stared at the tiny yellow crystals, and sucked in a long breath. Gingerly, I placed the vial inside. This was it. I had done it. Three hundred thousand dollars richer and now I could take care of my mother. I replaced the board and pushed the rusty nail back in to the end of the board, pegging it in place.

If the sample didn't work, we were . . . I didn't know. I'd have to come up with some kind of excuse. Some reason or detail that would make them want to work with me again. Without them, I was almost back to square one.

I let my eyes drift closed. *Please work. Please. Please. Please.*

My head swiveled from side to side as I stood, then spun around. No one seemed to be watching from any morning shadows. I ducked back out from under the fence and started up the sidewalk, peeling back the wrapper of my Snickers bar.

And that was it. Another big thing, just over and done.

I texted Stella so she'd know I'd made the drop, only I just told her I'd walked downtown. She'd know. Again, one foot in front of the other. All the way home.

The drive seemed like it took forever, but once I was home, all I had to do was sit and stare at the messages. Wonder if they'd made the pickup. Wonder about who had the funds for this kind of thing, and wonder where in the world they'd come from.

TWENTY-SEVEN

Twelve hours after the drop, and all I'd done was a few bits of schoolwork and stared at the computer screen. At the last couple messages we'd sent back and forth. The ones detailing where to drop the toxin. And since then, nothing.

Tonight would be following the same procedure as I had a couple of nights ago—sneaking over and changing heat and stuff. But if the sample hadn't worked, then what?

I slipped off the chair and flopped onto my unmade bed. Actually, it was always unmade. There was no point in pulling up the blankets if I was just gonna mess them up a few hours later. I stared at the ceiling of a crappy townhouse that wasn't ours, and as crappy as it was, it still looked and smelled and felt better than anywhere we'd lived since our military housing on the East Coast.

This was the way out. Sam's formula was the way out. It had to be. He couldn't have made something new, as a teenager, only to be turned into a quiet whisper of an unsolved case.

The computer beeped, and I jerked up so fast the room spun. I jumped into the chair and froze.

MPG: How did you make it?

I mean, did they want the whole process? Because *that* wasn't gonna happen. My fingers were moving the second my phone had flashed on.

Chuck: Stella, they're asking how I made it. Ideas on responses?

The three little dots shifted and shifted as I waited for her.

Stella: Maybe just ask them why they want to know? But don't pretend like there might be something wrong with it. We need to instill trust.

Chuck: thx

Stella: Keep me updated!

I turned for the computer again and placed my shaking fingers on the keys.

SAM: Why do you want to know?

And then I held my breath. No dots for me to know if they were responding or not, just that same stupid green cursor blinking at me.

MPG: Strain unknown. Stronger than anything we've seen. Worked faster than we have ever seen.

It worked!

Relief washed over me. Maybe the yellow crystals were the thing that made the difference. The piece of Sam's equipment that had made me the most worried had actually made this better. I was a master botulism creator.

SAM: Due to purity of strain, I'm going to need 500,000 for the 1.5.

I hit Send before allowing myself to think too hard. Too much was on the line.

We can't believe how quick it worked. What did that mean? I thought of Sam's cat and how he'd accidently killed it. Was that what happened here? Did someone mishandle it? An accident? Did *I* kill someone? I swallowed down the bile that had begun to creep up my throat. I couldn't think about that. These people were professionals. Maybe they just tested it at a lab, or on mice. Of course, how else could they test the purity? They had to be a university or something. I had to tell myself this because I had to save Mom. I had to get us out of this dump and into a life that wasn't counting pennies and still barely scraping by.

But still, what *were* they using it for? I stopped myself before I spiraled into a cyclical thought process. No, I would not focus on that. I'd think about Mom on the couch with oxygen on her face—a person who had done nothing wrong in her life, suffering for years.

No response. No response. No response.

> *Chuck: Can you come over? Now? I may have messed things up.*
>
> *Stella: Will find a way.*

Normally I worried about what Stella would have to go through to get here, but as I started to regret demanding more money, I didn't care what she had to do. Had I ruined the deal? Was I too forward? Stella was the only person who knew the details of what I was doing, and so she was the only person who could help.

The steps creaked. And then again. And again.

A cough.

Another cough.

I scrolled down until only my last message appeared, but I couldn't risk Mom seeing this. *Damn it.* The whole computer had to be shut down, and then I'd have to boot it back up again. I should have shifted the desk so she couldn't see the screen from the door.

Another round of coughing said Mom was at the top of the stairs. Oh. Monitor. I flipped it off and hoped they wouldn't message until I could answer.

Two knocks were followed by Mom, who immediately slumped against the door frame. There was no need to ask her how she felt. Her cheeks were sunken in. Purple lined underneath her eyes. Her shoulders drooped.

"I'm going . . ." she rasped. "I'm going to bed early."

I forced a partial smile. "Yeah, me too."

Mom scoffed, which sent her into a coughing fit. My legs tensed as if ready to push me out of the chair, but even if I were next to her, I couldn't stop this. We needed specialists. We needed insurance. "Don't tease, but selfishly, I'm glad you'll be here."

Because she was scared. Because anyone who had a hard time breathing would be scared often. "Me too."

And then she was out of my room, and I knew I'd keep that image of her in my doorway in my head as I moved forward. Because I wasn't stopping until I had the cash in hand. I flipped the monitor back on just as Stella texted.

> *Stella: Outside. Not sure how much trouble you're in.*

> *Chuck: Not in trouble. Gimme a sec.*

When I looked up, Mom had shuffled off to her room. I flipped on the monitor and tiptoed down the stairs. I wasn't sure how she would react to Stella being here—sneaking her in felt best.

Using two hands, I slid the chain off the door and slowly opened it. Stella ducked in under my arm, her hair damp and smelling like shampoo.

"Close the door, genius," she whispered.

Right. Because I was still standing in the open doorway, stunned again by Stella's nearness. I softly closed the door and replaced the chain with two hands. "Mom just went upstairs to nap."

She nodded once. "Can you feed me? I didn't take time to eat, just grabbed the keys and ran."

"You gonna get in trouble?"

"Probably." Stella shrugged.

I stepped around her into the kitchen. We were low on food, but there was always mac and cheese. But when I opened the fridge, the cream was gone. So much for making it edible.

"This is what we have," I explained as I filled a pot.

"Mom always buys the generic stuff. If you think this is bad, it's because you haven't tried that yet."

The chat slipped into my thoughts again. "I asked for more money."

"MPG?" she whispered, and then froze. "On the chat?"

I nodded once. "The toxin works fast, according to them—whatever that means."

"Oh!" And then her face fell, but there was a brightness in her eyes. That tinge of excitement that reminded me of my first days in Twin Falls when Brock said I should be careful.

I stared at the water, willing it to boil. And then determined to watch it until it did boil. Needing to prove the stupid saying wrong—*a watched pot never boils*. I wasn't going to move my eyes.

"Seriously?" Stella whispered. "Is it that interesting?"

"I'm conducting an experiment," I said, still watching the silver bottom of the pot, "now that I'm a chemist."

"Is this an always thing for you?" she asked. "Experiments?"

I shook my head, still not averting my gaze. "I guess maybe they are now."

Trial and error until something incredible happened.

Small bubbles began to form on the edges of the bottom of the pot. "It's working."

Stella stood next to me and leaned forward. "Riveting, Science Guy."

She backed up far too quickly. But I forced my attention on the water. On the small bubbles and then slowly growing to bigger bubbles until they began to break the surface in a rhythm.

"Conclusion, a watched pot *can* boil."

Stella snorted, and when I glanced up, she was leaning against the wall staring at me. "You're the weirdest."

Warmth spread up my neck and I just shrugged as I ripped open the box of pasta.

"But it's probably my favorite thing about you."

Well, that was something.

A few minutes later, Stella and I sat side by side in front of the old computer, staring at the chat with our crappy mac and cheese.

"No response yet," she said.

I didn't want to know what they were gonna do with the stuff, just that they were gonna give me money.

A cough rattled from down the hall, and I knew I was moving forward no matter what.

We finished our mac and cheese in silence, then the computer beeped again.

I flinched.

> **MPG: Funds confirmed. 2g not 1.5. In five days' time. 9:00 p.m. Fountain Square near library. I'm sending two people to pick up the package and deliver the money.**

"Tell them you're bringing your assistant." Stella leaned over my shoulder, looking at the screen.

"No." I shook my head. "That is not a good idea."

"You are not taking me out of this now, Chuck. No way." She grabbed my shoulder and forced me to face her. "Come on."

Stella could decide for Stella.

> **SAM: I'll be bringing my assistant.**

> **MPG: Bring your assistant.**

Five days. Five days to make more of what we'd just done. Following the *same* formula and same purity—moving forward. And I only had two days of suspension to follow the timing in. This was gonna be interesting.

TWENTY-EIGHT

Sneaking into a house that no one was using proved harder than I thought. I stood back on the pathway that connected the neighborhoods, waiting for the people in 2625 A to get the whole family in the car.

How someone got seven children in one of these tiny townhomes, I'd never figure out. How they got them in the family van . . . well, I was listening to a play-by-play of that one. It happened with some threats, squeals, and bribes. Fortunately, nothing was on a timer at the moment. I was just waiting for some of the bacteria to grow on the few cans of Big Boy Beans.

Once the van pulled out, I crept through the back gate. We should have picked one where the fence wasn't visible from any of the roadways. Too late now.

I tiptoed through the weeds and slipped in the back door.

The bacteria had grown nicely, so I flipped open Sam's journal—even though I basically had the process memorized. The world slowly faded as I began with one can of beans, and then another, and then another. Adding yeast and sugar. Then starving the culture so the whole thing would die, releasing the toxin. Patiently waiting for the solution to turn clear. Then came the yellow mud. Precipitate, purify, then dry. Set timers for the first short burst of mild heat—just enough to encourage growth.

A few minutes or an hour or so later, Stella slipped in the back door. "I got us a new door handle for the front." She let keys dangle from her index finger.

I wanted to replace the lock, but coming in the back was far easier if we didn't want to be seen.

"I see that face," she said as she started for the front door, peeked outside, and then began dismantling the doorknob from the inside. "Wear a hat or something. Someone seeing the supposed new owners of this place would be far better than someone using that unlocked back door and screwing everything up. There's a half mil on the line now."

My throat closed up. Half a million dollars on the line. It took Stella a scarily short amount of time to replace the old doorknob with the new one and to slip a key in my back pocket.

"You're so chatty today," she teased. "I can hardly get a word in."

"Where'd you get the handle?"

"Don't ask things you don't want the answer to." She grinned. "But they're the same knobs used on the houses on base."

Yeah, I probably didn't want to know.

"How are you here?" I asked as I wiped down the counter around the beakers. "Aren't you in trouble?"

"Aren't you?" she fired back.

Yeah, I was.

"I may have told my mom that you were borderline suicidal and that you couldn't get a therapist appointment for a few days and how your dad was mistreated in the military and left with PTSD because the VA near you had terrible leadership, and she went off on one of her rants and said she wasn't happy about it, but she understood how hard it was to make friends in new areas. And then I explained about your mom's health and how much you have going on, and that I could come and basically keep both you and your mom alive. So yeah. As long as I answer my phone, I can hang as much as I want until you talk to your therapist, and then Mom and I can revisit the policy."

This whole story was so very Stella. "Do you have a *need* to make up stories, or do they just come?" I was half-teasing, half-curious.

"Both." She shrugged. "But there was at least some truth in that one."

"Good stories always have a seed of truth—or more."

"Right, you're a reader."

I stepped back from the counter. "There's really nothing to do for a few hours, and I gotta check on Mom."

Stella moved out of the kitchen to the sliding back door and locked it. "Well, you're stuck with me today because I'm not going home, and I'm also suspended from school, so."

"So." So I was going to get to spend the day with Stella and maybe Mom, if she woke up, and hopefully it would help keep my mind occupied so I wouldn't just keep spinning around and around over all the things that could go wrong.

For two days, Stella and I made as much toxin as we could with the supplies that we had. We weren't fully finished, but we had what I guessed was a half gram from the first can, so once we were done, we should have what we needed.

Neither of us had a scale, and that seemed pretty

important, but I'd rather guess too high than too low, so we just kept working. I snatched naps between Mom and Stella watching true crime shows together—seriously, watching true crime while I was in the middle of a true crime was somewhat surreal, but my focus was almost fully on getting as much of the yellow crystallized toxin as possible.

If Mom was awake, she was on the couch with her oxygen mask on. When she was asleep, her coughing kept us both awake. Another boss would find an excuse to fire her—one who didn't make it look like they'd fired her because of her chronic illness.

We'd been through that before.

There was no way I could make it to school on Wednesday—not with my toxin deadline looming and not with Mom so sick. In the last few days, Stella and I had found a rhythm in the families who lived on the block of our toxin townhouse. She'd studied each house in turn to figure out who might be at home, just bored and watching, but never saw anyone. I kept my head down.

"Four-hour timer this time, right?" she asked. "Before we add another dose of heat?"

I nodded as I stared at the two small test tubes we had crystals in. The 1.5 grams wasn't a lot, but it was more than what we had so far.

"I'm gonna have a pizza delivered to your house. You cool with that?"

I just nodded in response as we went through our routine of leaving the house—Stella checking through the window, then through a crack in the door, and then us walking out to the path as fast as we could while also looking casual.

The idea that someone could see us walking out of this place and think that we were sharing it. Together. Even when I took care of Mom, I didn't feel quite as grown up as I did while stepping out of a stolen place with Stella.

Mom slept—well, sort of slept—on the couch while Stella and I watched YouTube videos on her phone. I still hadn't told her about the last few videos I'd made of Sam's stuff. They felt too . . . personal somehow. Or maybe they were reckless and stupid, but I didn't want to hear her echo what I already knew, or have her push me to publish them before I was ready.

The doorbell rang just as Mom's coughing grew louder. She was out of her room and probably heading down.

"I'll get the door. You help your mom," Stella said.

When I rounded the corner at the bottom of the stairs, I paused. Mom grasped the railing with two hands, taking the steps one at a time. I sprinted to her and grasped her pale hand. She was getting worse. And I was doing what I could, but nothing was happening fast enough. Mom needed expert help now, not next week or next month.

I supported her the best I could. Voices carried from downstairs, and all I could think was that of course Stella would strike up a conversation with the pizza delivery guy.

"No," she said. "I already told you that we're both here because Chuck is sick and his mom needs care, so I came over."

"That's a nice story," the man said.

Wait. Truant officer? Did they even have those here?

I real quick forced a sneeze and rubbed my nose with a free hand to redden it. Messed my hair. Mom's focus was still wholly on the steps. Just before we hit the bottom, I slouched as if the steps had just been too much for me.

Another coughing fit hit Mom as we turned the corner toward the kitchen and a guy with a shirt and tie and

ID card stood with his arms crossed. Only his attention wasn't on Stella, it was on us.

Mom wheezed again and blood spattered down her front.

"See?" Stella snapped at the guy. "You two sit. I'll get a washcloth for the bloody nose."

I helped Mom into a kitchen chair and then sat. She lifted her head to see the truant officer standing just inside the door. "Can I . . ." she rasped. "Can I help you?"

His attention moved from Stella to me, to Mom to me, and then back to Stella. "Just make sure that when Chuck comes back to school, you send him with a note."

A note. That jerk came all the way over here just to make sure that I'd come to school with a *note*?

"Yeah," I whispered, trying to make my voice sound scratchy.

Stella was gently holding the cool cloth to Mom's face.

The guy backed out of the house. "Hope you're all feeling better soon."

Mom managed a subtle wave but nothing more. The walk down the stairs had exhausted her. She should be at the hospital.

"I think the bleeding is almost done," Stella said. "Let's get your oxygen hooked up."

"Aren't you still suspended?" Mom asked slowly.

"The guy got the dates mixed up," Stella said evenly. "Let's get you on the couch with your mask."

We looked at one another over my mother, and maybe just now did Stella fully understand why I was doing what I was doing. Why I had to make this trade. Why this money was so incredibly needed.

TWENTY-NINE

Stella rolled out some makeup thing that she'd emptied. The vials of toxin sat sealed next to her on the counter.

"It's small, right?" she asked. "And like, who is gonna check a girl's makeup bag?"

She made a solid point.

"Don't touch those without gloves, okay?"

Stella sighed. "You've disinfected everything in here a ton of times, Chuck. It's fine."

I reached forward, but she'd already slipped the first vial in a narrow slot in her makeup bag.

"This is for my brushes," she explained as she set the next vial in a slot next to the first. "Works even better than I thought."

"We're gonna have to be careful," I warned, adjusting the bandanna and N95 mask on my face. "Like, if we move wrong, one of those could break."

"Don't you, like, need to ingest the stuff?" She peered over her shoulder through fogging glasses, her features as relaxed as they'd be if we were headed to school.

"Yes, true . . ." I trailed off. Because as much as I did know, there was a lot I still didn't know.

"It's already after dinner." She slowly rolled her padded case back up and wrapped some attached strings around the outside. "We need to head out."

"I can take that." I reached forward, trying not to think about the kind of people we were supposed to be meeting up with. Instead, I just chanted again, *five hundred thousand dollars.*

Stella whirled away from me, tucking the package in the top of her small backpack. "A dude carrying a flowered makeup bag is suspicious, don't you think? Should we spray-paint the outside or something?"

This was not what I'd planned at all. I was gonna hold the toxin, but I had to agree. "Fine."

"Oh *fine*," she teased as she wandered toward the front door. "So you're not annoyed or anything about how this worked out."

Even now, even in what was probably the biggest moment of my life so far, Stella had forced me to smile.

We moved out of the townhouse with purpose. I'd need to come back tomorrow and clean all this out. Though I hadn't yet decided what I'd do with it. Maybe they'd want more. Maybe . . . I didn't know. What did a guy do with the knowledge of how to create a new kind of botulism toxin? It wasn't something that ever came up in a career test at school.

Stella swung herself into the passenger's side, and I climbed in the driver's side. Two Snakes fired right up, and I released a breath. Hopefully this wouldn't take long. I hated leaving Mom home alone when she was feeling as terrible as she had been.

"Is it weird that I'm kinda sad this is almost over?" Stella asked.

I shoved the stick into reverse and backed out of the borrowed driveway.

"We have an hour," she said. "We're gonna be stuck in that awkward waiting time when we get downtown."

"I'm both terrified and relieved they wanted a public drop spot, though it's not like there are a whole lot of people downtown after everything shuts down."

We drove in silence, Stella staring out the window. I continually adjusted my grip on the worn steering wheel, my fingers running over the smooth nubs that were supposed to act like finger grips.

Town appeared around us both too fast and not fast enough. *Almost done. Almost over. Almost have five hundred thousand dollars.*

"I'm gonna park sort of behind the library," I said. "It's not like this truck blends."

"Twin has a lot of trucks." Stella shifted in her seat and faced me.

"There aren't a lot with golden snakes on the hood that look as if they may collapse from rust."

"I can see the road underneath me in a few places through the floorboards."

The truck shuddered to a stop, and I turned to face Stella. "If things get weird, promise me you'll just run."

"So chivalrous of you."

I shook my head. "There's a chance everything could go wrong here."

"They want the stuff. They like our stuff. They may want *more* of the stuff. So why would they kill the guy who can get it for them?"

I tugged my black baseball hat lower on my head. "Will you just promise that you'll run?"

She rolled her eyes. "I don't know why you think I'm less culpable than you are, Chuck."

"Just . . . please," I pleaded. "If things get weird, just run."

"I'll think about it."

And that was probably the best I'd get from her. "We have thirty minutes."

"Well, why not just go hang by the fountain for a bit?" she suggested. "That way it looks like we're out on a date."

"This would be your idea of a date, wouldn't it?"

"A shady exchange of toxin for a massive amount of cash?" She waggled her brows. "Definitely yes."

I leaned forward. "A kiss for luck?"

"How about a kiss just because I like you?" She leaned forward with a smile and pressed her lips to mine.

There was no way Stella was more than a piece of my life. She'd never hold her attention in one place for long. But she was a piece I would never forget, and I was going to enjoy every minute I had to spend with her.

We walked together, me hyperaware of the toxin in her backpack. Her hand slipped into mine. We moved up the quiet downtown street and then back around to the fountain across from the library. This library was already the home of a lot of pivotal moments for me. It almost made cosmic sense that the drop was here. Or was this a setup, and the cops got to the library computer? I shoved that thought deep down inside me. I had to risk it. For Mom. It was the only thing I had left to get her help.

Shops were closed for the night. Only a few cars still sat parallel parked. Main Street was for wanderers during the daytime, not for any kind of nightlife. Not that Twin Falls had much of a nightlife outside of a couple of dive bars closer to the freeway.

When Stella and I sat—our legs together, shoulders together—a strange calm came over me. I'd done all of Sam's steps. And while I didn't know the particulars of how his story had ended, it felt as if I were accomplishing something he'd worked toward but hadn't quite completed. Plus, my ending would be saving my mom.

And maybe one day people would write about me the way they wrote about Sam. Somebody besides Stella, who for sure would be writing about me. About us.

Stella swung her pack over her shoulder and let it rest on her lap. All I could think about was those few precious vials with crystallized toxin. "I think we need some luck," she said.

"Everyone needs luck," I responded.

She opened a small zipper and pulled out a penny. She held it between two fingers and raised it near my face. "Blow on it."

"What are you talking about?"

"You know, like people do on dice and whatever else they need luck for." She waved the penny in front of my face.

"How could breathing possibly help any—"

"Would you just do it already?" She laughed.

And so I blew on the penny in Stella's fingers. The lights around the fountain snapped on as the sky dimmed. A large truck rumbled down the quiet main street.

Stella placed her pack on my lap, and I cradled it as she paused in front of the fountain, pressed her lips to the penny, and tossed it into the water.

Same torn jeans. Same worn boots. A flannel tied around her waist. A white tank top with some random cartoon-like drawings on it. Every inch of her was pure Stella, and I hoped she never changed. Never turned into one of the people who got older and started to conform with whatever society felt was "normal."

Again, Sam's disappearance floated through my head. Disappearance, wasn't it? And I thought about the kind of people who would have this kind of cash and be on the dark web.

Then I thought about Mom at home on oxygen. Mom's bloody noses. Mom's tiny form in a hospital bed.

Stella grasped my hand as she sat down again, and we gripped one another in silence.

My head fuzzed and grew light. I had to do this—I'd come too far to back out now—but part of me wanted to take the toxin and run. Call the EPA or something and tell them I'd done this on accident. Beg for a job. But, yeah . . . no diploma.

"Your mom needs help now," Stella whispered, as if sensing my scrambled thoughts.

And she was right. She'd also spent days with Mom. Days when Mom couldn't move from one room to another without wheezing and coughing.

"Remember when we thought that guy in Ogden was scary?" Stella whisper-laughed. "Like, because he was one of a ton of people who carry a weapon? And now we're here?"

"Yeah," was all I could say.

Two young guys with duffel bags and baseball hats laughed and shoved one another as if they were friends. Outdoor T-shirts. Too-clean cargo hiking pants. One looked up and his eyes met mine with a sharpness that stopped my breath.

"That's them," I whispered.

"Hey!" One of the guys waved as he jogged our way. Like we'd known each other for ages. But there was something in the way he said that one word—a hint of him not being from here.

Stella waved back. I clutched her backpack more tightly.

"Relax," the man said as he got closer. And only now

could I make out their faces in the dim light. "We're on vacation in Idaho. For the hiking."

Russian? University scientists? Maybe?

The other guy stepped forward. They were both dressed just . . . off, like someone who wanted to blend but missed the mark. The hiking shoes were too new. The pants not quite right somehow—still had folded store creases.

"If you look like we're friends, that could help," one whispered with a smile.

"So great to finally meet some of Sam's friends," Stella chirped.

"You have something for MPG?" one of the guys asked.

I swallowed. Nodded. "And . . . and you?"

The guy sat on the bench next to me, slumping back as if we were longtime friends. The other guy dropped the bag next to the first guy's feet. They were both young. Like, older than me and Stella, but part of me expected old dudes in suits or something. But then, no one in Twin Falls would miss two men in suits who weren't from here.

"Your assistant?" the guy next to me asked.

Stella just nodded.

Two young guys in hiking gear? They'd blend anywhere in this part of the world. Well, if people weren't looking for something to be wrong.

I opened Stella's backpack and pulled out the flowered makeup case.

The guy next to me scoffed. "Serious?"

"Kept the glass from breaking," I explained. "At least you have giant pockets?"

The two guys looked at one another and the one on the bench pulled the rolled-up bag thing from my hands. He slowly opened it as he chatted about the weather and the town and the river, and I didn't hear a word because he was obviously covering in case anyone walked by.

"All good." He stood and turned. "So great to see the two of you." His accent still clung to his words. "Let's hike soon."

Or never. "For sure," I answered as I reached for the duffel.

"MPG would never short someone," the other guy said. "Peek, but don't pull anything out!"

His voice lowered on the last sentence.

The duffel wasn't nearly as big as I'd have thought for that much money, but when I opened the zipper, the hundred-dollar bills were bound together. There were so many. More than I ever thought I'd see in my life.

I just nodded once.

"See you on the trail!" one of the guys called over his shoulder as they walked away.

We had the cash. They had the toxin. We'd done it.

A rush like a flood of uncertainty flew from my head to my feet.

"Ready to get out of here?" I asked Stella.

"So very."

Someone across the street opened the door to their shop, closed it behind them, and locked it from the outside.

I slipped the duffel on my back, wearing it like a backpack. Who knew what kind of power these guys had. They could shoot us as we walked away and leave town. So many things could go wrong.

"Try and look normal, right?" Stella released a nervous laugh as she grasped my hand.

Once again, we held each other too tightly as we moved for the truck. Two Snakes was parked the same direction as the two men had been walking. When I'd parked, I thought out of the way would be smart, but now . . . now it just felt as if it was a good place for us to get shot.

"I gotta run," I said as I broke into a jog.

We sprinted around the last corner, raced for Two Snakes, and jumped in. My hands shook as I pulled off the duffel. Everything felt big and strange and terrifying. Two guys with foreign accents had come to this small town without me needing to tell them I was here. I had no doubt they could find me if they wanted to. They already had.

I fumbled with the keys and then finally stabbed the end of it into the ignition.

"Start it, and let's get out of here." Stella was breathing hard in the passenger's seat, her face pale.

Honestly, I hadn't been sure that anything could get to her. Guess now I knew what it took. Strange men willing to murder people and drop off hundreds of thousands of dollars to murder more people.

"When will I feel safe?" I asked as I put the truck in gear and drove back toward my home.

Stella sat sideways in the seat and stared out the back window. "No one's behind us."

That was something.

Still, my hands felt sweaty, and all I wanted to do was take the truck out somewhere and burn it. And burn everything we'd left in the empty townhouse. Not that glass would burn, but I had the cash. I wanted everything else gone. Done. Behind me. But then again, why add arson to my bio-toxin rap sheet?

There was no way I could do this again. *Or would I have to? Am I on the hook for life?* Only time would tell. Besides, the cash would have to last until I could find a better way to help Mom. I'd need to look into what degrees I could finish in three years if I did summer school. The ones that would pay the most when I finished. I had to scramble for the rest of the school year to get killer grades.

I put my foot down harder on the pedal.

A faint siren sounded behind us.

"Oh, suck!" I breathed quietly. We couldn't be caught. Not now. Not when I only had a few miles back to the empty townhouse.

Back to the place where I might just wipe the truck down and leave it to die.

The siren grew louder.

"Slow down," Stella whispered, as if her quiet voice would somehow lessen the tension.

I brought the truck back down to a steady fifty-five miles an hour. Exact speed limit.

Flashing lights appeared behind us in the dark.

How had we been caught now and not when the exchange was being made?

I grabbed four wads of cash out of the duffel and shoved them under the seat—in a strange pocket place behind the center seat. Maybe if we were caught, they wouldn't find those. Maybe . . . "Get those to Mom, okay?" I asked.

Stella just nodded.

Though it was a stupid thing to ask of her since she was with me now. I could always say that she had no idea. I mean, I knew that's what I'd say.

The cop car grew closer, and I released the gas, pushed down on the clutch, geared down, and moved to the side of the road. "I made videos," I said as the cop car drew nearer. "I made videos about Sam and what I know that the internet doesn't know. You saw some of them, but I did more. I need you to post them. They're in drafts."

The cop car was closer.

"So you just need to hit publish, so more people know more about Sam. Maybe they'll figure out what really happened with him."

"Are you serious?"

"I just need you to do this. You get into my phone by starting with the two and working clockwise until the dots are filled. Please?"

"Yeah. Okay." Stella nodded.

"Just not unless we know I'm getting arrested."

Just then, the cop car flew by us.

I put the truck in neutral and just sat on the side of the road, trying to find my breath. Trying to make the world around me stop spinning. My hands trembled.

"It's the release of adrenaline," Stella said as she rubbed her hands on her thighs. "That's what makes you feel so weird."

I flopped back until my head rested against the window on the back of the cab. "At the moment, I sort of wish I were the kind of person who got high."

Stella laughed. "No, you don't. Just take one of your mom's sleeping pills. Tomorrow this will feel like a lifetime away."

"Not sure how to explain to Mom where the money came from."

"You could tell her you used a fake ID to gamble," Stella offered.

It would make a lot of sense, really. Mom wouldn't want me to get caught. I had "won" the money honestly if that were the story. "I can't believe I hadn't thought of that before now. Like, all I cared about was getting the money. It never occurred to me how to explain it once I had it."

"Let's get this truck off the road, and then you can talk about money."

Yeah. That was probably the best idea. Still, my hands shook as we pulled back into the empty townhouse, and I slung the bag over my back again.

"My car's at your place," Stella said.

I concentrated on breathing as we got out of the truck. Each shadow seemed to hold the threat of someone after us. Of one of the two "hikers" waiting with guns, or . . . One thing was certain—I was not cut out for criminal anything.

THIRTY

A big weight had been lifted, but another had settled on my shoulders—the weight of knowing I'd sold enough toxin to *work faster than they had ever seen.* I slipped the key into the lock of the front door, grateful Mom hadn't thought to turn on the light.

I didn't need our neighbors knowing what time I'd gotten home.

"Can I use the bathroom real quick?" Stella whispered behind me.

I just nodded as I pushed open the front door.

Mom lay sprawled on the floor next to the kitchen. I froze. A pool of blood splayed around the front of her face.

Stella sprinted around me and fell to Mom's side. "She's barely breathing. Go get the truck!"

"I . . ."

"The truck!" Stella yelled.

I spun around and sprinted back through the same path, a whole new kind of terror ripping at me. Half of me wanted to call 911, the other half couldn't imagine just sitting and waiting next to Mom rasping while they came to us.

We'd get to the hospital in half the time it would take an ambulance to get here.

Two Snakes roared to life, and I sped around in front of my house.

Stella already had Mom propped up against her as they slowly moved for the truck.

The liquid-rasp said that she was probably beyond the point of having the strength to cough. My heart pounded as I helped ease her into the car. As Stella and I climbed in, we sandwiched her between us.

The money still clung to my back in the duffel, but instead of readjusting, I just put the truck in gear and hit the gas.

"She'll be fine, Chuck," Stella said.

But Mom wasn't fine. Nothing about this was fine. There was blood all over her front. Out her nose. And it looked as if blood had dribbled out of the side of her mouth as well.

I swiped at my eyes. This was too much. This whole night. This whole week. Everything was too much.

"What's on the videos?" Stella asked.

"What?"

"The videos you wanted me to post. What's on them?"

I couldn't wrap my mind around her questions and also around driving at freeway speeds on this back road. "Stuff," I said. "Like, how I found Sam's stuff. What I know. Thought it could add to what information is already out there."

"Cool."

Maybe. If I ever posted it.

"Why did you do that?" she asked.

"I'm gonna wait until this all settles. Until I feel safe posting. But I just wanted to put out there what I know. I kept the camera off my face, but I probably also should have disguised my voice. I don't know."

"That's always suspect, you know? And is it set up on your LegendCityVids channel?"

"Right now, yeah," I said. So adjusting my voice would have made no sense.

Mom wheezed again, and I pressed my foot harder into the floorboards, but the truck was already pegged.

We slid sideways into the hospital parking lot, and I screeched to a stop in front of the emergency entrance, immediately laying on the horn.

"Crap. I should have thought to call," Stella said as she leapt out of the car.

Mom was slumped against my side, bloody spittle dripping onto my lap.

This couldn't be happening. Not now. Not when I had finally gotten us set up. But I had the money now. We'd fix her. We were at the hospital, and she was still breathing.

"Let's get her out here," a nurse said from the passenger's side.

I gently eased Mom toward the open door as the uniformed nurse and Stella helped slide her into the wheelchair.

"Can you park the car?" the woman asked as they started for the door. "We'll take her straight to a room and get her on oxygen, but we need this space clear."

I just swallowed as I watched them wheel her away. Still feeling powerless. I gunned Two Snakes and put it in a parking spot before sprinting inside.

"We just have a few things for you to fill out," a woman said. "And then we can take her back."

Mom was slumped over, hardly moving. Stella at her side.

"Take her back now!" I yelled. "Look at her! She's barely breathing!"

"Now, young man," the older woman said. "I need

you to calm down. We need some information from you before we—”

“We can pay, all right?” I yelled as I jerked the duffel off my back. “I have money! We can pay!”

“Chuck!” Stella hissed. “Stop it!”

But I couldn’t. Mom was sitting next to me, slumped over, rasping terribly, and they hadn’t taken her to a room.

I dropped the bag and unzipped a corner before pulling out a chunk of cash. I slammed the stack of bills on the counter. “We have money! We can pay! Now save my mom!”

A woman nodded to another nurse, who got behind Mom and started for the doors.

“You stay here and fill this out.” Gray brows shot upward. “And then we’ll take you back to see your mom.”

Another nurse picked up a phone and looked at me sorta sideways.

Okay, yeah. I was a little off the rails, but who wouldn’t be after my night?

I snatched the clipboard off the counter. Mom had just been at this hospital. They should’ve had our info already.

A man and woman in suits strode into the lobby.

Stella sat next to me and hissed, “Give me your phone. Now.”

“What?”

But she’d already slipped her hand in my pocket and taken it out.

“Chuck Yarrow?” the woman asked as she stopped in front of me and then glanced at Stella. “And Stella Warner?”

I glanced up. There was something formal and tall or big or . . . something about the way the pair of them stood. Definitely no MPG this time.

“We’re FBI, and we’d like to talk to you two.”

Two nurses, one of them the gray-haired one, stood and stared.

The woman faced them. "We've been in contact with your local law enforcement."

One of the nurses nodded, but all I could do was stare at the agents in front of me.

Stella released a slow breath. "Can I use the restroom first? I've had to pee for like an hour."

"I'll help you get there safely," the woman said.

Safely?

Nothing made sense until everything made perfect and horrible sense. Stella and I had been caught. Someone, somewhere, in the government had found us. And I sat at the hospital with a bag of cash at my feet.

Stella had my phone.

Stella would have a moment in the bathroom stall.

"You wanted to talk to me?" I asked the man standing in front of me in a suit.

He shook his head once, his attention moving from me to the hospital door to the bathroom door where Stella had disappeared.

Part of me wanted to run. All of me knew I'd get nowhere. I should have hidden some money in the house. Or somewhere . . . on Mom's person or . . . There was only the small bit in the truck.

"How is my mom?" I asked around the man, my voice trembling, even to my own ears.

"We have her on oxygen," the older nurse said. "We'll keep you updated."

But the way her eyes shifted to the man in front of me said the same thing I already knew. I wouldn't be able to stay in this hospital while Mom recovered. The FBI was going to take all this money. Ask me a million questions I probably couldn't answer.

I swallowed. I needed my mom.

The best I could hope for now was a fate like Sam's. For someone to know part of this story. Anyone to know part of this story.

Stella emerged from the bathroom just before the female agent.

I hadn't filled out a single box on the form the nurses had handed to me.

Stella gave me a subtle nod.

"We're going to cuff you both because I don't feel like chasing down teenagers who feel the need to run," the woman said. "We'll figure out whatever your friend did on your phone while using the restroom."

The videos were up now. Anyone worth anything would screen capture those videos before someone knew to take them down.

I stood on shaky legs, and just as promised, the man cuffed my hands in front of me. I stared at the metal. Stared at the duffel of cash. I hadn't even had a chance to pay off anything. To even really look at all of it.

"I hadn't planned on this part of the story," Stella said. "I mean, I thought about it, but I hadn't planned it."

I looked at each agent in turn. "She really has nothing to do—"

"We're not talking now," the man said. "I'd be very cautious about whatever information you divulge."

The world around me felt as if it were falling away, piece by piece. The walls of the hospital. The worry. The fear. The everything . . . it was over. The whole adventure was over. And we'd lost.

Just as we stepped into the night air, Stella jumped my direction and gave me a quick kiss on the cheek. "It was worth it," she said. "It was all worth it."

SIX MONTHS LATER

Twin Falls Daily Sentinel

Couple Finds Eighty Thousand Dollars in Truck They Purchased at Auction

Deb and Harry Roady had literally just lost their farm, their home, their everything, when they purchased a truck with golden snakes painted on the hood while at the local auction. Their previous truck had been repossessed by the bank as part of their farming operation, and they needed transportation to stay with family in Arizona while they regrouped.

They were cleaning the vehicle to prepare for the drive when four wads of hundred-dollar bills were found shoved behind and under the center of the truck's bench seat. Because of the rules around the truck, which had been in an impound, and the authorities not finding the money, the Roadys are now eighty thousand dollars richer, which should help them get back on their feet after their devastating loss.

An act of God? Karma at its best? We'll leave it for you to decide.

WHEN THE CASE RUNS COLD:
WE PUT OUT THE INFO, AND HOPE YOU CAN HELP SOLVE IT.

This week's case is a puzzler, folks. In some places, an urban legend worthy of wild speculation. Are you ready?

COLD CASE FILE #524 – What Happened to Chuck Yarrow?

To fully appreciate this story, check out episode #316, and the "death" of Sam Miller, because we're all pretty sure they're related. This arrest happened more than ten years ago, but we still haven't been able to put all the pieces together. Maybe you'll do better than us.

On May 5, 2024, Chuck Yarrow posted an urban exploration video that he did while exploring the area near his townhouse—adjacent to the military base where Sam Miller lived. Not long after, a few videos were posted on this same account, detailing materials from Sam Miller that this guy had found. Because LegendCityVids never used his face, or his real name, it's a lot harder to track what happened to him after this.

But at almost the same time as this group of videos was posted, at about one a.m., a Chuck Yarrow was arrested in the town of Twin Falls, Idaho, but there are no records of him after that time. If that is our LegendCityVids— and most say it is—he spent two years trying to make it on YouTube to help his mom get medical care, but she died in the hospital on the night he was arrested. He did finally make several viral videos, many of them regarding Sam Miller, but he was never able to reap the benefits— at least not to our knowledge. YouTube won't comment, nor have they turned over any personal information on LegendCityVids.

Rumors range from him being abducted by aliens to him attempting to sell some toxin he found to spies from another country to him finding military secrets that were too sensitive to allow him to roam free—or maybe even live. Some say there's no way this dark web contact wasn't compromised from day one, in which case the argument is that he was always talking to the US government, who probably hired him to work for them once this was over.

The other theory is that Chuck legitimately sold toxins, and the FBI caught a lucky break in catching him. We prefer this story because it sounds cooler.

We do know that he was arrested, but there's no record of a trial—at least not in Idaho or the surrounding states. Everything has been buried. As far as we know, Chuck just up and disappeared after he was taken into custody by the FBI at the hospital. The similarities between this case and the case of Sam Miller, who supposedly died of alcohol poisoning, are startling.

With the release of Stella Warner's book after her five-year stint in jail, a few of the details were spelled out, but with her penchant for adding fiction to truth, no one is sure what within her story is true and what isn't. If you watch any of her interviews—both on mainstream media and some of our more trusted channels—she is beyond dodgy when it comes to revealing what is truth and what is fiction. While her dealings with Chuck Yarrow were unconfirmed, the one true thing we know is he was arrested, because Stella was too. It was laid out in her book, but she's never said definitively if he's also LegendCityVids.

But how could it be someone else when we have so much linking the two people?

She holds the key, so if anyone ever cracks the Stella code, we'd love to know. Though she spends most of her time writing on her island—yes, you read that right, on her island where the Son of Sam Law doesn't apply. But we don't recommend showing up there. Rumor has it that her dogs are well trained to keep people off the beaches.

Since the time of Chuck Yarrow's arrest, no one with that name and approximate birth date has shown up on any records anywhere within the United States. LegendCityVids never made another video after that night.

Coincidence?

We think not, but we'll leave it for you to decide. And as always, if you have information you think may help us all solve the puzzle of Chuck and LegendCityVids, or even Sam Miller? We'd love to have it.

The one thing we know. The one thing we always know. We have a lot more material to uncover.

EPILOGUE

The newly minted ID for Chuck Yarrow sat in the man's pocket as he stepped out of prison. His possessions were few—only the earnings from the anonymous LegendCityVids for the last fifteen years in a bank account he'd never used while free and a few items from his incarceration: a worn Bible, J.R.R. Tolkien's *The Lord of the Rings* series, a faded photo of him and his mom from when they first moved to Twin Falls, and a torn-out newspaper article titled "Russian Terrorists Caught at JFK Airport with Suspicious Vials of Botulism Toxin in Carry-On." The few items from the outside world he'd had on him on his arrest day were handed to him in a clear plastic bag.

Clothes for a sixteen-year-old kid, blood-stained shoes, and the leather journal that had gotten him here in the first place. It had been evidence, so many of the pages were missing, but the leather still felt familiar in the man's hands.

"And this is your last day of mail." The woman out-processing him reached forward with a package in her hands.

The man took it and pulled off the brown paper, recognizing the return address immediately. They'd sent each other a lot of mail over the years.

Within the Pages of Sam Miller's Journal—a signed

copy. Courtesy of Stella. The book was in its fifth printing. He'd read it already, of course, since they'd had a copy in the prison library. But still . . . He flipped open the front cover.

"Friend of yours send that?" the woman asked.

"Used to be," the man said gruffly as he skimmed over the sparse lines of text.

A hair over thirty, he'd spent almost half of his life behind prison walls. He got out on good behavior from his twenty-year sentence, and because his crime was committed as a minor, so he was charged as a minor. He felt horrible about the harm he had caused and hated that his mother had passed away, but it still wasn't worth becoming the "youngest bioterrorist"—according to the prosecutor—in US history. He didn't believe that and had served his time. He wasn't quite sure who he'd sold the botulism toxin to, and he had hoped and prayed that he didn't truly hurt anyone. And fortunately, the government had kept his and Stella's trials as hidden as possible.

The world had forgotten about Chuck Yarrow. It was time to be a responsible member of society. Get a job with his microbiology degree he had earned in prison and do all he could to educate the public. What he was drawn to—his calling in life—was to work with the government for a small-town health department.

He let his eyes drop back to Stella's book.

The familiar loops of her writing brought a small smile to his lips.

Heard you were out soon. They wouldn't let me publish this while I was in, and . . . I wanted you to have one. I know you said we didn't have to share the profits, but now that you're out, I think that was a stupid agreement. I won't share on my other books, but would love to share on this one. Pretty sure you lost a half mil at one point. Look me up when you're out. We both knew I'd get off easier, and I did. Feel like I have some ground to make up. Would love to see you. Pretty sure we have more to do,

Stella

Chuck closed the book and took a deep breath as he walked past the threshold of the outer door of the prison. He *did* have a lot of ground to make up.

THE END

As a kid, Tyler H. Jolley always had a knack for storytelling. When he grew bored of old fables, he created his own exciting and unique worlds. Many years later, he still had so many new ideas and stories swirling in his head, but with nowhere to share it. That's when he put his pencil to paper and let the creative juices flow.

His debut novel, *Extracted*, came out in 2013 and swiftly became an Amazon Best Seller and Spencer Hill Press Best Seller. *Prodigal and Riven*, the second and third books in The Lost Imperials series were released in May of 2015.

After a brief hiatus he restructured and returned to writing. His Adventurous Ali series has received much praise. To date, he's released four in the series.

When he's not writing, you can find him at his orthodontic practice, mountain biking, or on the hunt for the perfect doughnut.